ASK NOT WHY

Ask Not Why

Book One of
'The Corncrakes of Skye'

LUCY MONTGOMERY

ECOLE ALOUETTE

First published in Great Britain by Ecole Alouette 2018
Copyright © Lucy Montgomery 2018

ISBN 9781901870671

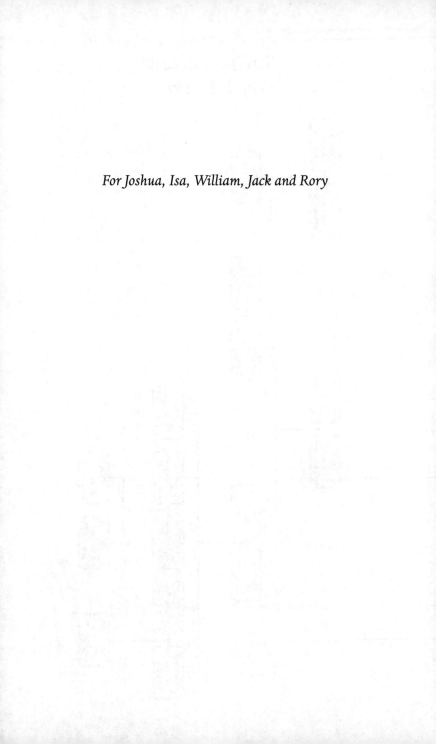

For Joshua, Isa, William, Jack and Rory

Tavish MacLeod
of Kilbackie

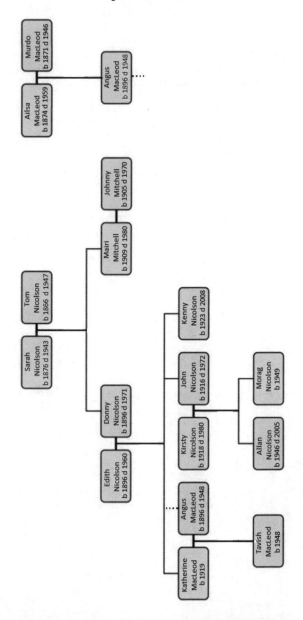

PART I

(1914–1921)

CHAPTER I

Kilbackie, Isle of Skye, August 1914

In an upstairs bedroom, a young mother sat quietly brushing her five year old daughter's long hair before attempting to make her look like Heidi, the girl in the story they were reading. Her two older daughters looked on as she plaited the hair and wrapped the braids over the child's head, pinning them firmly in place.

The result was so successful the three girls instinctively jumped off the bed, held hands and skipped gleefully round in circles enjoying the freedom to express a rare moment of merriment. This family time of simple pleasure came to an abrupt end when their father, the fiery, larger-than-life minister of Kilbackie, returned home from his morning visits expecting to walk into a silent Manse but instead he was greeted by the sound of giggling and thumping from somewhere upstairs.

Although longsuffering and compassionate to those who obeyed his teaching, he was prone to vengeance and cruelty when confronted with disobedience — the sounds of rebellion under his roof sent him into a state of uncontrollable rage.

He stormed unannounced into his youngest daughter's bedroom and confronted three joyful girls holding the ends of their dresses and dancing.

"What is going on here?" he boomed as the children released the hems of their dresses and ran behind the bed in terror. The minister had no interest in pursuing his daughters but he felt it his duty to humiliate his wife as a punishment for flouting the strict rule of silence he had placed throughout the house.

"Explain yourself, Sarah!" he shouted at the oppressed woman who sat on the child's bed failing to understand why her husband took so much pleasure depriving her of happiness.

"You, of all people, should know that noise is forbidden."

One by one his three daughters popped their heads over the top of the mattress and peered at their father who stood in the doorway waiting for a plausible explanation.

"We were trying to copy the picture on the dust cover of the book I am reading. It's about…"

The minister raised his hand in the air to stop her from continuing.

"You are reading a work of the Devil," he sneered, "And you have endangered our daughters' souls by turning them into harlots. Such ungodly behaviour cannot go unpunished. Do you understand?"

She kept her head bowed and nodded meekly.

"Be afflicted and weep: let your laughter be turned to mourning and your joy to heaviness," he announced in his overbearing preaching voice, adding: "From now on there will be no more stories or dancing."

Satisfied that discipline had been fully restored, Tom Nicolson returned downstairs to his study leaving his children glued to the spot in terror. Their mother turned round and smiled at the three ashen-white little faces staring at the door ahead, beckoning them to re-join her on the bed.

"Shhh, girls!" she said trying to comfort them. "There now! Everything's fine. Dry your eyes and reflect on your father's words. He loves us very much and wants to protect our souls by stopping us becoming vain."

Mairi, Ishbel and Effie sat snuggled together with their arms tightly linked trying to put on a brave face but the sound of heavy footsteps returning up the wooden stairs sent them scurrying back to their place of safety, arriving just as the minister entered the room brandishing a pair of scissors. He appeared particularly tall and menacing as he demanded his youngest daughter, Mairi, to step forward.

"Kneel down," he commanded the frightened girl who looked hesitantly towards her mother for help.

"Leave her alone, Tom," Sarah pleaded. "She's done nothing wrong. It was my idea to plait her hair, not hers."

Tom ignored his wife.

"Kneel!" he repeated harshly, untying the Heidi-plaits and hacking them off near the nape of her neck. Mairi's sisters looked on in horror as twisted strands

5

of flaxen hair dropped onto the bare floorboards.

"Next!" he called, oblivious to the gasps of horror in the room. One by one his daughters knelt on the floor and winced at the sound of the scissors slicing off their long, fair hair.

"The books please, Sarah," he continued, stretching out his hand. "I want all the children's books brought to me, now."

Sarah showed great dignity as she gathered up the story books that had given so much pleasure and handed them over to her furious husband.

"No more works of the Devil," he said relishing his power to judge and bully his family into submission.

With the minister's visit at an end, Sarah demurely fetched a dustpan and brush and swept up the piles of soft hair, allowing a few silent tears to roll unnoticed down her flushed cheeks.

When Donny returned home later that evening for supper and saw the state of his sisters' hair and his mother's distress, he confronted his father.

"What have you done to them?" he cried, clenching his fists.

"'If a woman be not covered, let her also be shorn,'" the minister quoted coldly.

Donny walked up to his father and standing a few inches away from his face, said without flinching, "Britain is about to go to war and I've decided to do my duty and join the army."

There was the merest hint of surprise on Tom Nicolson's face but he said nothing.

6

"And when I return home I will be stronger and fitter than you, sir. If I hear you have hurt my mother or sisters during my absence, I will give you a hiding you will never forget. Do you understand me, sir?"

No-one had ever threatened the minister in this way before and, for once, he was speechless. He stared into his son's green eyes and for the first time betrayed a hint of fear. He left his supper untouched and disappeared into his study.

"You're not really leaving us, are you?" Sarah said in a hushed voice, tiptoeing past the snivelling girls towards her son.

"I can't stay," Donny replied sorrowfully. "You of all people should know how difficult it is living with father — I need to get away before he does something he regrets. You and the girls will be fine because he only disciplines you with words but I can't take any more beatings."

He looked at his mother's worn face; her eyes were still blue but they had lost their sparkle and her hollow cheeks stood out against the dark circles around her eyes. This noble, downtrodden lady was the finest person he had ever known and he deeply loved and respected her.

"Before I leave," he whispered quietly, determined not to give his father a reason to return. "Will you give me your blessing?"

Sarah Nicolson held her son's face firmly in her hands and kissed his forehead.

"Go!" she said so faintly he had to strain to hear her

words. "The Lord bless thee and keep thee: The Lord make his face shine upon thee and be gracious unto thee: The Lord lift up his countenance upon thee and give thee peace."

Donny Nicolson wasn't the only young man from the Isle of Skye preparing to leave for war. His friend, Angus MacLeod had responded positively to a recruiting sergeant visiting the Kilbackie Estate where he lived. In elegant Gaelic, the sergeant pleaded for more recruits to join 4th Cameron Highlanders, fight German cruelty and return home a hero. Angus didn't need much persuasion to abandon the grind and monotony of subsistence living for an adventure overseas.

A few days before he was due to leave, his father, Murdo, surprised everyone by walking up the steep hill behind his croft and with his bare hands, dug out a particularly large rock. It was back-breaking work as most of the stone lay deep in the peaty soil below a layer of purple heather and green bracken but Murdo had never shied away from physical labour and after a huge effort, he managed to free the heavy stone and carry it down the hill where he placed it in the long grass next to his home.

"What are you up to?" his wife, Ailsa, asked curiously when he arrived home dripping in sweat.

He gave her no explanation but the next day he repeated the same exhausting process and after a week, the pile of rocks grew into a beautifully constructed cairn five foot tall and four foot wide. It was a labour of love which only a stonemason with Murdo's eye could have pieced so perfectly together.

On the eve of Angus' departure to join his regiment, his father sat in the heather holding the end of a length of thin wire which he deftly twisted into a small loop then fed the other end through the small loop to make a noose. He hung the snare from a frame made of alder twigs and placed it over a trail leading down to the rough grass beside the croft's dry stone wall. Once the snare was set, he carried on with his daily chores checking regularly to see if a creature had scampered into the noose. By early evening, he noticed a lifeless rabbit lying under the wooden frame. Very gently he eased it free of the noose and laid it on top of the cairn then knelt on the soaking grass with his head bowed and let the pouring rain trickle through his hair, over his face and down the back of his neck.

After several long, anguished minutes, he stood up, shook the water off his clothes and made his way back to the house where Ailsa and Angus sat waiting for him to share a passage from Scripture before retiring to bed. He picked up the family Bible and began reading the story of Abraham and Isaac, a story he had read countless times and knew by heart. His melodious voice resonated strongly round the room until he came to the words; *Abraham looked up ... and saw a ram caught by its horns. He ... took the ram and sacrificed it as a burnt offering instead of his son.* At this point his voice started to falter and crack until it was barely audible.

Oblivious to the presence of his wife and son, the faithful servant promised to sacrifice a rabbit a day to appease God's wrath if He would spare his only son, Angus.

CHAPTER 2

London and Inverness August 1914

August Bank Holiday 1914 was a glorious day when
the whole country basked in sunshine under a cloudless blue sky and thousands of families flocked by
train to the coastal resorts for their annual break.
Amidst colourful parasols, windbreaks and flags, hol-
iday-makers made the most of the bracing air,
promenades, piers and pleasure gardens and relished
the freedom to stretch out on golden sand, explore
rock pools, eat greasy meals out of newspaper, treat
their children to ice-creams and donkey rides and
laugh at the antics of Punch and Judy.

The noise of hungry seagulls mingled with the
irrepressible squeals of excited children nagging their
parents to buy something from the pedlars who
touted their wares, trying to be heard above the
marching sound of the brass bands in the bandstands.

Elsewhere in the Kingdom, the sound of leather on
willow echoed across beautifully kept village greens,
narrow lanes, hedgerows and cornfields. Those
fortunate enough to be at the Oval witnessed Sir Jack
Hobbs score a magnificent double century for his
county, Surrey against Nottinghamshire.

These were exciting times of growing leisure and

prosperity in an industrialised country built on steam and innovation with an Empire spreading over a quarter of the globe and the largest navy in the world.

In London, the full Cabinet met in sombre mood to discuss the worsening European crisis. The German government had refused to accept Belgium's neutrality and demanded passage through their country but the Belgium Government stood by their right to remain neutral and denied them access. Britain was still bound by the 1839 Treaty of London to protect Belgium in the event of war.

As the ruby sun slipped spectacularly below the London sky-line, ending a perfect summer's day, Sir Edward Grey looked out of his window onto St James's Park where the gas lamps were being lit and remarked, 'the lamps are going out all over Europe; we shall not see them lit again in our lifetime.'

A deep sense of foreboding hung over the Prime Minister Herbert Asquith as he listened to Big Ben strike eleven and by the time the great bell fell silent, he had to announce with the utmost reluctance and with infinite regret that His Majesty's Government had been summoned to put Great Britain in a state of war with Germany who for generations had been a friendly Power.

All eight units of the Territorial Force were immediately mobilised, including 4th Cameron Highlanders which formed part of the Seaforth & Cameron Brigade in the Highland Division. Close to six hundred and fifty fit young men from the North of Scotland had already volunteered and were assembling in Inverness to start their military training but more were urgently needed to bring the battalion's fighting force up to the thousand men required to be sent to France.

On Wednesday 12th August, Angus MacLeod and Donny Nicolson travelled to the Portree recruiting office on the Isle of Skye and took their Oath of Allegiance, promising to defend His Majesty, Heirs and Successors against all enemies. With the formalities over, they were ordered to take the ferry to Kyle of Lochalsh and from there, make their way by train to Inverness. The journey across the Highlands from Skye to Inverness was a huge first step for these naïve young men who had never yet been so far from home and as they tried to settled back in their seats and relax, the knots in their stomachs grew tighter. The clacketty-clack of the rotating wheels on the single-track should have lulled them into a dozy sleep but the seats were uncomfortable and the carriages shuddered and swayed from side to side as the huge engine spluttered and coughed its way through the mountains and glens, spewing sulphur and stream into the summer air. Their jangled nerves were a far cry from the jolly bonhomie of the first guns of the season lying hidden in the butts, waiting for a covey of rapid-flying grouse to dart into the firing line. Before long the peace of the Highlands was shattered by the sound of guns firing lead into feathers and flesh. Scores of dead grouse tumbled to the ground where they lay motionless in the flowering heather but those who made it through the barrage swooped down to the ground where they rested until eventually being flushed out by keen-nosed dogs and driven towards another line of butts.

For the last few miles of the journey east, the train cruised along the southern bank of the Beauly Firth until eventually it came to a halt in Inverness.

"Where do we go from here?" Donny shouted, trying to be heard above the noise of hundreds of young men thronging the railway station and spilling aimlessly out into the town.

"I've no idea," Angus replied, never having seen so many people assembled in one place before. The crush was suffocating.

"I can't stand this," he added, lifting his small bag above his head and shoving his way through the crowd. "Come on, Donny, let's ask where we're meant to be."

They wove their way deftly round a bottleneck of recent arrivals who were milling aimlessly on the platform, thoughtlessly blocking the exit. The whole town seemed to have erupted into a state of chaos but eventually the two friends managed to break through and find an officer who was standing on the kerb holding a clipboard.

"We're looking for Perth Street," Donny said in Gaelic.

"What's that you said?" replied the officer in English.

"You'll have to speak up. With this noisy racket going on, can't hear a word you're saying."

"We're looking for Perth Street," Angus repeated in English.

The man glanced down at his list of names.

"Perth Street. Yup, here it is. You must be 4th Camerons. Go straight up Academy Street and on into Chapel Street, then take the third turning on the left. You can't miss it."

Inverness was teeming with soldiers and civilians criss-crossing its narrow streets looking for their Regimental Headquarters and billets. It took Donny and Angus over twenty minutes to reach the tall, granite building, by which time a queue had formed outside. When eventually they arrived at the front door, they were ushered into a side room and told to strip naked, six at a time.

There was no question of refusing the order, so reluctantly the six new recruits took off their clothes and sat down in a state of shock, deeply embarrassed by their public nakedness. When the Medical Officer finally opened the door, he was faced with a row of shivering boys with hunched shoulders and arms firmly crossed across their laps in an attempt to cover their private parts.

"Stand to attention!" he barked. "Straight backs and hands by your sides."

There was a moment of agonising shame as each recruit revealed his full naked body to everyone in the room.

"You there, get off your arse!" the officer cried, spotting a young recruit who had refused to stand up. "You're about to go to France, not the Garden of Eden, so don't expect anyone to hand you a fig leaf!"

The humiliated lad stood up and began to cry but the Medical Officer ignored him.

"Angus MacLeod of Kilbackie!"

"That's me," came the soft, sheepish reply.

"It's 'Yes sir!' to you, boy," barked the officer.

"Yes, sir!" Angus repeated, standing to attention.

"Speak up, lad! I can't hear a word you're saying."

"Yes, sir!"

Angus felt extremely exposed standing in front of the officer who didn't seem to notice anything unusual and began writing up his notes:

Birth – Kilbackie, Skye
Age – 18
Next of Kin – Murdo MacLeod – father
Occupation – crofter
Height – 5 feet 8 inches
Weight – 9 stone 8 pounds
Colouring – blue eyes / black hair

The doctor proceeded to carry out a full public examination, feeling down his spine, listening to his chest and lungs, testing his eyes, checking his teeth and inspecting his legs.

Angus could hear the other recruits giggling as he

hopped across the room, first on one leg, then on the other.

"Stop the giggling," the doctor said dryly. "This is no laughing matter. When you miserable specimens reach France, you will have to say 'Auf Wiedersehen' to privacy and get used to eating, sleeping and crapping in front of each other. Size won't matter, but survival will. And for those who don't know what 'Auf Wiedersehen' means, ask a German when you meet one!"

There was a deathly hush.

"Next!"

Donny was far less self-conscious when his turn came to be examined and once they had left the room, he turned to his friend.

"You should have seen your face, Angus, when you were told to strip off in front of everyone. You looked really shocked!"

"I was," Angus replied. "I had no idea becoming a soldier would involve taking off my clothes!"

Donny burst out laughing as they made their way to an adjoining room where a sergeant asked if they were willing to sign Army Form E624, giving their consent to fight in France or anywhere else overseas.

Without hesitating, both boys signed the form and were then led next door to be kitted out from piles of uniform lying on long trestle tables.

Here they were measured and handed a Cameron of Erracht kilt, a khaki jacket, a blue-grey cotton shirt and finally, a webbing belt complete with ammo pouches, water bottle, bayonet and helve carrier. They were also issued with leather studded ankle boots, khaki hose, garters and spats.

Pinned on their Glengarry was the battalion's emblem of St Andrew holding the saltire and surrounded by a wreath of thistles.

By the time Donny and Angus walked out of Perth Street, they had been transformed into uniformed soldiers of 4th Cameron Highlanders and a week later sixty seven troop trains packed with 17,000 Highland soldiers of the Territorial Force arrived in Bedford for three months' training.

CHAPTER 3

Bedford, October 1914

The skirl of bagpipes could be heard throughout the town as the new arrivals marched in formation down Bedford High Street. Large crowds lined the streets as a mark of the town's appreciation and the mayor and local dignitaries warmly welcomed the troops with a few short speeches. Tradespeople were pleased with the extra business and landladies made sure their young lodgers, many of whom had never been away from home before, were well looked after and given regular hot meals and baths.

Donny and Angus were billeted with Mrs Wilson and her two children, Annie aged nine and Frank aged seven whose father, Eric, a reservist in the 3rd Battalion, the Bedfordshire Regiment, had already been sent to Landguard Fort, Felixstowe to provide coastal defence against the threat of invasion. Mrs Wilson's marriage was one of convenience which many thought would fail but having been born poor and blessed with beauty, this extremely attractive Cockney from Cheapside taught herself 'received pronunciation' and took a pride in her appearance, effortlessly playing the role of the bank manager's wife and charming the clients with her wit and good humour.

Mr Wilson's pride in his beautiful wife only lasted until the children were born. Selfish and emotionally needy, he demanded his wife's undivided attention and when she focussed on the needs of Annie and Frank, he became unreasonably moody, withdrawing to the front room to read his newspaper and complete the daily crossword.

Gradually he began to go out more after work and it didn't take long for Mrs Wilson to suspect that he had found a mistress but in her pragmatic way, she accepted this arrangement as long as her husband continued to provide for her and the children.

Starved of attention and romance, she quickly became fascinated by the enigmatic young men from the rugged North with their colourful kilts and mournful music. Stories of murder and passion in the glens and castles of their remote Highland homeland spread like wildfire among the housewives of Bedford whose monotonous lives had grown dull with daily chores and marital neglect.

She knew she should have consulted her husband before billeting the Highlanders but fearing a negative reply, she decided to go ahead without his permission.

It was her first act of rebellion as a dutiful wife.

Many times during the small hours of the night, her mind would drift into forbidden territory and she wondered what life without Eric would be like. She dreamt of moving to Devon and running a small guest house overlooking pristine white sands where, every morning, she would wake up to the wild cries of seagulls and the sound of waves lapping on a deserted beach. Her cottage would be thatched with an enchanting garden full of hollyhocks, stocks, sweet Williams and foxgloves and on summer days, she would serve cream teas in the shade of an old apple tree.

Divorce was out of the question but if something awful were to happen to her husband during the war, she wondered if she would have the confidence to leave Bedford and fulfil her dreams with the children in Devon.

When eventually Angus and Donny knocked on the door of her neat terraced home, she knew they were home-loving, well-brought-up boys who were used to work and wouldn't cause her family any trouble. Apart from finding their accent difficult to understand, she appreciated their smiles and good humour and welcomed them warmly into her home.

"Your room is up here," she said, leading them up a steep flight of wooden stairs. Moving along the narrow landing, Mrs Wilson opened the first door on the right.

The two boys stared in amazement at the small, sparsely furnished bedroom with glazed windows.

"Come this way," she added, squeezing past her two guests and opening the door onto a glistening, white bathroom.

The white bathtub, basin and lavatory shone in the

shafts of sunlight that streamed through the east-facing window onto the lino floor.

Modern living in Bedford was a far cry from the dark, airless homes they had left behind on Skye and it didn't take Donny long to immerse himself in Bedford's recreational life. He adored films and spent most of his free time in the lively Empire Cinema with its plush interior and comfortable red upholstered seats.

It was a magical world of fantasy and humour; a place where he could relax and escape the memories of his father.

His favourite film, 'Kid Auto Races at Venice' never failed to make him laugh — in fact it was so funny he watched it five times with his latest girlfriend, Edith Taylor. It featured a small-moustached, derby-hatted, bamboo-caned Little Tramp, played by Charlie Chaplin, who wore oversized shoes and kept getting in the way of the camera and interfering with the baby-cart race.

The funny films helped him forget the past but the tense cliff-hangers in the series 'The Perils of Pauline' left him clinging to the edge of his seat in a state of heightened anxiety.

Angus, on the other hand, had no interest in the cinema. He relished solitude and took great pleasure walking along the towpath by the River Great Ouse as it meandered its way through Bedford before spreading out over the water meadows. He loved the pastoral villages where thatched whitewashed cottages nestled around historic stone churches and ancient pubs.

Although the wild flowers were fast fading, there were still a few red campions, ragged robins and yarrows adding colour to the weary grass. Swallows and martins gathered in their hundreds ahead of their migration south and the first wigeon and hen harriers had arrived to overwinter in the marshes.

Angus had no desire to exchange this idyllic world for war.

The routine of army life suited him and he used his free time to explore the English countryside, visit the Public Library and write long letters home describing the minutiae of his daily existence. As he grew more content, he became increasingly aware of a rift growing between himself and Donny.

Bedford offered a wide selection of distractions to the soldiers billeted in its midst; and recruits like Donny, embraced their new-found freedom by flocking to the hostelries, dance halls and cinemas. As the days turned to weeks, many young Presbyterians began to fear God less and love life more.

Things came to ahead one morning at breakfast when Donny shuffled sleepily into the kitchen after a heavy drinking session the night before. He had flouted Mrs Wilson's house rules by returning home late and drunk and to make matters worse, he crashed his way upstairs waking Annie who screamed in terror convinced the Germans had landed and were going to kill her. The uproar woke Mrs Wilson and

Frank and it took much of the night to persuade the children they were safe and the Germans were nowhere near Bedford. Gradually the panic died down and the soothing words of their mother lulled the children back to sleep.

Angus insisted Donny should apologise to their landlady for the unseemly midnight disturbance but he was met with a shrug of the shoulders and a bowed head.

It was then he noticed the torn kilt.

"What's happened to your kilt?" he asked but Donny pretended not to hear and dragged his chair noisily across the floor to the breakfast table.

"Your kilt, Donny! What's happened to it?"

"Nothing," came the blunt reply.

"Well, it looks as if someone's taken a chunk out of it," Angus continued, looking at the frayed edges of the tear.

"Why would anyone do that?"

"I don't know, you tell me," Angus seethed, beginning to raise his voice. "Don't lie to me, Donny. Something's not right and I want to know what it is."

Before he could get an answer, Mrs Wilson came in carrying a full coal scuttle.

"Is everything all right?" she asked.

Donny put his arm around her waist. "Everything's fine; now let me help you with that," he said, lifting the heavy scuttle over to the range.

"You're not cross with me for tearing my kilt, are you, Mrs Wilson?"

His good looks and charm made her laugh and there was the tiniest hint of a blush.

"Of course not," she replied, gazing down at his knees and torn kilt. "If you like, I'll mend the rip and make it look as good as new. It shouldn't take long. Just leave the kilt with me when you're not wearing it."

Angus prayed Donny wouldn't make a suggestive remark, but to his credit he held back and, with a smile that lit up the room, he thanked Mrs Wilson for the generous offer.

"Has anyone told you you're an angel?" he chuckled, keeping his arm around her waist.

"Flattery will get you nowhere," she replied, clearly delighted that her offer to mend the kilt had been accepted.

"Before you go," Donny added, releasing his grip, "I just want to warn you to be careful when you go out shopping. There are Russians in town."

"Go on with you, you little scamp," she giggled, "there aren't any Russians in Bedford."

"Oh yes there are," he replied. "A man walked into the post office the other day and the postmaster asked where he was from and he replied 'Ross-shire!'"

The two of them roared with laughter and even Angus had to smile.

"Ah Donny, you'll be the death of me, you will, with all your stories," she cried and left the room with a slight spring in her step.

"Well?" Angus persisted. "Now Mrs Wilson has gone, perhaps you'll tell me what really happened to your kilt?"

"Let's just say a young lady wanted a keepsake and leave it at that."

"But what's going to happen at the next inspection when the Colonel sees that a chunk of your kilt is missing? He'll probably put you on jankers." Angus said earnestly. "Joining the army is no joke, Donny."

"Well, let's just hope he doesn't notice," Donny replied casually. "The kilt aprons we were issued with last week should hide the damage and with any luck no-one will be any the wiser."

Things came to a head the next morning when Angus woke at five-thirty and discovered Donny's bed hadn't been slept in.

Disbelief turned to fury and within five minutes, he was dressed, out of the house and tearing down the street, taking in short sharp breaths of frosty air as he ran.

He needed to find Donny before the six-thirty roll call, to stop him being confined to barracks and having to endure a dawn-to-dusk timetable of punishment parades, kit and uniform inspections and menial tasks.

The school playing fields were slowly filling up with sleepy Highlanders, heads bowed and arms wrapped firmly around their chests in an attempt to keep warm.

By six-twenty Donny still hadn't been found and Angus was on the verge of giving up when he saw a familiar figure leaning against a tree, casually smoking and talking to a pretty young girl with long brown hair. He looked up and caught Angus' eye, waving as if he hadn't a care in the world.

Angus sprinted over to where Donny stood and, without giving the girl a second glance, grabbed his collar and hauled him onto the parade ground.

CHAPTER 4

"You left in a hurry this morning," Mrs Wilson remarked brightly, placing a cooked breakfast on the table.

"I had an early duty," Angus lied. "I hope I didn't disturb you."

"No, no," she said. "I was already awake."

She fussed around the table making sure there was enough toast and tea then left the room.

"Well?" Angus quizzed. "What happened to you last night?"

"I don't think it's any of your business," Donny replied with a mouth full of bacon and egg.

"Now pour me out a cup of tea, Angus, there's a dear."

His flippant manner and strange mood put Angus on his guard.

"Look, Donny, I don't want a fight but I think you owe me an explanation."

Donny put down his knife and fork and stared directly into his friend's concerned face.

"I'm in love Angus and have found the person I want to spend the rest of my life with."

"Who is she?" Angus asked, trying to disguise his astonishment.

"Her name is Edith Taylor. She's eighteen years old

and works for the Adkin family who own the gun shop in the High Street. There isn't much else to say, other than that I intend to marry her."

Angus thought very hard before commenting — he knew Donny had a volatile temper and wished to keep the conversation as civil as possible.

"Listen to me, Donny. I believe you when you say you're in love but we're soldiers, billeted in a town hundreds of miles from home and in a few weeks we'll be leaving for France. This is hardly the time to talk about marrying a girl you've only just met."

"She's not a girl, she's a woman and her name is Edith," came the terse reply.

"Well," Angus said, determined to keep the peace. "Think hard before you raise Edith's hopes. Have you thought of the changes she would have to face if she returned with you to Skye?

"If you're seriously thinking of marrying her, don't you think you should sit down and explain some of the differences between the crofting way of life and Bedford, after all, it's only fair she has some idea what to expect.

"Perhaps you should tell her that the wet weather makes our houses damp, there's no internal sanitation or running water, fuel has to be dug out of the ground by hand, food is hard to grow and the diet is limited and repetitive.

"She should also know that dancing, pubs and other forms of entertainment are frowned upon."

"I don't see why she should know all that," Donny

gibed, shifting restlessly on his chair as his anger increased.

Angus ignored his tetchiness.

"Because love doesn't conquer everything and no matter how much she thinks she loves you, she will have to work hard on the land in all weathers, learn Gaelic and endure your father's temper. Remember, once she arrives on Skye she will have no means of returning home."

Donny put his hands to his ears, determined not to hear truths that might ruin his chance of happiness.

"Since when have you become such an expert in love?" he asked.

It was true that Angus had no experience of love but he was a great observer and listener.

"Why not wait until the war's over and then ask her to marry you? You won't have long to wait; they say the war will be over by Christmas.

"If she's half as good as you say she is then you are a lucky man," he said, giving his friend a good-natured punch.

Donny kept hold of his fork and pushed the last mouthful of bacon and egg restlessly around the plate. Eventually he stopped playing with his food, took a sip of tea and said, "I envy you, Angus."

Angus couldn't think of anything enviable about his life and waited for Donny to explain.

"You're always so calm and in control. I wish I had your peace of mind instead of the mess that's in my head. I'm so scared, Angus. Scared of being a soldier and scared of my own company. Does that sound silly?"

Angus shook his head.

"No, it doesn't sound silly," he replied, remembering the times Donny had arrived at school covered in bruises. The whole community knew about the violence in the Nicolson family but chose to turn a blind eye, considering it a private matter between the minister and his wife. Although weeks of training had helped erase many hurtful memories, Donny still had panic attacks at night and felt frightened during the day.

By early December, 4th Cameron Highlanders had been transformed into a fit, fighting unit ready for action. The Germans had begun their offensive in September and were determined to capture as much ground as possible before taking Paris but were halted by the French at the river Marne. The Allied and German armies spent the autumn months of 1914 trying to outflank each other as they fought their way north towards the Channel ports.

Both sides had consolidated their Front Lines by digging trenches, building reinforced concrete emplacements and laying miles of barbed wire.

As the people of Bedford prepared for Christmas, the soldiers living among them focussed their minds on moving across the Channel to help the British Expeditionary Force break the impasse.

CHAPTER 5

A week before Christmas, Angus woke up shaking and sweating. His eyes stung and every muscle in his body ached as fever set his flesh on fire. He tried to get out of bed but collapsed back under the blankets shivering.

At two in the afternoon, there was a gentle tap and Mrs Wilson timidly poked her head round the door.

"I don't want to seem nosy," she apologised, "but you weren't down for breakfast this morning and I didn't hear you leave for training. I was wondering if everything is all right."

Angus looked at her with half-closed eyes and sighed.

"I don't feel very well but don't worry, I'll soon be back on my feet," he said. "Thanks for your concern."

When Donny walked into the bedroom later that evening, he knew something was wrong.

"You look awful," he said, picking up the glass of water Mrs Wilson had placed on the floor next to the camp bed. "Try to lift your head and take a sip."

He held the glass up to Angus' parched lips and encouraged him to drink, but Angus turned his head away and let out a long moan. All the glands in his neck hurt and he found it difficult opening his mouth.

"I can't move," he whispered.

The sight of his distress unnerved Donny and he began to panic, calling downstairs to Mrs Wilson who was reading all about the German bombardment on Hartlepool in which over a hundred and thirty civilians had been killed and hundreds more injured. Mrs Wilson had bought a copy of the *Daily Express* and was horrified to read that enemy warships had fired over a thousand shells on the town just as parents and children were leaving home for work and school.

"It's barbaric," she muttered, gazing across at Annie and Frank who were playing a quiet game of Ludo. "I hope our brave boys give those savages a jolly good hiding!"

Donny's cry for help broke through her thoughts and she dashed upstairs to find out what was wrong.

"It's Angus!" he fretted. "I think he's really ill."

Inside the dimly lit bedroom, the air was musty and acrid and smelled of fever. Mrs Wilson had already nursed her children through scarlet fever, mumps, chickenpox and measles and knew exactly what to do. She adopted an air of authority, left the room and returned a few minutes later with fresh bed linen, a sponge and a face flannel.

"Hold these for me," she told Donny, who was standing by the wall in an inactive state of shock. "I'll let you know if I want any help but at the moment there is nothing you can do."

Mrs Wilson took control of the situation in a wonderfully calm way. She rolled Angus gently onto the floor, stripped the sweat-soaked sheets off his camp bed and replaced them with clean ones, ignoring his cries of pain as the winter air cut through his burning body. With all the tenderness of a mother, she whispered soothing words to coax him back onto the bed. Taking it in turns, she cooled his face with a damp flannel and moistened his lips with a sponge.

"What are you doing?" Donny asked, more sharply than he meant. "Can't you see he's in pain? Why don't you leave him alone and let him sleep?"

"He'll only be able to sleep if he's cool, so I'm trying to bring his temperature down," she explained calmly.

"What's wrong with him?" Donny asked, trying to hide the panic in his voice.

"I'm not sure, but it looks like measles. Apparently there's been an outbreak in Bedford and several of my friends' children have already been struck down."

She looked across at Donny's crestfallen face.

"Don't look so glum," she continued, trying to sound comforting. "It's a horrid thing to have but it's not the end of the world — now I'm going to fetch the doctor," she added, passing the flannel and sponge over to Donny. "Keep dabbing his face to cool him down and if the flannel gets too warm, run it under the cold tap. Don't forget to trickle water into his mouth with the sponge and keep his lips moist."

By nightfall, Angus's fever continued to ravage his body. He showed no signs of improvement, in fact, the high temperature triggered a delirium which distorted his mind, creating terrifying dreams.

"I don't want to let my parents down by dying," he cried out in distress. "Please someone, help me!"

Eventually, at eight-thirty, the doctor arrived and examined his patient.

"It's definitely measles," he announced solemnly. "There's been an epidemic sweeping through the camp and as the virus is unknown in the Western Isles, the Highland regiments have been particularly badly hit. I've seen scores of fit young men like you two brought to their knees and they have all taken weeks to recover.

I'm afraid I'll have to send you to the Goldrington Road hospital where you will be properly looked after and your friend here will have to go into quarantine at Howbury.

"You can be sure of one thing: it'll be at least three weeks before you'll be fit enough to go to the Front."

The doctor was right. It took Angus four weeks to regain full strength and he was one of the lucky ones. Fourteen of his comrades died in the epidemic: many of them were buried in Bedford's Foster Hill Road Cemetery and were never repatriated to the Highlands.

It wasn't until the early evening of 19th February 1915 that 4th Cameron Highlanders finally sailed from Southampton to Le Havre.

The long drawn-out goodbyes to Edith, Mrs Wilson and Bedford town had been particularly painful for Donny and it didn't take him long to confide in Angus that he no longer wanted to be a soldier. Bedford had shown him, albeit briefly, the happiness and security he had craved but never knew existed.

As they boarded ship, Angus sensed his friend's deep melancholy and decided to give him space to brood.

It was obvious that leaving Bedford had badly affected Donny's morale, and not even the sight of his battalion with their heads held high and chests puffed out, marching in perfect formation to the sounds of a full pipe and drum band, could shake him out of his depression.

To make matters worse, the seven-hour channel crossing was rough and by mid-way the wind had strengthened to Gale Force 9, pounding the troop ship and forcing her to pitch and roll like debris in an inky void.

From time to time, a large moon slid silently under the storm clouds and beamed its luminous rays onto the ship's decks before being swallowed back into the black night sky.

Donny had never liked boats and his stomach heaved every time the ship's bow climbed a threatening wave before sliding over its crest and crashing into the darkness, spraying the deck with white foam and ice-cold water.

"I can't take any more of this," he moaned, clutching his empty stomach.

"Leave me here to die, Angus," he added, spluttering bright green bile over his kilt and bare knees. "At least France won't be as bad as this."

The ship's movements continued to make Donny throw up and retch until he had nothing left to give.

"War won't be worse than this, will it?" he repeated, clutching the hem of Angus's kilt to steady himself.

Angus had no words of consolation. His mind was full of the recurring dream that had recently started to haunt his sleep. He dreamt he was back in Kilbackie, walking the meadows on a beautiful spring morning. Lying ahead of him in the grass was a solitary lamb surrounded by hundreds of hooded crows, all frantically hopping up and down as if performing a ritualistic dance.

Angus desperately tried to reach the distressed animal but the cackling crows ruffled their feathers and blocked his way, stabbing the air with their huge pointed beaks. The nearer he got to the lamb, the heavier his walking became until finally he could only move by dragging one foot slowly in front of the other.

The lamb's agonized bleating continued as Angus' movements became more laboured.

"I'm coming! I'm coming!" he wanted to shout, but no noise came from his mouth.

When, finally, he reached the poor creature, he cradled it in his arms and sang it Gaelic lullabies in hushed whispers until the bleating and twitching stopped.

It was only as he laid it back among the bluebells and clover that he noticed its eyes and tongue were missing.

He looked up and saw a black cloud of fluttering

wings hovering over his head and an army of beaks preparing for the kill.

Angus tried to protect his face with his hands, but they remained pinned to his side and, with tears streaming down his cheeks, he waited for the first pecks to reach his eyes.

He always woke up at this point, drenched in sweat and trembling like a leaf.

CHAPTER 6

Northern France, February 1915

Weak and shaky, the Cameron Highlanders disem-
barked from the troop ship at one o'clock in the
morning of 20th February and immediately started
the four-mile march to No. 1 camp where they were
quartered in white bell tents, each sleeping fifteen
men.

The unfamiliar sounds of the wind beating against
the canvas and the ghostly hoots of an owl in the
nearby wood unnerved those who weren't used to
sleeping out of doors. The cold night air soon began
to fill with the sound of anxious men coughing.

"You awake?" Donny whispered.

"Aye," came the reply.

"D-do you really think the Front is going to be
bad?" he stuttered.

"Get some sleep, Donny. We've got a five-mile hike
to the railway station tomorrow."

By midnight, a deep silence hung over the camp
and the north-easterly gale finally blew itself out,
leaving a clear sky ablaze with a million stars.

At two-thirty in the morning all fitful dreams and
restless movements were abruptly interrupted by a
lone bugle sounding the Reveille.

Bemused and bleary-eyed, the young recruits gathered their possessions and, after a quick brew, marched with little enthusiasm to the station, where they sat huddled under the platform roof waiting for a train to take them to Merville.

Minutes turned to hours and the weather steadily deteriorated.

No explanation was given for the long delay.

Eventually, Donny stood up and walked over to Iain MacKinnon, the piper from Glendale. He whispered something in his ear and before long the haunting sound of the lone piper filled the air and through the rain and mist, Angus could once again hear the plaintive cries of curlews on the Kilbackie estate and the mournful mewing of buzzards above Rosvaig Head.

Donny started to sing in a clear, quiet tenor voice:

"There's many a man of the Cameron clan
That has followed his chief to the field
He has sworn to support him or die by his side
For a Cameron never can yield
Tis the march of the Cameron men
'Tis the march, 'tis the march
'Tis the march of the Cameron men.
I hear the pibroch sounding, sounding
Deep o'er the mountain and glen
While light springing footsteps
Are trampling the heath.
Oh proudly they walk but each Cameron knows

He may tread on the heather no more
But boldly he follows his chief to the field
Where his laurels were gathered before."

Men, crammed together on the platform, were moved to tears as the music brought back memories of the glens and islands they had recently left behind.

In the silence that followed, green shoots of fear began to take root.

They had joined the Territorial Army in their thousands, fired up by tales of valour and Scotland's proud military history. Stories of Germans mutilating Belgian babies and raping young girls spread across the Hebridean townships and overnight, boys seemed to turn into men, willing to fight to the death to defend their Highland way of life.

Donny had never wanted to fight.

He had left Skye to escape his father's temper and hoped adventure would numb his pain and block out his memories. Despite his fear, he always felt brave in his uniform and wore it with pride, reckoning the Cameron of Erracht tartan was the smartest on parade. Thanks to Mrs Wilson's neat needlework, the tear in his kilt didn't show as he marched, cheered on by enthusiastic crowds waving small flags and handkerchiefs.

Army life in Bedford had transformed him from an underweight, nervous boy with dark circles round his eyes and bruises over his body into a fit, well-fed soldier who had met the girl he intended to marry.

He would never forget the way the town had changed his life and given him hope.

The stirring sound of the pipes soon began to work their magic and as the music seeped into his soul, Donny began to crawl out of his melancholy.

Standing upright next to Iain, he drew the cold, damp air deep into his lungs, shut his eyes and started to sing:

'Speed, bonnie boat, like a bird on the wing
Onward! the sailors cry;
Carry the lad that's born to be King
Over the sea to Skye.

Loud the winds howl, loud the waves roar
Thunderclaps rend the air;
Baffled, our foes stand by the shore
Follow they will not dare.

Many's the lad fought on that day
Well the claymore could wield;
When the night came, silently lay
Dead on Culloden's field.

Burned are their homes, exile and death
Scatter the loyal men;
Yet ere the sword cool in the sheath
Charlie will come again.'

By the time he had sung the song through twice, everyone was joining in, swaying from side to side with linked arms. The singing completely transformed the atmosphere on the station platform and when, at last, the train finally arrived, morale was high.

"'urry up boys," a sergeant shouted. "Get yeselves inside. Come on now, more can fit into this wagon."

One by one, they scrambled into the enclosed box-cars and edged forward as more followed behind. The crush was unbearable and Donny shouted at the sergeant that they were full, but he took no notice.

"Don't talk daft," he replied. "You're only 'alf full. Keep going, lads. You there, step on board, there's plenty of room."

Eventually forty men were packed tightly into the windowless wagon and the doors closed.

Tempers could easily have flared during the long, monotonous journey but everyone seemed optimistic and bore their discomfort with admirable patience.

Eating, singing, smoking and telling jokes helped pass the time and kept spirits high.

"Did you hear about the young lad from Harris who decided to wash his dirty underwear and socks?" asked Donny, trying not to laugh.

"No, we haven't heard about the young lad from Harris who decided to wash his dirty underwear and socks," came the chorus reply.

"He put them in a china bowl, gave them a good scrubbing, then watched in horror as they swirled around the bowl and disappeared."

"Why did they disappear, I hear you ask?" he continued, then paused before answering.

"He pulled the chain!"

There was a roar of laughter from everyone except George Mackay, who showed no sign of being amused.

"The china bowl wasn't a cup of tea, George, you fool," Donny explained, when the chortling had died down.

George looked po-faced.

"It was a piss pot!" he chuckled and again the whole carriage broke out into hysterical giggles.

Much to everyone's amusement, humourless and dour George Mackay had never experienced teasing before and it soon became obvious that he didn't like it. The son of a Free Presbyterian minister, he lacked empathy and compassion but earnestly believed that God had set him apart from the sinful world in which he lived. There was something insufferably irritating about the young zealot's beliefs, but to his credit, he showed remarkable discipline and never once compromised on his daily prayer and Bible study.

Swearing and blasphemy were a complete anathema to George and whenever he heard someone swear or blaspheme in his presence, he would rise up in indignation and chastise the offenders, warning them against the perils of sin, hell and damnation.

When eventually the train drew into Merville station, the exhausted soldiers staggered out and stretched their aching bodies.

"About bloody time!" John Ross cursed within earshot of George. "I suppose we've now got to march another bleedin' four miles to reach our billet."

"Don't swear, Ross," George chided. "May God forgive you and save your soul from hell."

"I'm in bloody hell!" came John's furious reply, "so what difference does it make? You answer me that one, holy bloody Mackay."

CHAPTER 7

Northern France, May 1915

The huge Allied bombardment started at three o'clock in the morning. Thousands of shells screeched from behind the British trenches, exploding with devastating effect in or behind the German lines. Twisted wire, body parts, guns and horses were thrown into the choking air filled with clouds of green, black and white smoke.

Angus sat huddled in a waterlogged trench with his eyes closed, trying to remember his life back in Kilbackie. His nerves were jangled and the thuds and explosions were slowly destroying his mind. He hadn't slept for days and was physically and mentally exhausted, living unwashed in a cramped ditch overrun with rats.

He thought back to the times he sat in Kilbackie's little whitewashed church and listened to sermons on God's vengeance, not understanding what it meant until he reached the mudflats of France where he witnessed the true horrors of Hell opening wide its gates and the Lord descending like a whirlwind, unleashing his fury on all flesh and killing many.

Traumatised by the events unfolding around him, he glanced down the trench and noticed a distraught soldier sitting with his head buried in his hands, sobbing inconsolably. His body jerked so violently he looked as if he were having a fit.

"Donny?" Angus enquired, edging his way towards the broken boy.

The reply was a whimpering sniffle.

"Donny, it's me, Angus. Come on now, no more crying, we've got work to do."

His kind words were lost in the noise of battle so, very gently, Angus put his arm round his friend's heaving shoulders and drew him close, comforting him by stroking his hair as a mother would her child.

After a few minutes, he leant over and shouted, "Come on, Donny, we've got to get ready for the attack so whatever you do, keep your head down."

"I can't move," the young soldier replied, his vacant green eyes staring blankly into the distance. "My legs hurt."

Angus helped his friend onto his feet and together they stumbled to join the line.

"I'm not a coward," Donny sobbed. "It's just I've got a splitting headache and pains in my legs."

"I know you're not. You've got trench fever, Donny, and should be in hospital. You're one of the bravest men I know and after this charge, I'll make sure you are properly cared for."

Angus experienced an intense, unexpected flash of anger, which made him cry out and punch the soft earth with his bare knuckles. He riled against the injustice of sending a sick man into battle.

He blamed the government, the army and God and ached for peace.

Peace once again to hear the skylark sing above the early purple orchids and tufted vetch in the Kilbackie meadows.

Peace to hear the silence of the night sky ablaze with constellations and to watch the Aurora Borealis spread its swirling green and blue lights over Lewis.

"When we're told to charge, Donny," he shouted, "run straight across the open countryside towards the enemy trenches and think of the times we used to run up to Craggy Broch at sheep gathering time and disturb the grouse. Do you remember how their wingbeats whirred as they flew up from under our feet, giving us the fright of our lives? Concentrate on familiar sounds, Donny, and don't forget to listen out for corncrakes."

He gave his friend's cheek a gentle pat, then moved forward keeping his head down.

"First line, charge!" barked the command.

The first row of men scrambled 'over the top' to the rousing music of the pipes played by Iain MacKinnon.

Kenny MacLean fell back with a bullet through his forehead before he had time to clear the trench and young Lachlan MacKenzie lost half his face as he sprinted across the battlefield.

Donny was next.

"Second line, charge!"

He clambered over the top and started to run aimlessly into the enemy fire. Bullets, shrapnel, bone and flesh whistled past him but he kept running, praying that death would be instant and painless.

"Keep going," he repeated to himself over and over again. "It'll soon be over, just keep going."

By the time Angus went over the top, his friend was nowhere to be seen.

Darting at full speed like a grouse on the moor, Angus ran forward then flung himself onto the ground, pausing for a few seconds before continuing.

The Allied bombardment had not been as successful as planned. Despite the huge amount of shelling, some of the German artillery and machine-gun emplacements were still intact and had opened up a murderous barrage against the Cameron Highlanders.

Angus continued running across the boggy marshland until he reached an open ditch full of thick, brown water. It was too wide to clear carrying a heavy backpack, although some taller, stronger men had tried and succeeded. The only way for Angus to clear the ditch was to half-wade and half-swim to the other side, then clamber up the slippery bank and carry on the attack.

At the top of the ditch he heard what sounded like the terrifying night screams of a red fox but as he crawled forward, he became aware that the agonising noise came from a crumpled body writhing in the crimson mud, its severed, twisted leg lying a few feet away.

The soldier was struggling to breathe and was bleeding profusely.

"Help me!" he shrieked. "For God's sake, someone help me!"

Angus paused, recognising something familiar in the voice.

"Donny?" he asked, unsure if the mud-splattered face was indeed his friend.

"Angus? Is it really you?" the young soldier cried, stretching out his hand to feel his friend's face. "It's my leg, Angus, I can't feel it. What's happened?"

"You're fine," came the reassuring reply, "but I need to get you out of danger and patch you up a bit."

Behind them lay the water-filled ditch where drowning and wounded men pleaded with God not to abandon them. Most harrowing of all were the whimpering gasps of the contorted and disfigured bodies who, through their tears, begged their mothers to hold their hands and stop the pain.

One by one their voices faltered and became fainter until they were no more.

Theirs was the silence of a terrible death but eternal peace.

In front of Donny and Angus lay the lethal German machine guns which raked everything that moved.

Angus slithered low across the grass and, straining every muscle, hoisted a dead soldier into a sitting position then dropped him on top of an extended corpse to form a protective wall of flesh and kit.

Working quickly, he untied one of the dead soldier's belts and was on his way back to Donny when he noticed a couple of drones sticking up through the quagmire.

"Oh dear Lord," he cried. "Not Iain. Please don't let it be Iain."

He wiped the dirt off the soldier's face and saw the cloudy eyes of Iain MacKinnon staring back at him. Life back home without good-natured Iain was unthinkable; his prodigious talent brought gaity and mirth to every family celebration in Northern Skye and no ceilidh was complete without his lively playing of reels, waltzes and jigs.

Angus dug out the shattered pipes with his bare hands and tucked the bag gently under the dead piper's head, letting the drones and chanter hang away from the enemy's fire.

"Watch over Donny for me, Iain," he implored, blinking away the tears. "Don't let him die."

Donny's cries were becoming more urgent as he struggled to stay conscious. Angus wrapped the belt tightly round the jagged stump that had once been his leg and twisted it tighter and tighter until the tourniquet gripped the flesh and stemmed the flow of blood.

As long as Donny stayed out of the muddy water, he had a chance of survival.

"Donny, listen to me," Angus shouted. "I'm going to drag you behind the pile of bodies over there where you should be safe from bullets and shrapnel. Help will come, I promise, but you may have to wait until the battle has died down before the stretcher bearers can reach you."

He took two bottles of water and a couple of boxes of cigarettes from the dead soldiers and left them next to his friend.

"Don't leave me, Angus," Donny cried, tugging helplessly at his friend's sleeve. "Don't leave me here to die alone."

Angus lit a cigarette and placed it in Donny's mouth.

"Take a few puffs," he said encouragingly, "Then look into my eyes and nod if you understand what I am saying.

"You're not going to die, you're going to live, and when this awful war is over, you will marry Edith and take her home with you to Skye. You'll probably have ten children together and live to see your grand-children grow old."

Through tears of pain, he managed to fix his gaze on Angus and give a weak nod.

"And while you're waiting," Angus added, "listen out for a corncrake."

There was the merest hint of a smile as the young Highlander remembered summer days filled with the repetitive, rasping sound of corncrakes hiding in the rough grass and nettles around the crofts, their necks stretched high like blackbird pie funnels.

It was ludicrous to think of these shy, secretive grassland birds running across an open mud-filled battlefield.

"That's better," Angus said, thankful that Donny had managed a smile. "Stay focussed on that irritating little bird, Donny. Stay focussed and you'll survive this terrible war."

CHAPTER 8

Angus continued to crawl through the mud, trying to keep his head down and avoid the corpses that littered the battlefield. He had grown used to the sight of dead bodies, even the most mutilated ones, but he never got used to the heart-rending cries of the injured and dying. The terror and pain of their lonely deaths reminded him of the recurring nightmare that still haunted his sleep.

Every instinct in Angus' being wanted to comfort the dying but he knew the rules and proceeded to advance towards the barbed wire fence that separated him from the enemy. The first wave of soldiers to reach the fence faced a contorted, impenetrable mass of twisted metal. The only way to cross the barrier was to cover the spikes with trenchcoats and crawl over the top but the process was slow and the murderous rifle and machine-gun fire never let up. The advancing line of Highlanders grew thinner as the injured and dead fell onto a land devoid of compassion and humanity.

Many of the dead hung grotesquely on the wire 'like crows shot on a dyke'.

The high number of casualties suggested that a way through the wire had not yet been found and any attempt to cut a safe passage would end in further tragedy.

Every soldier capable of moving an arm or leg wriggled towards the safety of the ridge, without which the entire company would have been wiped out.

The survivors couldn't believe they were still alive.

"Bloody lice!" gasped John Ross, scratching his midriff as he lay prostrate on the mound next to George Mackay. "They'll be the death of me!"

Gordon Hamilton roared with laughter.

"Lice may eat you but they won't kill you, unlike those bloody Germans," he cursed, pointing to the other side of the mound. "If you want to experience death, be my guest and crawl to the top of this slope with your head held high!"

George MacKay gave the two men a disapproving scowl.

"Stop the swearing, you two," he pleaded. "It's vulgar and offensive. God will judge you for your sinful ways."

"Judge us for our sinful ways!" mimicked Hamilton. "Don't be so bloody righteous, George. Just because your father's a minister, it doesn't mean you have to be so high and mighty."

George looked at the two friends with an air of disdain but they ignored him. Life was too short.

They closed their ears to the relentless sound of machine guns hunting down their comrades and stretched out on a patch of green grass before drifting into a deep sleep.

Life in the cramped, rat-infested trenches was hard enough but the retching stench of decaying bodies, open latrines, vomit and sweat was unbearable and, to make matters worse, the filthy conditions provided the perfect breeding ground for lice. They lived in the pleats of the unwashed kilts and burrowed deep into the seams, clinging onto the wool with their claw-like legs.

Hopping freely from body to body, they feasted on blood, leaving blotchy red marks that itched. Many of the lice were infected with *Bartonella quintana*, a bacterium which spread disease through their faeces. If a soldier scratched a louse whilst it was feeding, he could inadvertently rub the infected faeces into the bite wound and go down with trench fever.

The symptoms of this debilitating disease were intense headaches, dizziness, painful shins and a raging temperature and although not fatal, it was serious enough to confine a sufferer to hospital for several months.

The lice were difficult to eradicate, but during quiet spells soldiers would remove their kilts and either run a lighted candle along each pleat or crack the lice between their thumb and index finger.

Lieutenant Colonel Sir Hugh Hollister had taken command of the unit at Merville and had been with his men every moment of the attack. He had miraculously survived the machine guns and the artillery onslaught and had been one of the first to reach the safety of the knoll where he immediately took control of morale and encouraged every survivor to rest.

Quietly spoken and unassuming, he was morally, spiritually and physically tough and there wasn't a man in the battalion who wouldn't have given his life for the Colonel.

"I want to thank each of you personally," he commended, in a firm, confident voice, "for the professional way you have performed your duty today. As Territorials you have chosen to leave home to assist the regular army in the defence of our country and your supreme effort and sacrifice has not gone unnoticed. We now need to regroup for one final push and pray the victory will be ours.

"We will stay here tonight and make a surprise attack on the enemy trench early tomorrow morning. Get as much rest as you can."

He took out his Bible and read part of Psalm 69 as the evening prayer.

'Oh Lord, deliver us out of the mire,
And let us not sink;
Let us be delivered from those who hate us,
And out of the deep waters.
Let not the floodwater overflow us,
Nor let the deep swallow us up;
And let not the pit shut its mouth on us.'

Angus' anger was still raw and although he repeated 'Amen' at the end of the psalm, he hadn't listened to a word the Colonel had said.

The mood of the men sheltering behind the knoll

grew sombre and tense as they rested ahead of the signal to charge.

"Campbell, Rennie and Macaulay," the Colonel whispered loudly. "May I have a word?"

The sleepy men rose and stumbled towards him.

"I want each of you to take a pair of bolt cutters and form a wiring party. Your objective is to widen the gap in the barbed wire between here and the enemy's trench so we can crawl through during tomorrow's attack. We've already lost enough men over the past twelve hours and I have no intention of losing any more unnecessarily.

"You will be working under cover of darkness and the Germans won't be expecting you, so as long as you keep very quiet and act quickly, you shouldn't come to any harm."

One by one the men slipped into the night across no-man's land and started cutting through the twisted wire that separated them from the enemy. It was nerve-wracking, painstaking work and the slightest suspicious sound or movement could easily have given their position away and ended their lives. The rain had thankfully stopped but the ground was wet and slippery and a cold wind blew, numbing their fingers. Progress was slow but eventually the exhausted Highlanders completed their task and returned to the knoll to find a patch of grass where they could lay their heads and close their bloodshot eyes. They could have slept forever, but after a couple of hours, just as daylight was breaking, the soldiers were woken and told to form a line ready for the attack.

When the signal finally came, Colonel Hollister and his men broke cover and stormed towards the enemy trench, uttering blood-curdling cries and brandishing fixed bayonets. The sight of marauding, kilted Scots caused panic among the few remaining Germans who were short of ammunition and whose Commanding Officer lay dead beside them. They started to abandon their trench and by the time 4th Camerons had breached the wire, it was empty, except for two very scared, wounded soldiers crouching with their hands held high above their heads.

"Keep your hands up," the Colonel ordered in a steady voice. "Stay exactly where you are and don't try anything foolish."

Colonel Hollister was tall and lean with thick, dark, wavy hair and soft brown eyes. He was only son of a baronet, an old Harrovian, a wrangler and a Cambridge blue and people found his natural self-confidence and courteous manner attractive.

To the casual onlooker, he was a privileged aristocrat who enjoyed all the advantages of an upper-class education but unknown to most, his family's estate was heavily in debt and existed on a knife-edge.

Hugh had no wish to fight and conflict wasn't in his nature but he had been brought up to believe in right and wrong and had a strong sense of duty. He was determined to sign up as an officer in a Highland regiment to honour his grandmother,

Annie MacKenzie who, at seventy-two, still lived on the Applecross Peninsula, where Hugh had spent many summers pursuing his passion for natural history. Immediately after war was declared, he had joined 2nd Battalion Seaforth Highlanders and moved to Harrow before being mobilised on 22nd August 1914 and sent to Boulogne. He saw action with the British Expeditionary Force at the Battle of the Marne and would have stayed with the Seaforths had he not been promoted to Lieutenant Colonel on the battlefield at the age of twenty-two and transferred to the Cameron Highlanders.

"MacGregor," he commanded his batman, "disarm those two Germans over there and check them thoroughly for hidden grenades or weapons. Watch their every move and don't trust them an inch. Take your time. We don't want any trouble."

The tousled, red-headed lad from Beauly did as he was ordered and cautiously approached the young Germans. He picked up their rifles and threw them back to where his fellow Highlanders were watching with bated breath. Having disarmed the men, he proceeded to pat their uniforms, feeling for hidden weapons.

It was the first time he had seen a German face to face and instead of the evil child molesters and rapists he had been told about, he saw two fair-haired, blue-eyed, pale and freckled young men about eighteen years old who could easily have been called Ruairidh or Angus.

Everything about them looked familiar and for a brief moment he forgot he was staring at the enemy and lowered his guard. This short lapse of concentration was all it took for one of the Germans to whip out a hidden revolver and take aim.

Still staring into the German's face, John MacGregor became aware of a grey muzzle pointing directly at his chest and realized that Fritz or Hans or whatever his name was, was going to kill him.

The bullet struck at point-blank range.

There was a gasp, followed by a stunned silence, as the tall, muscular man slid silently to the ground, never to breathe again.

Before Colonel Hollister could take full charge of the situation, Hamish Smith and four other soldiers took aim and emptied their magazines into the young Germans' chests, shoulders and heads.

Within seconds, three bodies lay in a twisted heap in the muddy trench and Colonel Hollister was furious.

"Smith, Buchanan, Hamilton, Ross and Rennie!" he shouted. "Pick up your spades and if need be use your bare hands to dig two graves for these young Germans. We may be at war but there is no excuse for barbaric behaviour. Do I make myself clear?"

There was a weak murmuring.

"Do I make myself clear?" he repeated, looking directly at the four men concerned.

"Yes, sir!" came the loud reply.

"Make sure every tiny speck of flesh, gut and brain

is buried with them. I don't want a trace of their death left inside this trench and when you've finished, tie together two crosses and place one on each grave along with the correct dog tag.

"MacLeod, you and I will dig MacGregor's grave. Take good care of him and treat him gently for he was a good man and a fine soldier."

When the digging was over the Colonel inspected the trench, and only when he was completely satisfied that his orders had been obeyed were the men allowed to put down the spades and finally rest.

The company stood nervously round the freshly dug graves with their heads bowed, waiting for the Colonel to start the short service.

He took out his well-thumbed Bible once again and read Psalm 25.

The words of the psalm and the Colonel's beautiful, melodious voice were deeply moving and several men felt remorse for what had happened to the two young Germans.

John Ross kept his distance from George Mackay.

As soon as the final grace was over, the Camerons went to work shoring up the trench walls and preparing to defend their newly-captured territory, but it didn't take long for the Colonel to realize that they were isolated from their comrades and in desperate need of support.

Pounded by German artillery on one flank and mistakenly bombed by their own side, 4th Camerons' position had become untenable.

Colonel Hollister summoned his men together.

"We can no longer defend this trench without reinforcements," he said grimly. "It looks as if our company was the only one to make it and we seem to be surrounded by the enemy on all sides. I have sent messages back to Headquarters requesting urgent assistance but haven't received a reply. It appears none of the messages got through.

"I have no choice but to command you all to vacate this trench and retreat back across the mud flats to the large dyke which I've reliably been informed leads to our own line."

Each soldier listening to the Colonel hung his head, aware that luck was no longer on his side.

"I wouldn't ask you to make this perilous journey if it weren't your only chance of survival.

The entire stretch of land between this trench and the dyke is covered by German machine guns and snipers from the outer flanks, so keep your bodies low and your heads down."

The retreating 4th Camerons became easy targets as they dragged themselves back towards the large dyke. Angus kept his head low and wriggled forward on his stomach, hoping to find Donny leaning against the two dead soldiers but there was no sign of him. Just before reaching the dyke, he came across the body of a young soldier curled up in the foetal position with a gaping hole in his back.

It was George Mackay.

Respectfully, he lifted the flap of his jacket and

pulled out his well-thumbed King James' Bible. There
wasn't a scratch on its fine leather cover.

"Don't worry, George," he reassured the lifeless
disciple. "I'll make sure your Bible gets back to your
father." And with those words, he closed the soldier's
eyes on the sinful world he had tried to save and left
him to the care of the God he had faithfully served
throughout his short life.

Able-bodied soldiers crawled past and slithered
over the side of the ditch like rats in a sewer, leaving
the maimed and dying convulsing where they had
fallen.

Angus crawled towards the ditch and joined the
remnant of his battalion in the water-filled trench,
which in places, was so deep he had to use his rifle to
keep afloat. After a terrible struggle, drenched and
coated in filth, he found himself once again behind
British lines.

CHAPTER 9

During a lengthy pause in the fighting, Hugh Hollister
sat at the makeshift table in his dugout and began the
grim task of jotting down a series of coded letters
against the name of every missing and dead soldier
under his command:

b (brave), c (conscientious), dow (died of wounds),
gf (God-fearing), ka (killed in action), t (trusted),
mw (mortally wounded), snp (suffered no pain),
wl (well-liked), mpd (missing presumed dead),
sm (sorely missed), r (respected), nrc (never
regained consciousness)

These symbols would later form the basis of a letter
of condolence which would be sent to the parents or
wife of the deceased. When it came to writing the
name, John MacGregor, the Colonel paused. A few
scribbled symbols seemed disrespectful and demean-
ing to the memory of such a loyal and enthusiastic
recruit whose endearing smile and alert eyes never
missed an opportunity to serve. John was everything
an officer hoped to find in a junior soldier and had
first come to Hugh's attention when he volunteered

to join a small group of stretcher-bearers to look for a wounded soldier trapped in no-man's land. It took the party four hours to locate the badly injured man and another four hours to carry him back to the dressing station. The constant fear of being shot or drowning in the flooded shell-holes never left them and working under cover of darkness, they were hampered by the appalling mud which sucked their boots into the sticky quagmire.

Miraculously the wounded soldier survived his ordeal and was back serving at the front three months later.

Hugh recognised MacGregor's extraordinary self-discipline and stamina and wasn't surprised to hear that he had been a talented athlete before joining up, with dreams of representing Great Britain in the 400 metres. He trained whenever he had the chance and willingly became the Colonel's runner and batman.

His sudden and unexpected death had particularly affected the Colonel, who cared deeply for every soldier under his command and tried to set aside a short time of quiet every morning to remind himself that life still had value despite the madness of war.

"I should never have asked him to disarm the enemy," he sighed, pausing to think of meaningful words to write to John's parents and aware that every word would be pored over and interpreted in the months and years to come.

He picked up his father's Parker pen and started to write in his usual fluent style.

Dear Mrs MacGregor

It is with deep sadness that I have to inform you of the death of your dear son John, who died in the course of duty, disarming the enemy to protect his Battalion.

He was the finest of soldiers in every sense of the word and an outstanding Highlander, selfless, god-fearing and resourceful. As you can imagine, a man like John quickly became an invaluable friend to many and he will be sorely missed.

I know words are of little consolation to you and your husband but it is important for you to know just how highly John was regarded and how badly his loss has affected everyone.

He died a patriot and a believer and I pray he is now at peace with his Saviour.

I remain, Yours Sincerely
Hugh A. C. Hollister Lt Col

Hugh read and re-read the letter then folded the sheet of paper and slipped the dry sprig of heather found in John's breast pocket into the envelope.

It needed no explanation.

CHAPTER 10

"Private MacLeod, the Colonel wishes to see you."

A week had passed since Angus found his way back from the captured enemy trench and his clothes were still damp. The matted wool of his kilt rubbed against his skin causing severe chaffing and sores which were slow to heal.

He saluted the Colonel and stood to attention.

"Stand at ease, MacLeod," the Colonel ordered, in his quiet commanding voice.

There was a respectful silence between the two men.

"I hear you have been trying to find your friend, Donald Nicolson, who was injured in the advance on the German trenches at Festubert?"

Angus nodded.

"Well, a strange thing happened to me a few days ago as I was travelling to Divisional Headquarters at Bray Farm on the Rue du Bac.

"I was passing an old stone barn when, totally unexpectedly, I heard the repetitive, rasping call of a corncrake coming from inside. As a Skye man, I expect you are familiar with this sound."

"Yes, sir," Angus replied with amusement.

"Well, these shy birds have fascinated me ever since

I first heard them behind the crofts at Canusterrach in Strathcarron.

"Intrigued by what I had heard, I opened the barn door and saw twenty injured men lying on the floor listening attentively to the extraordinary corncrake sounds made by a one-legged soldier propped up against a straw bale.

"The call was so realistic, I paused before entering.

"The man imitating the corncrake so perfectly told me his name was Donald Nicolson from Kilbackie on Skye.

"During our conversation, he told me he had lost his leg in the attack at Festubert and was in a terrible state before his friend Angus MacLeod found him. Angus saved his life by tying a tourniquet around the bleeding stump and dragging him behind a makeshift wall of dead men.

Private Nicolson also recounted how his friend had made him promise to stay alive by listening out for a corncrake, a shy bird that only calls from summer meadows. This light-hearted comment made him smile and probably saved his life. Determined to make the Hebridean corncrake sing on a French battlefield, he set himself the task of imitating its rasping call."

Here the Colonel paused.

"Do you like birds?" he asked.

"Very much, sir!" Angus replied.

"Well, as you know, my batman, John MacGregor, was shot when we captured the German trench and I am looking for someone I can trust to replace him.

I was wondering if you would consider taking on this responsibility."

Angus stared at the man sitting in front of him and felt enormously proud at being considered a worthy choice.

"I'd like that very much, sir," he replied, "very much indeed!"

"Splendid!" the officer answered. "I can't offer you many privileges or protect you from the Front but you will receive a few perks. Probably the one you will most appreciate is the chance to wash and dry your clothes and get rid of some of the lice which are no doubt crawling all over you and driving you mad.

"I can also arrange for you to see Private Nicolson."

Within an hour, Angus was sitting by Donny's bed in the field hospital, where he had been moved at the orders of Colonel Hollister.

He looked relaxed and in good spirits, with a fresh dressing on his stump and a bandage round his face covering a superficial flesh wound.

Angus couldn't help noticing his clean uniform.

"Colonel Hollister has taken charge of everything," Donny explained. "Nothing is too much trouble for him."

There were tears in his eyes as he struggled to thank Angus for saving his life.

"As soon as I recover from this bout of trench fever, I'm being sent back to Scotland," he said, pointing to his missing leg. "My fighting days are over, Angus, and as far as the army is concerned, I'm a bloody nuisance and a useless cripple."

Angus listened, silently amused at the effortless way his friend swore.

"It's a strange world," he continued. "I never enjoyed being a soldier and was scared stiff of fighting but now I have permission to return home, I don't want to leave my friends."

Angus clung to the hope that one day, he too would be free to return to Skye and walk through the gentle Kilbackie meadows and over its barren moorland.

"What are you thinking about?" Donny asked.

"Nothing much," came the reply.

"Go on," Donny persisted. "I know you well enough to know when something's troubling you."

Angus thought hard before answering.

"Every night I used to have nightmares," he said, "but now I dream of the snow-topped Black Cuillin and rugged coastline of Skye, I feel the wind on my face and listen to the silence of the long winter nights."

He paused.

"So what's the problem?" Donny asked, "apart from this bloody war!"

"I don't think I'll ever return," Angus replied.

"Why not?"

"The violence and suffering we've witnessed has changed me and I'm no longer the same person I was six months ago. Don't ask me to explain, Donny, because I can't. All I know is that if I survive this war, I've got to get away."

Donny stretched out his hand and grasped Angus' arm.

"I've also got something to tell you," he admitted sheepishly, keeping his eyes firmly on the bedcovers. "I meant to tell you before we left for France but I didn't have the courage."

The two friends looked at each other warily.

"While you were in hospital with measles, Edith and I secretly got married!"

"You did what!" Angus exclaimed in total disbelief. "I thought I told you to wait."

"You did," Donny replied, "but you were ill for such a long time, I grew lonely and looked to Edith for support. Then one day I knew I couldn't live without her, so we got married in St Paul's Church with Mrs Wilson and Ian MacKinnon as our only witnesses. It was the happiest day of my life and now I am a useless cripple.

"Do you think she will still love me?"

Angus shrugged his shoulders.

"I have no idea what women think," he replied honestly. "You may be lucky!"

CHAPTER II

Dover, December 1918

When the war finally ended, Angus was sent to a tran-
sit camp in Calais and eventually he found his way to
Dover where he hoped to transfer to a dispersal centre in Kinross.

He was twenty-two years old, discharged from the
army with a railway warrant in his hand and free to
travel back to Skye, the place that had inspired his
survival.

Instead of feeling ecstatic, he was full of self-doubt.

Sitting outside a Nissen hut overlooking the great
Norman castle guarding the White Cliffs, he turned
his travel warrant over and over in his hands, wondering what to do next.

"Are you off home, MacLeod?" a voice next to him
wheezed.

He looked up and saw the Colonel, or at least he
thought it was the Colonel, standing next to him.

"Do you mind if I sit down?" the gaunt man asked.

Angus shuffled along the bench and tried not to
stare at the burns on the Colonel's face and the crusts
around his eyes. The hideous effect of mustard gas
had aged the poor man beyond recognition and his
once fresh complexion was now sallow and grey and

his sparkling eyes had turned dull and sunk deep into their sockets.

"To be honest, sir, I'm not sure what I'm going to do," Angus replied truthfully, waving the warrant in his hand. "I don't know if I'm ready to return home just yet."

The Colonel fidgeted and looked uncomfortable. The war had not been kind to this exceptionally brave and talented man.

Angus remembered clearly the fateful day.

* * *

The Colonel had ordered a stretcher party to go into no-man's land to rescue Duncan MacKenzie, a young Cameron Highlander from Portree. His pitiful cries for help had continued all night and were so disturbing that men were praying someone would hurry up and put him out of his misery. There was something about Private MacKenzie's lonely suffering that had moved the Colonel to volunteer as a stretcher-bearer.

He and James MacKinnon made the perilous journey across no-man's land to where the soldier lay trapped in rolls of tangled barbed wire, with a bullet lodged in his thigh.

He was still conscious but had lost a lot of blood.

Colonel Hollister carefully cut through the wire and pulled back the jagged strands of metal that were lacerating MacKenzie's tender flesh.

"Gas! Gas!" came the warning cry from the English

line but he was so engrossed in freeing the young man, he never saw the faint yellow cloud silently creeping towards them.

James panicked and fumbled for his gas mask. In his terror he forgot about everyone but himself and stumbled back to the British trenches, leaving Colonel Hollister on his own to tend the wounded soldier.

Undeterred by the encroaching sickly-coloured gas, the Colonel persevered in peeling back the twisted wire and freeing MacKenzie. He hurriedly placed his own mask over the boy's ashen face and spoke to him encouragingly.

"Breathe in slowly, MacKenzie, and take your time! I'm going to get you back in one piece, just breathe gently and trust me."

With great tenderness, he lifted the traumatised soldier over his shoulder and began the long, slow walk back to the trench. An eerie calm fell over the battlefield as both sides watched this extraordinary act of compassion and bravery.

Not a single bullet was fired during the rescue but no-one could stop the poisonous gas from attacking the unprotected officer.

Safely back behind British lines, Colonel Hollister ordered the hapless James MacKinnon to take MacKenzie to the medics, then he sank to his knees, gasping for air and rubbing his eyes.

Duncan MacKenzie made a full recovery and served in the army right to the end of the war, but Colonel Hollister wasn't so lucky. He received a Mention in

Dispatches and was promoted to full Colonel but needed to spend several months in hospital, suffering from the effects of burns to his skin and eyes and developing chronic respiratory problems. He was reluctant to leave his men for a desk job at Army Headquarters, but his new rank demanded his withdrawal from the Front.

★   ★   ★

"Come back with me," he stuttered, nervously. "There's plenty of room in the house and it would be a privilege to show you all the places we've talked about. I'll take you to see the dunlins, reed buntings and snipe where I live."

For the second time, Angus replied, "I'd like that very much, sir, very much indeed!"

CHAPTER 12

Shottenden, December 1918

Nothing could have prepared Angus for his first sight of Shottenden Park.

A chauffeur sat waiting for them at the station and once the luggage had been packed into the Armstrong Siddeley, they set off along narrow country lanes, eventually slowing down outside a pair of magnificent wrought-iron gates, topped with gilded fleur de lys finials. Guarding the entrance of the long drive was an octagonal Gate Lodge with lattice windows and overhanging eaves. Grey smoke poured out of a chimney into the crisp, winter air.

The car crawled down an avenue of mature beech trees silhouetted against a weak winter sun and came to a halt outside a Georgian mansion built of local limestone which had mellowed over the years. It had long sash windows, a low roof partially hidden behind a parapet and a pair of chimneys on each side of the house.

Angus stared transfixed at the beauty of the elegant house and would have happily continued staring had he not been distracted by a noisy border terrier tearing out of the house and down the steps, yapping with obvious delight. Hugh lifted the excited dog high into the air then smothered it in a warm hug, nestling his injured face deep into its grizzle and tan coat.

"Gosh, I've missed you, Tats!" he cried, keeping hold of the small quivering bundle.

Amidst the excitement of the Colonel's return, Angus noticed an elderly liveried man, wearing white gloves, walking slowly and discreetly down the short flight of steps to where Hugh was standing with his dog still wrapped in his arms.

"Good afternoon, Sir Hugh," he said calmly. "It's good to see you home again."

The butler gave no hint of surprise at the deterioration in his master's health.

Years of service had trained him to focus on the job and not concern himself with the behaviour or appearance of the family.

His loyalty was unswerving.

"It's wonderful to be back, Huntley," the Colonel exclaimed and turned towards his guest who was being escorted out of the car by the chauffeur.

"This is Angus MacLeod from Skye, who will be staying with us for a while."

The butler inclined his head but said nothing. The chauffeur collected the luggage and followed Hugh into a magnificent marble entrance hall, where their footsteps echoed in its vast cavernous space.

"Welcome to Shottenden!" Hugh enthused. "Huntley will show you to your room and then we can have tea in the drawing room."

Huntley picked up Angus' kitbag, led him up a sweeping staircase and then along a corridor to a large comfortable bedroom with two long sash windows, cushioned window seats and heavy drapes.

He placed the bag on a stand and left without saying a word.

The huge bed was covered with a dark green and red counterpane and all around the walls hung oil paintings of Highland scenes and portraits. Despite the bitter weather, the room was warm, heated by a coal fire burning in the grate, its flickering flames dancing in shadows on the ceiling and walls. Folded neatly on the bed were a pair of new pyjamas and a warm shirt.

Angus felt he had entered another world.

He washed his hands with huile d'olive French soap before making his way downstairs to the drawing room where Hugh was sitting on a comfortable sofa, talking to an exquisitely dressed lady.

Tats lay curled up at her master's feet, determined never to let him out of her sight again.

The woman was ample in size, with porcelain skin, greeny-brown eyes and dark hair swept up in a chignon. She wore a silver-grey silk dress with three strands of pearls and a light tartan shawl over her shoulders. Her elegant presence charmed the room and completely overwhelmed Angus, who had never met anyone so regal.

Hugh stood up as soon as Angus entered the room.

"I hope you've found everything you need in your room," he said. "Mother, allow me to introduce Angus MacLeod from Kilbackie on Skye."

Angus approached the lady, who remained seated, and took her raised hand in his.

"Pleased to make your acquaintance, your Ladyship," he mumbled awkwardly, catching a waft of huile d'olive as he released her hand.

As soon as he opened his mouth, he regretted his stilted, rather strange choice of words and blushed at the thought of letting the Colonel down by sounding ignorant. He was out of his depth and had no idea how to talk to such a beautiful, sophisticated lady.

She didn't appear to notice his awkwardness and continued talking in her soft, attractive voice.

"Ah, Skye!" she sighed. "My mother lives on the Applecross Peninsula where Hugh used to spend his summers roaming the hills, stalking and birdwatching. Everything he knows about natural history, he learned from the crofters of Applecross. It's such a beautiful place."

She paused, lost in thought.

"Do you have a croft?"

"Yes, my Lady," Angus replied, not knowing how to address Hugh's mother but thinking 'my Lady' sounded better that 'your Ladyship'. "My father has a croft on the Kilbackie Estate."

"How nice!" she replied sweetly and then made it quite clear that her conversation with the crofter's son from Skye was over.

Rather abruptly, she turned back to Hugh, leaving Angus standing alone, unsure what to do next. He gazed out of the large windows onto the immaculate lawn which swept out towards a ha-ha, below which sheep grazed in the fading light of day. In this secluded, privileged world, everything appeared orderly and he felt at peace.

His thoughts were interrupted by the silent, gliding steps of a young girl with large, innocent blue eyes and thick golden hair tied up under a small white cap. She wore a dark high-necked dress and white apron and was very pretty.

"Shall I set the table, Lady Hollister?" she asked demurely.

"Thank you, Violet."

Violet closed the buttery-yellow curtains, muffling the evening song of a blackbird.

She spread a starched white tablecloth over the drum table in the bay window and set three places using the family's finest porcelain and silverware.

A shy girl, no older than fourteen, brought in a three-tier cake stand, laden with freshly-prepared finger sandwiches, delicious white scones and a variety of mouth-watering mini wafers, tarts and cakes. She placed it on the table next to a tray of homemade jam, clotted cream, milk, lemon and sugar.

The French mantel clock struck four o'clock.

Violet picked up a vase of fragrant winter-flowering honeysuckle, irises and jasmine to place in the centre of the table and gave an unexpected cough.

"Is everything all right?" Lady Hollister asked.

"I'm fine, thank you, my Lady," she replied, looking flushed. "I just suddenly feel rather hot and breathless."

The cough returned and she placed the vase back on the side table in order to cover her mouth with her hand.

"Come and sit down for a moment and catch your breath," said Sir Hugh gallantly. "You don't look at all well."

"Do stop fussing the girl, Hugh," Lady Hollister retorted rather haughtily, moving across the room to the tea table. "She'll soon be as right as rain, won't you, Violet? Now, how about tea?" She patted the chair next to hers and invited Angus to sit down.

Violet glanced anxiously at Sir Hugh, then picked up the vase. She had only managed to walk half way across the room when there was a loud crash and she slumped to the floor, shattering the vase and scattering the fresh flowers over the carpet.

"Oh, those beautiful flowers!" Lady Hollister exclaimed, horrified. "You've ruined them, Violet!"

"Mother, do be quiet!" Hugh urged, trying to help Violet to her feet. "Can't you see she's unwell?"

"Nonsense!" Lady Hollister replied. "She's been as right as rain all day, haven't you, Violet?"

The young girl was unable to stand and remained crumpled on the carpet, coughing and holding her throat. However robust her health might have been earlier in the day, it was clear she was in a bad way and was having trouble breathing.

"Daisy!" Lady Hollister instructed the serving child. "Go and fetch Mrs Davies and explain that Violet is unwell, then come back and serve tea."

CHAPTER 13

By ten o'clock Angus was exhausted and in need of solitude. He had spent the entire afternoon and evening being ignored by Lady Hollister whose selfishness had shocked him. The Colonel, on the other hand, had remained as courteous as ever, showing immense sensitivity, especially to the unfortunate maid who had fallen ill.

After the slightly strained dinner, at which Lady Hollister refused to talk and Angus felt out of his depth, Hugh announced it was time to retire. With huge relief, Angus climbed the imposing staircase and entered his room, surprised to discover someone had already been in to stoke the fire and light the oil lamps.

He stood with his back to the fireplace and let the heat from the glowing embers soothe his tension. The neatly folded pyjamas and shirt still lay on the bed and he had no idea whether they were for him to wear or had been left there by mistake. Unsure what to do, he laid them on top of the chest of drawers beside a small vase of delicate winter jasmine and slipped naked between the soft linen sheets, pulling the covers up under his chin.

Cocooned in luxury, he closed his eyes and drifted into a deep sleep, only to be woken a few hours later by the sound of running footsteps outside his door and loud hushed whispers. He tried to hear what was going on but only managed to catch a few words: urgent, doctor, tragic.

The commotion eventually died down and apart from the distant sound of sobbing, all was eerily quiet.

The church clock struck four o'clock.

By six-thirty Angus was wide awake and ready to explore the estate. He drew back the curtains and peered onto a frosty lawn lit by a huge silver moon.

It was as bright as mid-day.

Despite the early hour, the domestic staff were already on the move, folding back the shutters, dusting and sweeping the breakfast room and cleaning the hearth. The kitchen was bustling with activity and the large dining room table was being set for breakfast.

He crept unnoticed through the front door, walking briskly down the crystallized drive.

Turning left by a large oak tree, he continued along a well-worn track leading to a small village where he could just make out a fine mediaeval church, some stone cottages and stables, all immaculately maintained and painted the same shade of arsenic green. The rural community reminded him of the Bedfordshire villages he had loved visiting in his free time before being posted to France.

Angus leaned over a gate admiring the winter view and wondering how many other demobbed soldiers were fortunate enough to return to an English scene as idyllic as this one. His thoughts were abruptly interrupted by a flurry of pheasants rising out of the beech trees behind him, frantically beating their wings and squawking in alarm in an attempt to evade a prowling fox. The russet-coloured predator slunk back over the crisp, dead leaves, having failed to catch his prey.

'Take cover!' he told himself, dropping to the ground with his arms covering his head. The green and coppery birds with long tail feathers flew high overhead, then slowly glided down into a neighbouring field where they pecked at the frozen earth in a futile attempt to find food.

Angus' panic attack profoundly shook him and he remained crouched on the icy ground, waiting for the burst of gun fire that would finish him off.

Death no longer frightened him but for the first time since the war he badly wanted to survive.

He waited but all was quiet.

As his pulse rate stabilised, he remembered he was staying with Colonel Hollister in England and the war was over. He took a few deep breaths and stood up to continue his walk. The milking parlour was only a stone's throw from where he had flung himself to the ground and the sound of lowing cattle drew him closer. He peered in through the door.

Six lean, honey-coloured cows were standing patiently on the straw while two girls, sitting on wooden stools, eased the milk from them.

"Good morning!" one of the girls purred, keeping her cheek closely pressed against the belly of the cow.

"We don't usually get visitors at this time of the morning, do we, Ethel?"

They giggled and blushed.

"Can we help you?" they gushed in unison.

Now it was Angus' turn to blush.

"No, everything's fine, thank you," he replied. "I'm staying up at the big house. Sorry to have bothered you."

"Where're you from?" Ethel asked curiously. "You're not from these parts with an accent like that."

"Shhhh!" the other girl hissed. "Don't be so rude, Ethel. You're embarrassing the poor man."

"I'm from Skye," Angus replied, and the girls nearly fell off their stools laughing.

"Well! If you're from Sky, I must be in heaven," Ethel chortled.

"Would you like a drink of milk?" she asked, lifting one of the cow's teats and aiming it at Angus.

"No thank you," he replied, wishing he'd never set foot in the shed.

"If you don't like cow's milk, perhaps I can offer you something more tasty," she insisted mischievously, unbuttoning her top to expose a plump white breast. "How about this then?"

"Ethel! Stop it!" the other girl scolded. "Stop being so cheeky and get back to work before Mrs Woodman catches you. You won't 'alf get a telling off if she catches you like that."

Ethel thought carefully, then did as she was told and buttoned up her blouse.

This was Angus' chance to escape and he quickly left the sweet smelling shed and started walking back to the house. Coming slowly up the track to meet him was the Colonel.

"I see Shottenden's magic is rubbing off on you," he beamed, gazing back at the magnificent house radiating its opulent grandeur.

"It is the loveliest place I've ever seen," Angus replied truthfully.

"I rather hoped you would feel that way. Perhaps if you've finished your walk, we could return to the house. There's something I want to show you."

A clear bright sun was slowly rising over the trees as the two men ambled back, pausing several times for the Colonel to catch his breath and steady himself.

As soon as Angus opened the front door, Tats appeared and scampered enthusiastically across the hallway. She tore round her master in circles, yapping for his attention and refusing to leave his side until he picked her up and made a fuss of her.

"What am I going to do you with you?" he smiled, stroking the dog's oily coat. "You're incorrigible!"

He put the terrier down and led Angus past the dining room to a closed door. Tats followed at a short distance but no longer demanded to be picked up.

"Don't worry, we'll eat soon," the Colonel said, sensing Angus' hunger. "But first I want to show you this room."

He took a bunch of keys from his pocket and unlocked the door.

ASK NOT WHY

"You've probably noticed how breathless I've become even after the briefest stroll. Our short walk up the drive was almost more than I could cope with, so very regrettably I am unable to keep my promise to show you the dunlins, reed buntings and snipe on the estate, but I hope this room will make up for my limitations."

The door opened into a totally dark room in which it was impossible to see anything.

"Stay there while I open up," he commanded, walking over to the full-length windows and unfolding the wooden shutters one at a time until shafts of sunlight poured into the freezing room.

"My mother locked this library the day I left for war and I've only just found the key. Having already lost her husband in the Boer War, she was frightened of losing me, her only child, and couldn't bear to be reminded of the happy times I used to spend here. To me, this is the most wonderful and exciting room in the world."

Fine clouds of dust floated across the room, irritating the Colonel's lungs and sending him into an uncontrollable fit of coughing.

Desperate to regain his composure, he placed a hand on Angus' shoulder and kept it there until the coughing spasm had died down. It was the lightest of touches, nothing more than the steadying hand of a sick man, but it made Angus feel uneasy.

"Angus?" the Colonel began, but for some reason couldn't continue. He appeared uncomfortable and frail and Angus couldn't help feeling sorry for him.

"It doesn't matter," he continued. "Another time, eh?"

Angus had no idea what he was talking about but was relieved when the hand was finally removed from his shoulder.

"I'll leave you to browse through the books," the Colonel wheezed, staggering out of the room.

Angus was left alone to take in the full glory of the sunlit library.

Its carved bookcases reached to just below the ceiling and resembled a classical facade with pilasters and gilded egg and dart moldings running across the top. The leather-bound books were arranged in themes and included some rare first editions.

He went to the natural history section — birds, butterflies, wild flowers, eggs and insects — and carefully and respectfully pulled out a large book on British birds, placing it on the reading desk in the middle of the room. Turning the pages, he discovered a number of exquisite paintings which left him spellbound. He was so absorbed in the illustrations that he failed to hear Hugh return and, once again, felt a steadying hand rest on his shoulder.

"Let's go and have something to eat. I'll leave the library unlocked so you can make full use of the books whenever you want."

Angus closed the book and gently replaced it back in the bird section before re-joining the Colonel.

"I'm afraid the household is in turmoil this morning," the Colonel explained. "You remember

Violet, my mother's maid, who was taken ill yesterday tea-time, well, she died quite unexpectedly in the night and now little Daisy is ill. The doctor has diagnosed influenza and Huntley, who is normally so measured and calm, has gone to pieces, fearing Daisy, his only grand-child, is going to die. I've given him some time off but I hope for all our sakes, she gets better.

"As you can imagine, Mother is terribly upset. She had grown particularly fond of Violet for whom nothing was too much trouble. It is rare to find such a cheerful and modest servant who works hard and takes a pride in her work. Violet is going to be very difficult to replace."

Despite the bleak description of chaos, Violet's untimely death hardly seemed to affect the daily routine of the house. Breakfast was still laid out in the dining room and the sideboard was laden with dishes of eggs, bacon, kippers, kidneys and mushrooms.

Colonel Hollister sat at the head of the table reading his newspaper and opening the post whilst Lady Hollister sipped her tea, unwilling to talk. She was clearly annoyed at the inconvenience of losing Violet and hoped Daisy would pull through, as good staff were so difficult to find.

After placing his neatly-folded copy of *The Times* on the table, the Colonel gazed intently at Angus, tentatively broaching the subject of his future and asking if he had ever thought of travelling abroad.

"I have often thought about it, sir, but with no qualifications or contacts, I wouldn't know where to begin. When you say 'abroad' did you have a particular country in mind?"

"India," came the unexpected reply.

Angus looked aghast.

"India!" he exclaimed. "Why would I want to go to India, Sir Hugh?"

"I've just received a letter from James Patterson, a Cambridge friend of mine who owns the Kirriemuir Tea Plantation near Darjeeling. He is looking for a disciplined, hardworking manager and I immediately thought of you. I think you would be an ideal candidate for the job and a couple of years overseas might help you clear your mind."

Angus put down his knife and fork and looked across the table.

"I don't know what to say," he replied. "I'd love the chance to travel and see the world and I've heard India has much to offer, but as I've already said, I don't have the right qualifications to be a manager."

"Give it some thought," the Colonel said kindly. "Personally I think you would make an excellent manager and any business would be lucky to have you. You showed outstanding leadership qualities in the war, you are fit and have a wonderful way of gaining people's trust."

Angus was touched by the Colonel's generous support and kind words and promised he would give the matter some thought.

CHAPTER 14

Angus spent most of his time at Shottenden Park reading in the library and birdwatching on the estate. He took full advantage of the Colonel's hospitality and the estate's seclusion to rebuild his mind and contemplate the future.

The Colonel didn't seem concerned about the differences in their backgrounds and education and expected him to stay on after dinner to smoke, drink and discuss farming.

At first Angus felt uneasy about the arrangement but in time, he realized that the Colonel's hospitality was sincere and he genuinely enjoyed challenging Angus to think for himself and recommending books for him to read.

He was a compassionate, tolerant man with a strong belief in prudence, fortitude and justice.

Angus spent the short winter days alone in the library, surrounded by the comforting smell of leather, paper and wood smoke. When the weather was particularly cold, the Colonel had the fire lit early so he could settle down and read in comfort. During these quiet times of discovery he began to question everything he had ever been taught.

Far from being alone with his doubts, he was encouraged to discover that the great minds of the age were also challenging 'received teaching' and publishing their theories and thoughts in the face of ridicule and opposition.

One evening whilst sitting by the fire with a glass of whisky in his hand, the Colonel told Angus about an Austrian neurologist called Sigmund Freud.

"I don't have any of his books for you to read but he has recently established a discipline called psycho-analysis which explores the conflict between the conscious and the unconscious. Freud states that repressed memories can materialize in the form of mental or emotional disturbances, such as neurosis, anxiety and depression. Some of our thoughts and feelings are too painful to bear, so we banish them from our minds and send them to the unconscious where they fester."

Angus listened intently to the Colonel's explanations of Freud's theories and wondered if Donny's erratic behaviour was the result of repressed feelings from his violent childhood.

During the weeks that followed, Angus became engrossed in the novels of Sir Walter Scott, Charles Dickens and Sir Arthur Conan Doyle and through their story-telling, he visited places, met people and felt emotions he never knew existed.

Then, quite unexpectedly one morning at break-fast, he received a short letter from Reverend Nicolson to say that his father had been taken ill and he was needed at home.

"Not bad news, I hope?" the Colonel asked when

he saw Angus fold the letter and place it meticulously back in its envelope.

"No, Sir Hugh, everything's fine. It's just a letter from home," he replied. "It's come at just the right time because it has forced me to think about my future.

"You will never understand how much Shottenden means to me, sir. I have grown to love the place dearly but I feel it's time to go home."

"You can't go back to Skye," the Colonel exclaimed. "You'll be throwing your life away! At least consider the job in India; I believe you'd be the perfect candidate."

"Don't think I haven't thought long and hard about India," Angus replied. "I've struggled to know what to do for the best but in the end I need to be true to myself and not pretend to be someone I'm not. I speak the language of Skye, my kinsfolk live on Skye and I belong to its collective memory - I need to return."

"You can't leave without some sort of plan for the future!" the Colonel responded, looking desolate. "Think of the waste if you don't have access to a library. How are you going to feed your mind?"

"To be honest, sir, I've no idea what I'm going to do but I need to return whatever the cost."

He picked up the minister's letter and turned it over in his hand, wondering how to bring up the subject of George Mackay's Bible, something that had been on his mind since first arriving at Shottenden.

"Can I ask a favour, Sir Hugh, before I leave?" he asked, flushing a little.

"Of course you can!" came the instant reply.

"Do you remember George Mackay who was in our battalion in France? He was deeply religious and lived his life strictly in accordance to the teachings of the Bible. As far as I remember, he never once failed to read his Bible or pray during the short time he was on the Western Front. His iron discipline was inspirational."

"I'm not sure I do remember him," the Colonel replied. "Why do you ask?"

"During the retreat from Festubert, I found him lying in the mud with a gaping hole in his back; he had been killed instantly but the Bible in his jacket was totally unmarked. I promised him that I'd get the book back to his father, the Reverend Alasdair Mackay at Craighallin but I'm not sure where Craighallin is."

The Colonel was sensitive enough to know why Angus hadn't been able to post the book back to the Highlands himself and felt a duty of care towards George's father.

"If you give me the Bible," he said graciously, "I'd be happy to post the package to Reverend Mackay with an accompanying note. Should I send it to The Manse, Craighallin?"

Angus nodded, relieved that his promise to George would be honoured and he didn't have to talk about money.

"Have you any idea where Craighallin is?" the Colonel asked.

"No. It's not on Skye so I reckon it must be somewhere in Wester Ross."

"I'll look it up on a map," the Colonel assured him, keen to solve the problem.

"Thank you, sir," Angus replied.

"Don't forget that there'll always be a home for you at Shottenden," the Colonel added. "When Arthur Woodman retires in a few months' time, I'll be looking for a new stockman. Bear that in mind, Angus. You would be totally independent and have your own cottage on the estate."

"That's very thoughtful of you, sir, but I need to go home."

CHAPTER 15

Skye, April 1919

The train drew into Kyle of Lochalsh station early on a cold, misty April day nearly five years after Angus first left Skye.

He took his time walking the short distance from the station to the ferry, determined to savour the feel and smell of the cool, moist air that blew across the Strait of Kyle Akin.

"Angy MacLeod of Kilbackie?" came a quiet voice, speaking in Gaelic.

Angus stopped short and looked hard at the old man's ruddy, weather-beaten face.

"I'd have recognized you anywhere," he continued.

"Duncan!" Angus cried, warmly grasping the old man's hand. "Duncan MacIver! I'd have recognized *you* anywhere. How are you doing now?"

"Not bad," he sighed, shaking his head sadly. "You'll be returning from the war I take it. 'Tis tragic that so many of our lads will never catch the ferry again nor see this grand land of ours."

Duncan had crewed the ferry for as long as anyone could remember and there wasn't a person on Skye he didn't know. It was obvious from the dejected look on his face that he had been deeply affected by the loss of so many boys.

One soldier returning home alive was a triumph.

Angus sat on a bench and looked across Loch Alsh towards the snow-topped Cuillin range. The mist cleared just long enough for a shaft of sunlight to illuminate Eilean Bàn and transform the tranquil waters from gunmetal grey to cobalt blue. The intensity of the colours set against the mountainous backdrop was a stark reminder, if he needed one, of the beauty of his island home and hearing Gaelic spoken once again filled him with unexpected emotion.

By the time he reached Kilbackie it was dark. He lifted the latch of the low door and walked into the cosy, oil-lit room he knew so well. Wafts of peat smoke swirled around the fire place and mingled with the smell of potatoes, turnips and fish being prepared by his mother. As usual, his father was smoking in the corner, seated in a high-backed chair.

"I'm back!" he shouted with enthusiasm but before he could utter another word, his mother put down her knife and flung her arms round her son, hugging him as if she would never let him go.

"Good to see you, son," was all his father could say, leaning down to stroke Peg, his favourite border collie.

Ailsa MacLeod wiped her hands on her apron and stood foursquare in front of her son with proud, glistening eyes.

"Let me touch you to make sure I'm not dreaming," she grinned, cupping his face in both hands and kissing his forehead.

"Murdo, don't just sit there, make yourself useful and add more peat to the fire. We've got something to celebrate."

Murdo MacLeod did as he was told and reluctantly raised himself out of the chair to place another brick in the grate, then slumped back with a long drawn-out sigh and deep-throated cough. He had aged since Angus last saw him and appeared much frailer but Ailsa, on the other hand, was as active as ever and hadn't changed at all. She loved the crofting way of life and thought nothing of working long hours making hay, planting potatoes, gathering sheep, milking, spinning and waulking.

"It's time to eat," she announced, looking lovingly at her husband.

Murdo eased himself out his chair and took his place at the table. He closed his eyes and gave thanks to God for all his goodness.

There was no mention of his son's safe return.

Angus' home was a black house which his grandfather, John, had built stone by stone as a wedding gift for his wife. The herculean task had provided them with a secure dwelling and winter accommodation for their livestock.

It was constructed with a double dry stone wall infilled with peat and topped with a layer of clay to prevent water seeping through. As trees were scarce on Skye, John MacLeod had spent many hours scouring the foreshore for driftwood to form a sturdy roof. He thatched it with heather and overlaid the frame with rushes, covering the entire roof with fishing net attached to large rocks. The weight of the rocks held down the thatch and prevented the roof from blowing away in a gale.

Every year, Murdo would re-thatch the roof and use the old straw and soot as fertiliser on the land. He had improved the black house by building a fireplace on the end wall to reduce the build-up of smoke in the living room and across the chimney he added a cross-bar and chain for Ailsa's large family kettle and cooking pot.

The house was cosy and well insulated and, thanks to the chimney, it never became too smokey or blackened by soot. Standing out among the simple furnishings was Ailsa's pride and joy, an exquisite brass and enamel French carriage clock which her mother had left when she died. Rumour had it that an Italian commercial traveller had fallen deeply in love with her mother and asked her to elope with him. When she refused, he gave her the clock as a small memento, telling her that its ticking represented the beating of his broken heart.

Angus remembered its hypnotic sound during the long, winter evenings when his parents sat round the fire, spinning, weaving or mending creels.

The MacLeod family was materially poor but proudly self-sufficient. They owned a few cows for milk and butter, half a dozen laying hens, a few sheep and a pig. Fish was always in abundant supply and small areas of barley were grown for winter cattle feed.

During the long summer months, potatoes, carrots and turnips grew plentifully in the rigs and strong breezes swept across the land, drawing moisture out of the stacks of cut peat. Fresh water springs bubbled out of the rocky land and ran down ditches and burns to the sea, supplying water for the crofters' daily needs.

Angus sat with his parents by the peat fire watching the flames reduce to glowing ashes.

Murdo and Ailsa's marriage had been founded on mutual trust and contentment and neither saw a reason to talk when they had work to do. The intimate proximity of life round the fire satisfied their emotional needs whilst the Bible and prayer satisfied their spiritual needs.

Angus shuddered at the thought of spending the rest of his life in silent ignorance, governed by a church unwilling to accept alternative thinking or personal interpretation.

That night he settled into his wooden box-bed and ran his fingers over the innocent words he had carved as a child — 'gannet' 'adventure' 'friend' 'lonely'. Each word told its own story and as he closed his eyes, he remembered the dreams and fears that had shaped his childhood and he knew that his mind would decay if he remained on Skye.

Early the next morning, he woke to the familiar sound of the cockerel crowing on the thatched roof above him. His mother was already outside hanging the washing on the line but there was no sign of his father.

Everywhere he looked, families were hard at work, making the most of the fine dry weather; preparing the soil, hoeing, sowing seeds and planting early potatoes. They were thankful to have survived the long, dark winter when the earth ceased to yield fruit, the sun hardly rose and the days were short.

Angus eventually found his father where he thought he might be, visiting the stone altar he had erected just before Angus had left for war. The top of the cairn was heavily stained with rabbit blood and its sides splattered with the white excrement of eagles, buzzards and hooded crows who over the past four and a half years had feasted daily on fresh meat.

"Come and help me, son," the old man panted, lifting a bloodied stone off the top of the altar and placing it on the ground. "I'm not as strong as I used to be and I promised your mother I'd repair the walls of the sheep-pen if you ever returned home alive."

Murdo's daily re-enactment of the story of Abraham and Isaac had served its purpose and his son's life had been spared. Now he was going to honour his wife by mending the fank.

CHAPTER 16

A few days after his return, Angus received the expected visit from Donny's father, the Reverend Tom Nicolson.

"How's your father?" he asked. "He hasn't been at all well, which is why I wrote to you."

Angus assured the minister that his father was all right and had been examined by the doctor who said he would soon be fit enough to work the croft.

Tom Nicolson accepted the explanation but appeared restless as if spoiling for a fight.

"And you?" he goaded, showing neither grace nor empathy. "Have you a good reason for not attending yesterday's service with your parents?"

"Yes, Mr Nicolson," Angus replied, trying to contain his anger.

"Well?" came the curt response.

It was obvious the two men were never going to have an easy conversation as neither respected the other.

"I no longer believe in *your* God," Angus said, trying to sound measured and choosing his words with care. "So attending church would make me a hypocrite."

Never in thirty years of devoted ministry had anyone questioned the minister about the existence of God.

He stared furiously at Angus.

"What do mean 'you no longer believe in God'?"

"I didn't say, I don't believe in God," Angus replied, not wanting the conversation to last any longer than necessary. "I said, I don't believe in your God."

The subtlety of this distinction was lost on the minister.

He sat in Murdo MacLeod's chair by the smoldering peat fire, staring in disbelief at Angus who was sitting uncomfortably on a low stool.

"The wages of sin is death," he scowled, wagging his finger. "If you don't repent, you will be cast into an everlasting pit of suffering and torment."

The minister's silver tongue and polished words produced a masterful hellfire sermon aimed at terrifying Angus into submission, but hours of reading in the Shottenden library had given Angus confidence in his new beliefs.

"How do you know what hell's like, if you've never been there?" Angus asked, already tiring of the minister's bullying rant.

"I trust the Bible," came the confident reply. "It states that hell is a place of never-ending pain and suffering where sinners are punished in the flames of everlasting fire."

Angus looked at the pompous man sitting in front of him and wondered if he had ever known the true meaning of love.

He got up off his stool and looked down at Donny's bombastic father, sitting smugly in the chair.

"I've been to hell," he continued, "and it was full

of the bravest, most courageous people I have ever met. As far as I could tell, they weren't there because they had sinned but because they trusted foolish, ignorant leaders who promised them glory and told them God was on their side. It all turned out to be a lie and God was nowhere to be found in the carnage and suffering on the Western Front.

"I cannot believe in a God who hides his face, then condemns us for not finding him.

"Now, if you'll excuse me, I have work to do for my father."

Angus got up and walked out of the house into the fresh air, leaving the stunned minister to regain his composure.

On the road he came across Donny who was hobbling the best he could on a pair of crutches. He looked tired and sallow-skinned and lacked the impish optimism that had made him so attractive before the war.

His dream of settling in Bedford with Edith had not worked out.

Depressed and homesick, he decided to move back to Skye to run his grandfather's croft and be near his mother. Fortunately for him, Edith was looking for her own adventure and was willing to return with him and make Kilbackie her home.

Tom was still hard on his son and showed him little affection but the violence had stopped and the two men seemed to have come to a tense yet bearable truce.

"Hi Donny! It's good to see you," Angus said, placing his hand firmly on his friend's shoulder. "How are the corncrakes?"

Donny didn't smile. He was clearly in no mood for humorous banter.

The two men walked side by side with nothing to say, then, out of the blue, Donny started talking.

"I hear you've been staying with Colonel Hollister on his English estate. That must have been nice."

Angus didn't want to be drawn into a conversation about Shottenden.

He just nodded.

"The Colonel was the bravest man I've ever met and I often think about him," Donny continued cautiously. "If it hadn't been for him, I'd probably have died of infection. But being alive has come at a huge cost, Angus. I am in constant pain and sometimes it is so bad I think about ending it all. It may sound strange, but the only thing that keeps me alive is thinking about Colonel Hollister and the way he coped with his burnt lungs and blisters. I don't expect you've ever heard him complain or seek sympathy."

Angus didn't know how to reply. In the end he just agreed with Donny and changed the subject.

"How's Edith?" he asked, choosing what he hoped would be a neutral topic.

"She's fine. Come and meet her," Donny replied, showing very little emotion. "She's outside planting early potatoes."

The two friends walked down the track to Donny's croft where Edith was kneeling on the freshly turned soil with a basket of seed potatoes by her side.

She was heavily pregnant.

Beside her, playing in the dirt, was a flaxen-haired toddler aged about three.

"Edith!" Donny called out, ignoring the child. "You remember Angus who shared a billet with me in Bedford and fought with me in France."

She looked blankly at both men and said nothing.

"For God's sake, Edith, what's the matter with you!" he hissed. "You must remember Angus. He's the one who got so angry when I stayed the night with you and nearly missed the morning roll call."

Edith's face glazed over and she showed no sign of recognition.

Angus wondered what the matter was with her.

He watched Donny lean over to help her onto her feet and noticed her flinch at his touch.

They walked back to the house and sat outside on a bench, enjoying the fading warmth of the sun and admiring the view over the Minch to the Outer Hebrides. The ruined walls of an abandoned village on the off-shore island were just visible in the low light and seagulls and oyster-catchers flew over the tranquil waters of an incoming tide. A large gangly heron took off from the rocks and flew round the bay squawking like a prehistoric bird.

"You've got a lovely spot here," Angus praised,

trying to break the tension between husband and wife. "This used to be your grandparents' croft, if I remember rightly."

Donny nodded, not wishing to engage in conversation.

The silence was broken by a small child's chatter.

"John go digging," the young boy prattled, waddling away from his parents and heading back towards the potato bed.

"Come back here, John," Donny shouted, but the child ignored his father and tottered down the path towards the basket of seed potatoes.

"Come back here, at once!" Donny screamed but his son took no notice and continued walking.

"Leave him," Edith whispered. "He'll come to no harm. He enjoys playing outside."

But Donny was furious at his son's disobedience and having struggled to get up, he limped towards the contented child playing in the freshly-dug earth.

The unequal fight that followed was pitiful to watch.

Donny pulled his small son up by the scruff of his neck and smacked him hard on the bottom, whereupon the child howled and bit his father's hand.

"You'll do as you're told, you little bugger," he shouted, carrying the terrified boy up the path and into the house. John struggled to free himself from his father's firm grip and cried out for his mother. Angus and Edith could hear the belt being unbuckled and then the sickening thwack of leather on tender skin.

There was a deathly silence, then John let out a piercing scream.

"Dear God!" Edith shrieked, making a huge effort to stand. "This time I really think he's going to kill him. Angus, for God's sake do something!"

Angus had already leapt to his feet and by the time Edith arrived to rescue her sobbing son, he had managed to wrestle the belt out of Donny's hand and sit him down.

"What's got into you?" he asked his friend. "John's just a child, Donny. Look at him! He can't be more than three years old. Think back to when you were young and how your father beat you, do you really want John to suffer what you suffered as a child?"

Donny buried his face in his hands and wept.

"It's the pain, Angus. I can't cope with the pain in this bloody leg any more. I don't know what to do. If only you and the Colonel had left me to die in France."

Angus knelt beside his friend but there was very little he could say or do.

The horrendous shrieking eventually died down and with John now safely back in his mother's arms, they returned outside just as the final rays of the setting sun disappeared behind Kilbackie Point.

Angus was at a loss to know what to say and Edith was too shocked to talk, so they sat in silence whilst she stroked John's fair curls and reassured him with gentle words.

"Shhhh! There now, it's all right. Mummy's with you," she cooed, rocking him in her arms.

Then, without warning, she let out a long drawn-out moan and doubled up over her son.

"Angus!" she cried, grabbing his arm. "Go and get help. My baby's coming!"

CHAPTER 17

Donny became a transformed character after his daughter Katherine was born on 20th April 1919 and much of the change was due to Edith's furious ultimatum after the incident with John and the potatoes.

"Either you reform or I leave Skye for good and take John and Katherine with me," she screamed. "It's up to you, Donny, because if ever you touch one of our children again, I swear I'll leave you."

Edith's outburst was vicious and left Donny in no doubt that he needed to turn his life around.

The first step on his road to recovery was to take church more seriously and attend the three o'clock service every Sunday, the second was to visit the Princess Louise Scottish Hospital for Limbless Sailors and Soldiers in Renfrewshire to see if Sir William Macewen could fit him with a comfortable artificial leg, the third was to give up drinking and the fourth was to take positive steps to control his temper.

He embraced his new-found faith with passion and soon became a zealot, bringing him into direct conflict with Angus.

His father was delighted with his conversion and took him aside one day to suggest he trained for the ministry, something Edith and Donny had already talked about.

With his face firmly set towards study and a place at theological college, Donny decided it was his mission to draw Angus back into the church.

"What's the matter with you?" he asked one day, sitting by the fire in the MacLeod's croft whilst Angus listlessly poked at the peat.

"You were always so content with your life but now look at you! You're edgy and have managed to distance yourself from everyone who cares for you. You've got to sort yourself out or else you'll end up friendless and damned to hell."

Hell was the church's favourite tool to threaten and terrify the community into submission. It was preached from the pulpits, backed up by scripture and so eloquently described that most of the congregation walked miles to sit in a pew as an insurance policy against possible eternal pain and suffering.

Angus had no fear of hell but his friend was right, he was miserable.

He wrote a brief letter and posted it back to England.

"Life is not working out as planned and my mind is deteriorating. Is vacancy for stockman still open? Angus."

A reply came back by return of post.

"Yes. Immediate start. Hugh."

Angus had little idea how his life at Shottenden would work out but he knew he had to go back. The train from Kyle of Lochalsh steamed along the single gauge track to Inverness, passing orange and yellow lichen-covered rocks, and shallow pools of brackish water in salt marshes.

Time on his own to relax and sit with nothing to do was still a luxury and he was determined to make the most of the journey, observing every small detail of the glorious varied countryside that flashed past his carriage window.

In a secluded cove, an old clinker boat rocked gently to the repetitive rhythm of lapping waves, and silver birch trees clung precariously to craggy rocks.

Black Highland cattle roamed the hills of Wester Ross and red deer grazed quietly by clear, shallow burns which meandered their way through tussocky grassland towards Loch Carron.

Circling the turquoise waters of the loch, the train continued its way east, taking Angus further into the unknown. Through puffs of steam, he caught sight of Sgorr Ruadh towering over the barren landscape.

At Attadale, the train followed the long, low perimeter wall of Baron von Schröder's great estate with its beautiful gardens and newly planted Wellingtonias. A tumbling burn cascaded down the hill, pouring over boulders before spreading out over a gravel bank into Loch Carron. The hill shimmered in the late morning sunshine and the lochs sparkled more brilliantly than the finest sapphires and diamonds.

The carriages rocked from side to side to the soothing sound of the wheels clacketing over the tracks. The rhythm seemed to calm Angus' nerves but nothing could take away the knot in his stomach which tightened every time he thought about his decision to leave Kilbackie.

The engine whistled and hissed its way through the landscape, pouring sulphur and soot into the fresh spring air. When it stopped at Achnashellach — with its abundance of rhododendrons and imposing Scots pines — men leant out of the windows selling newspapers and letters were posted in the Royal Mail box on the side of the carriage.

Beyond the lush vegetation of Achnashellach, the train climbed slowly towards a bleak, desolate moor where there were few trees, and strange hillocks appeared like goose bumps out of the rushes and stagnant bog.

Past Achanalt, two golden eagles with outstretched wings spiralled in the vast, shimmering sky as they searched for prey.

Angus finally arrived at Inverness where he changed onto the southbound train. He was acutely aware of the huge decision he had just made to leave his parents and all that was familiar but deep down he knew it was the right decision.

CHAPTER 18

Shottenden, May 1919

Captain Charles Middlethwaite walked confidently into the estate office, smartly dressed in a tweed suit and polished brogues. He looked at Angus, who had arrived a few minutes earlier, and hesitated.

"Oh I'm sorry," he apologised in a rather clipped voice. "Have I come to the wrong place? I'm here for a meeting with Sir Hugh."

"No," Angus replied. "This is the right place. Sir Hugh asked if I would sit in on the meeting."

Charles Middlethwaite gave Angus a withering look, privately annoyed that Sir Hugh had invited his stockman to one of their monthly meetings.

Having joined 2nd Battalion The Yorkshire Regiment as a private soldier in August 1914, he arrived in Ypres on 14th October the same year.

During the 1st Battle of Ypres, his battalion faced some of the fiercest fighting of the war with officers and men being killed in their hundreds and survivors having to shuffle up and down the line to fill the places of those blown out of the trench.

Of the thousands of soldiers who took part in one of the greatest ordeals of history, only a small number survived and Charles Middlethwaite was one of those.

He had limped, dazed and hollowed-eyed, back to his billet in the small Belgium village of Locre, too exhausted to celebrate his promotion to sergeant.

Captain Middlethwaite was academically gifted, with a particular interest in maths and law, but the war and his working-class background had denied him the chance to go to university, something he had never forgotten or forgiven.

Hugh employed him as the estate's Land Agent, more on the strength of his war record than his knowledge of farming, but Captain Middlethwaite soon showed his worth, organizing the office, keeping the ledger books up to date and making sure rents were paid on time. His attention to detail took the pressure off Hugh, who was finding it increasingly difficult to walk and see.

Hugh arrived soon after Charles and sat heavily in his usual chair, struggling to catch his breath.

"Thank you, Charles, for coming at such short notice," he said, somewhat ruffled. "We have a brief but important agenda to get through but before we start, I'd like to introduce you to Angus MacLeod, who has recently taken over from Arthur Woodman."

Charles showed great discourtesy by refusing to make eye contact with Angus or shake his hand.

Hugh saw the tension and gave a slight cough to get their full attention.

"Item 1 on the Agenda," he said, keen to get started. "Tenant farms. What do you think about their long-term future, Charles?"

"Well, Sir Hugh," he replied, rather pompously, "cereal prices are high at the moment and if the estate intends to increase its farming interests, it may be wise to bring all the tenanted land back in hand and sell off the housing."

Hugh thought long and hard before replying.

"I agree the estate would benefit from bringing the land back in hand, but perhaps it would cause less pain if we phased in the transition. After all, many of the families have lived on their farms for generations. The estate could certainly do with an injection of capital, so how about we sell one of the smaller farms first?"

"Matchings Farm is the obvious one to sell," Charles continued. "It's the one furthest away from Shottenden and I'm sure Mr Mitchell would be keen to buy the freehold, if he were given the chance."

Angus listened in awe as the two men discussed estate business. He had little understanding of what they were talking about and felt out of his depth, something Captain Middlethwaite quickly exploited to his advantage.

"How many acres would the estate lose if we were to sell Matchings?" Hugh asked.

"About four hundred and fifty, Sir Hugh," Charles replied. "Unfortunately Matchings is one of larger farms but in the present climate it should sell well."

"Have a casual word with Tommy Mitchell and see if he would be interested in buying the freehold," Hugh concluded.

Charles scribbled down some notes and looked very pleased with his contribution to the future of Matchings.

"Item 2," Hugh continued. "The Jersey herd. Angus, what do you think we should do about our small Jersey herd? Should we increase it?"

"I'm not sure I'm the right person to ask," Angus hesitated, feeling his lack of experience. "I'm only used to the crofting way of life which is completely different to farming here at Shottenden. My parents only have two dairy cows and we are entirely dependent on them for our livelihood, as they are on us for their survival."

Charles let out a stifled snigger.

"That's exactly what I want from the Shottenden herd," Hugh replied, rubbing his hands together with glee and ignoring Charles. "If we look after our Jerseys, add value to their milk by making butter and cheese, they could repay us fourfold. What we need is a first-class herd, high-quality grazing and a nutritional programme for maximizing milk yields."

Hugh's passion for farming was infectious. His sore, red eyes glinted with pleasure.

"I learned so much from my exceptionally wise grandmother, Annie MacKenzie, but when it came to cows, her answer was always the same. Ask a crofter."

Charles coughed to interrupt the conversation and bring the discussion back to his comfort zone. He had no idea what a croft was.

"Are you sure it's sensible to expand the herd whilst

cereal prices are so high?" he asked, scowling at Angus before turning to face Hugh. "It might be more profitable to plough up the pastures and sow more wheat and oats."

"I can see your point," Hugh replied cautiously, "but we need to think long term, Charles. Last December's Agricultural Act guaranteed farmers a four-year minimum cereal price, but after that, who knows where prices will be? Being naturally prudent, I think we should spread the risk.

"As you rightly say, wheat and oats are being subsidized by the government for the next four years, so I suggest we increase our cattle numbers and try to make our milk profitable without relying on financial assistance. An auction mart has recently opened at Leyburn and they have a sale next week. I want you, Angus, to go and buy twelve in-calf heifers."

Angus responded enthusiastically. He knew little about Jerseys but was determined to repay Hugh for the faith he had placed in him.

At the next meeting Charles informed Hugh that Mr Mitchell was keen to buy Matchings Farm and if the Estate were still willing to sell, he would draw up a sales agreement and proceed with all the necessary arrangements.

On 16th June 1921, Matchings Farm was put out to tender and bought by Cressida Holdings Ltd, an unknown company which had offered well over the asking price.

Hugh had been very disappointed not to have visited

Tommy Mitchell ahead of the sale and was surprised when he heard that Tommy had been unsuccessful in his bid to buy the Matchings freehold. Unfortunately, after suffering a serious chest infection, he had taken his doctor's advice and stayed at home to rest.

"He's an honourable and innovative tenant, always paying his rent on time and taking a pride in his beef herd. It would have been a wonderful opportunity for him and his family to have bought the farm."

"The decision to sell to Cressida Holdings wasn't an easy one," Charles said gloomily. "I know how closely the estate works with its tenants and I assure you, Sir Hugh, under normal circumstances, we would have accepted Mr Mitchell's lower offer but if the estate is to diversify into milk production, it needs the capital to invest in new dairy facilities and Cressida's offer was one we couldn't ignore."

Hugh decided to leave the subject alone but couldn't help but show his intense disappointment.

"Fill me with hope, Angus, and tell me how the dairy is progressing," he implored.

"The herd is producing good quality milk," Angus said with enthusiasm, "which we have started to sell door-to-door but if we are to increase production we need better quality pasture.

"Our main problem is access to grass. The fields within walking distance of the milking parlour are not as fertile as the ones at Sevenscore but unfortunately it is impossible to get the herd over to the best pasture and back again in time for milking."

Hugh declared himself delighted that the dairy business was showing signs of success and encouraged Angus to do more research and find solutions to the problems he was facing.

The 1920 Agricultural Act had promised to under-pin the price of wheat and oats in order to encourage farmers to take risks and invest more heavily in arable farming. It was hoped that a confident agricultural sector would employ more people on the land, halt the haemorrhage of workers from the country to the towns and reduce dependency on foreign food imports. By spring 1921, the government had grown increasingly alarmed at the tumbling cereal prices and it became apparent that the cost of guaranteeing a minimum price for the entire British harvest was more than the Treasury could afford.

Hugh and Angus spent many hours discussing the Act and agreed to take a more cautious approach to farming.

"Have you heard of Turnip Townshend?" Hugh asked one evening as they sat drinking whisky in the library after dinner.

Angus shook his head.

"He was an eighteenth-century viscount who introduced the English to a four-field crop rotation, producing wheat, barley, a root crop and clover.

The clever thing about the system is that the root crops can be harvested for animal fodder and the cows can graze directly on the grass and clover mix, allowing manure to accumulate in the soil and improve its fertility. If we are going to increase the dairy herd, continue to keep pigs and sheep and aim for quality high yielding cereals, it may be worth putting the whole farm into the four-field system. What do you think?"

Angus considered the question carefully.

It seemed the perfect way to farm the estate, if only he could solve the problem of getting the dairy herd to the clover enriched grass and back to the yard in time for milking.

"I think we should give the four-field system a go," he replied.

"Splendid!" Hugh replied. "I rather hoped you would agree with the plan."

The estate put its four-year plan into action and planted the fields with wheat, barley, turnips and clover, leaving the pastures unploughed.

In July, Angus was having breakfast when Hugh entered the dining room, shouting and waving his newspaper in the air.

"Look at this!" he cried, shoving the paper in front of Angus.

"Government reneges on Agricultural Act

The government has abolished the Act, with immediate effect, ignoring its promise to give four years' notice...."

The 'Great Betrayal' proved to be an agricultural catastrophe.

CHAPTER 19

"May I have a word, Mother?" Hugh requested one morning after breakfast. "It's about Huntley."

Lady Hollister was sitting on the sofa in the morning room reading the Court and Social section of *The Times* and sipping at a cup of orange pekoe tea. It was her favourite time of day when the early morning sun shone through the large window, bathing the soft furnishings in warm light.

The war had changed so many lives, and large houses like Shottenden were finding it hard to recruit and retain loyal staff. Huntley had served the Hollister family faithfully for over fifty years and his reserved personality and impeccable manners never once betrayed his inner thoughts or feelings. On several occasions since returning from France, Hugh had observed the elderly man grimace as he ascended the main staircase and his once upright posture had become noticeably stooped.

"What about Huntley?" Lady Hollister replied, closing the broadsheet and finishing her tea. "I hope he isn't ill. Losing Huntley would be a disaster for us all. He's irreplaceable."

"As far as I know, he's fine in himself," Hugh said, taking a seat next to her, "but he is having serious problems with his legs and his hands are beginning to shake. I asked Dr Phillips to have a look at him last week and he has just come back to me and suggested that perhaps the time has come for Huntley to retire. The constant to-ing and fro-ing up and down the stairs has definitely made things worse for him and the prognosis isn't good. He needs to do a few more tests but at the moment he thinks Huntley may have Parkinson's disease. Have you any idea how old he actually is?"

Lady Hollister thought for a while. "He joined us as an under-footman on 1st June 1867."

"Goodness, how on earth did you remember that?"

"I may be old but I'm not as decrepit as you some-times think," she chided. "When Huntley first arrived at Shottenden, he was a tall, pale lad of about sixteen. His father was a hewer at Oaks Colliery and was determined to spare his son the same fate but, with no other employment in the village, the young Huntley had to start work down the pit as a coal driver.

"Although the work was dirty and the conditions cramped, Huntley developed a close bond with his Shetland pony, spending up to eight hours a day walking him from the coal face to the bottom of the pit head.

"In December 1866, as he and his father were walking to the colliery to start their shift, a huge explosion ripped through the mine, killing 361. The mine was sealed to extinguish the fire and both men found themselves out of work in a small community which had been literally torn apart by the tragedy. His father never recovered from the trauma of surviving and died a few months later. Huntley heard through family connections that we were looking for an under-footman at the time and applied for the job.

He has been a loyal, devoted and much valued member of staff here ever since.

"He never spoke of the accident, his father's early death or the loss of his beloved Shetland pony, preferring to bury his emotions as deep as the mine itself."

"If he were sixteen in 1867, he must have been born in 1851," Hugh calculated, "which now makes him seventy. It's time we started to plan for his retirement so that he can spend more time with his pigeons and family. The reason I mention it is that a cottage in the village will soon become vacant and I'm thinking of offering it to him. What do you think?"

"Do what you think is right," came the terse reply.

Hugh knew how much his mother disliked the changes to her life at Shottenden. She resented the reduction in staff and the lack of formal entertainment and although she would never admit it, she regretted her son's celibate state and his aversion to hosting dinners, house parties, shoots and balls.

"I'll talk to him after dinner," Hugh suggested. "But I think the time has come for him to retire fully. The news should make Daisy happy. They've always been very close."

At first, Huntley appeared shocked when Hugh

mentioned retirement but on reflection, he saw the advantages of moving into the village near his family and the shop, and it was true his legs and hands were playing up and giving him pain. On his last working day, Hugh presented him with a magnificent pigeon loft for his new garden. Huntley's fondness for these birds started after the death of his pony in the colliery disaster and he would spend most of his free time stroking and talking to them and racing them whenever he could. They somehow managed to bring out the tender, more loquacious side of his reserved character.

Much to his relief, Huntley's retirement took him away from daily contact with Charles Middlethwaite; a man who took pleasure in goading and humiliating the elderly retainer and other member of staff, reminding them of his superior position at Shottenden. He was deeply disliked and mistrusted. As far as Huntley was concerned, the Estate Manager was a cocky social climber who only cared about himself.

As soon as the presentation was over, Hugh withdrew into his study to contemplate life without a butler. His passion for agriculture kept him focussed on the farm but he was conservative by nature and disliked the changes he was having to make to the household.

Huntley had come to personify the glories of the pre-war days when life seemed jollier, the grass greener, the air sweeter and the future brighter.

Hugh's lapse into nostalgia made him deeply

depressed and he sought solace in the only way he knew how; reading the poem 'In Memoriam' by Ewart Alan Mackintosh. Somehow the haunting words helped comfort him when he felt worn out struggling to cope with past memories and present pain.

'So you were David's father,
And he was your only son,
And the new-cut peats are rotting
And the work is left undone,
Because of an old man weeping,
Just an old man in pain,
For David, his son David,
That will not come again.

Oh, the letters he wrote you,
And I can see them still,
Not a word of the fighting,
But just the sheep on the hill
And how you should get the crops in
Ere the year get stormier,
And the Bosches have got his body,
And I was his officer.

You were only David's father,
But I had fifty sons
When we went up in the evening
Under the arch of the guns,
And we came back at twilight

O God! I heard them call
To me for help and pity
That could not help at all.

Oh, never will I forget you,
My men that trusted me,
More my sons than your fathers
For they could only see
The little helpless babies
And the young men in their pride.
They could not see you dying
And hold you while you died.

Happy and young and gallant,
They saw their first-born go,
But not the strong limbs broken
And the beautiful men brought low,
The piteous writhing bodies,
They screamed "Don't leave me, sir",
For they were only your fathers
But I was your officer.'

His melancholy was interrupted by a knock on the door.

"Can I have a word, Sir Hugh?" Angus asked, hesitating to enter. "Or is this not a convenient time."

"Of course," Hugh replied wearily, but pleased to have company. "Come in! Come and sit down."

Angus drew up a chair, wondering if it were the right time to talk about farming.

"I hope you are here to bring me good news," Hugh said. "I need to believe in a better world after so much suffering."

The collapse in cereal prices and the withdrawal of the government subsidy had put huge financial pressure on the estate and had also destroyed the lives of a few of his neighbours.

Hugh did everything he could to keep his tenants' rent low but the strain was beginning to show.

"I think I have solved the problem of moving the dairy herd to the outlying pastures," Angus informed him. "I've read about a Wiltshire farmer, Arthur Hosier, who has invented a portable milking plant that moves over the fields to where the cows graze. Would you allow me travel down to his farm and take a look at the machine to see if would be suitable for Shottenden?"

Hugh was keen to hear more about the Open-Air Dairy and encouraged Angus to visit Mr Hosier.

"If it's as cost effective as you say, we may buy one for the estate," he enthused.

The portable milking machine surpassed all Angus' expectations and he returned to Shottenden elated.

"It's an incredible system, Sir Hugh," he explained soon after his return. "The Open-Air Dairy reduces TB and calf scouring by keeping the cows in a clean, outdoor environment, unlike our cows which spend too much time in warm sheds full of dung and urine, inhaling each other's breath.

"Apparently, one man and a boy can milk and feed seventy cows in winter compared with a conventional milking system which requires a team of seven men to bring in the fodder, clean the sheds, wash the cows, cart the manure back to the land and spread it over the fields."

Hugh tried to take everything in.

"What about costs?" he asked. "The estate is under unprecedented pressure at the moment, so any purchase would have to improve its profitability."

"Mr Hosier was keen to point out that farms can no longer rely on subsidies and have to face up to foreign competition by producing milk and milk products as cheaply as other countries. He is managing to produce milk cheaper than the average cost of production in Denmark and New Zealand."

Hugh looked genuinely impressed and congratulated Angus on his research.

"Let me read through your notes and we can discuss the Open-Air Dairy at our next monthly meeting."

It didn't take Hugh long to read the paperwork and rather than wait, he gave Angus permission to buy a Hosier's portable milking parlour.

Some months later, Angus attended the Leyburn Auction Mart to buy more Jerseys for the expanding dairy. A dishevelled man approached him outside the ring.

"Mr MacLeod?" he asked, staring at the ground.

"Aye."

"You've never met me, Mr MacLeod, but I'm Mr Mitchell from Matchings Farm," the old man lamented.

"Ah! Mr Mitchell, how good to meet you at last," Angus said, shaking the man's scrawny hand warmly. "How are things going?"

"Bad!" he replied, trying to keep his voice steady. "Very bad! Mr MacLeod, I'm here to sell my entire herd and I have to vacate Matchings by the end of the month."

Angus looked kindly at Tommy Mitchell whose thin cheeks showed the familiar signs of hunger and fatigue. It was heartbreaking to witness a good man fall on hard times and lose his livelihood but unfortunately he wasn't the only farmer at the sale having to sell up. Depressed prices and high wages were making it difficult for new owner-occupied farms to keep up their monthly mortgage payments.

"Tell me what's gone wrong," Angus said with compassion, moving away from the large crowd that had gathered round the auction ring.

They found a quiet corner, where Tommy Mitchell gradually opened up and told Angus the full story of the farm since it was sold by the estate.

"When Sir Hugh put the farm on the market, I put in an offer slightly above the asking price," he confided. "You can imagine my surprise and disappointment when Captain Middlethwaite announced we hadn't got the freehold. Knowing how fair Sir Hugh is to his tenants, we had hoped the estate would accept our offer even if there had been a higher bid. Our new landlord remained a mystery but I continued paying the rent and farming the land just as my father and grandfather had done before me.

"A few weeks ago, I received a visit from a Mr Walters, who represented our new landlord, Cressida Holdings. He wished to look round the farm but only stayed a couple of hours, making detailed notes on the house, outbuildings and land. He refused a cup of tea and I never saw him again. He left without even saying good-bye.

"Not long after the visit, we received a letter informing us that our present rent had been re-assessed and would, with immediate effect, be increased by 30%, in line with current values. We struggled to find the extra money and asked for time to adjust to the large increase but Cressida Holdings were unyielding and, after six months, terminated our lease."

There was little Angus could say to comfort the ruined man but deep inside, he was furious at the injustice inflicted on the Mitchell family. He made it his mission to find out how much Cressida Holdings had paid for the farm, but he couldn't carry out the research without first telling Hugh the whole sad story.

Hugh was deeply upset when he heard about Tommy Mitchell's plight and financial ruin and suggested he and Angus put aside an entire afternoon in the estate office to sift through the relevant farm ledgers, deeds and correspondence. He hoped they would find a clue, however small, about the sale of Matchings Farm and Cressida Holdings. Angus was spurred on by the defeated look he had seen on Tommy's face and Hugh was determined to root out any injustice that might have taken place in Shottenden's name.

With daylight failing, they were beginning to lose hope of ever finding any evidence.

"I think I've found it!" Hugh finally cried, waving a file triumphantly in the air.

"Where was it?" Angus asked, delighted that some evidence had been found.

"That's the puzzling thing," he replied, slightly bemused. "It was hidden at the back of the filing cabinet in a file labelled 'General Plumbing Works'."

He opened the folder and spread its contents on the desk. Both men eagerly pored over the papers.

"Look!" Hugh exclaimed. "It shows here that Cressida Holdings Ltd paid below the asking price. I thought you said Tommy put in an offer matching the asking price."

"No," Angus replied. "Tommy told me he had put in an offer slightly *above* the asking price."

Hugh stared at the sale agreement and buried his damaged face in his hands, letting out a long, agonizing moan.

"Oh Angus!" he sighed. "I think the estate has been defrauded."

He checked the ledger book again and again, hoping the evidence would go away but the truth kept staring him in the face and there was nothing he could do about it. Cressida Holdings had paid below the asking price for Matchings Farm.

Things came to a head at the next monthly meeting, when Hugh confronted Charles Middlethwaite.

"Tell me about Cressida Holdings," he fumed, keeping his eyes firmly fixed on the young agent's surprised face.

"I don't know much about them," Charles replied, unsettled by Hugh's unaccustomed, cold manner.

"Liar!" Hugh barked, thumping his fist on the table, hardly able to contain his anger. "The company belongs to you and before you try to deny it, I have a letter here from Companies House confirming that you and your mother are the directors of Cressida Holdings which, by the way, was named after your mother, Cressida Hardwick. And what I find unforgiveable is that I have discovered from the War Office that you are nothing more than a NCO and a mere sergeant at that! All this pretence at being a Captain is scandalous and an insult to all those brave fellows in your regiment.

"You had the audacity, *Mr* Middlethwaite, to put in a low, anonymous bid for Matchings Farm which, as the Shottenden Land Agent, you accepted, regardless of the fact that Tommy Mitchell had put in a higher bid.

"Tommy is a faithful, honest man, whose family has farmed Matchings for over a hundred years, whilst you, sir, are a dishonourable scoundrel, who has taken advantage of your position and ruined an innocent man. I've a good mind to sue you for professional misconduct and insider dealing and don't expect me to shed a tear if you are sent to prison.

"Kindly clear your desk, leave the premises with immediate effect and never set foot on Shottenden soil again. Do I make myself clear, Mr Middlethwaite?"

Charles stared at his employer in astonishment but showed no sign of remorse. He calmly gathered up his papers and stuffed them into his briefcase, then walked out of the office closing the door behind him. No-one ever saw him again but several years later, Hugh received news that he had left England and was making a name for himself in Australia.

There was little Hugh could do for Tommy Mitchell as the estate no longer had the funds to buy back the farm nor did it have other land to offer him. He blamed himself for the Mitchell family's downfall and promised in future to check the accounts regularly and keep a closer eye on the estate's affairs. He asked Angus to take on more estate business and become his eyes and ears.

The following day, Sir Hugh drove over to Matchings Farm and offered young Johnny Mitchell the job of dairyman on the estate and a cottage.

Hugh became quieter and more withdrawn. He had become increasingly unwell and the Matchings incident severely shook his faith in human nature. He felt the loss of a world where honour and truth were valued and he wasn't sure he had the energy to embrace the modern, more abrasive, postwar era.

Angus continued to work hard, improving the soil, expanding the dairy and perfecting the four-field system which was serving the estate so well. There were times he felt lonely and longed to return to Skye and speak his native Gaelic but he was thankful for all he was learning, his access to the library and daily discussions with Hugh as well as the opportunity to be at the forefront of modern farming.

PART 2

(1946–1952)

CHAPTER 20

Skye, 1946

The letter Angus had been expecting for twenty-seven years finally arrived.

His mother was brief and to the point.

Murdo MacLeod had died peacefully, but unexpectedly, in his favourite armchair beside the fire.

He had returned home from checking the cattle during a particularly wild summer storm and complained of feeling tired. Ailsa hadn't taken much notice, as he regularly complained of aching bones and weak limbs.

She busied herself in the kitchen making him a cup of tea, with an extra spoonful of sugar to give him added strength, but by the time she placed the cup on the table beside him, he had already slipped away.

His father's funeral was to take place at Kilbackie on Thursday 13th June 1946 at ten-thirty.

Angus caught the train back to Skye and spent much of the long journey reflecting on the choices he had made in his life. A group of demobbed soldiers joined him in the carriage and he couldn't help overhearing their banter.

"Did you ever receive Red Cross food parcels in your camp?" a young man asked his neighbour.

"Yup! Every fortnight regular as clockwork: bully beef and milk, cocoa, biscuits and cigarettes and I hope I never see another bloomin' tin of beef in my life. God, it was awful! Just the thought of all that meat and jelly makes me feel sick!"

The young man sitting next to Angus chuckled and nodded in agreement.

"Do you know what I'm looking forward to when I get home?" he sniggered.

The lads in the crowded carriage started laughing, then burst into an uncontrollable fit of giggles.

"Not that, you idiots! Something much better," he replied.

"Is there anything better?" they cried, wiping away the tears rolling down their cheeks.

"Of course there is; clootie!"

"Mmmm!" cried the young Scots, winking at each other. "Are you quite sure it's better?"

Some of the carriage occupants had no idea what was going on and looked bemused.

"What's clootie?" one asked.

"You don't know what clootie is?" came the raucous voice of a ginger-headed lad sitting opposite Angus.

They shook their heads.

"It's a spicy dumpling made of dried fruit, wrapped in a cloth and left to simmer for hours. A cloot is Scots for cloth and my mother's clootie is the best in the world."

The soldiers continued chattering about home, food and their mothers while Angus leant against the window, thinking how little he knew about his father and now it was too late to find out.

"I should have stayed longer in Kilbackie after leaving the army," he thought bitterly, but at the time, it had seemed right to return to Shottenden and he never once regretted his decision to turn down the job in India in favour of becoming Shottenden's stockman and later its manager.

He arrived at Kilbackie on a glorious June day when the sun's rays lit up the orchids, tormentils and eyebrights flowering in the early summer grass. Corncrakes could be heard rasping their repetitive call in the tall vegetation, skylarks soared high into the sky singing their joyful songs and cuckoos repeated their two notes from the trees that clung to the soil under the cliffs.

A light, salty breeze blew through the washing lines anchored in unkempt garden plots which were covered in buttercups and daisies.

Ailsa saw her son approach the croft before he had started climbing up the hill and, like the father of the prodigal son, she hurried down the road to greet him, throwing her arms round his waist.

She had lost height since he last saw her and was very slender but her thick grey hair was still neatly tied up in a bun and her vigour showed no sign of flagging.

Her tender touch awoke in him a longing for intimacy and, for the first time in twenty-seven years, he felt an overwhelming desire to love and be loved.

"It's good to see you again, Angus," she said, holding her only son's hand. "Your father would have been so proud to see you looking well."

There was no guile in her voice, only a genuine longing to have her child back with her. Although nothing had ever been mentioned, Angus knew he had been a disappointment to his mother and it hurt him to think of the gossip she must have endured as a result of his behaviour and decisions.

He had rejected her church, turned his back on her way of life and denied her the joy of grandchildren and yet despite everything, she continued to shower him with love.

Ailsa MacLeod sat down beside her son on the bench outside her blackhouse and, without a trace of self-pity, asked him all about his life in England.

Over the next few days, they managed to catch up with each other's lives and become closer than ever. Their bond had always been special and Angus had found it easy to relax in his mother's company.

The huge funeral was taken by Donny, who had returned to Kilbackie as its minister some ten years ago. He had taken over the living from his father who had retired in 1934. Predictably, he exploited Murdo's funeral by delivering a barnstorming sermon on the wages of sin and the agony of hell. His preaching was so intense, he barely mentioned Murdo, who lay forgotten in his coffin, waiting patiently to be returned to the soil he had tilled all his life.

Angus listened furiously, as Donny abused his

ministerial position and used the funeral as a platform for his own glory. Trapped by his mother's grief and the crushing crowd around him, Angus had no alternative but to listen to the minister's long, unintelligible rant. He let his eyes wander round the packed church and became aware of a beautiful, slim woman whose auburn hair shone like gold in the sun's rays streaming through the windows.

She wore a rather jaunty black hat and a dark skirt which seemed to float with each graceful movement of her body when she stood up for the prayers. At one point during the service, she glanced shyly in his direction and gave him a broad smile which lit up her freckled face.

"Mother," Angus whispered as they followed the coffin out of the church. "Who is the beautiful woman standing next to Mairi?"

His mother held onto his arm and replied, "Surely you know who that is, it's Katherine Nicolson, Donny's daughter."

CHAPTER 21

Angus had spent the day on the moor helping the crofters rearrange the rows of peat slabs by lifting them upright and leaning them against each other like pyramids of playing cards. The increasing warmth of the spring breezes blowing off the Minch would help dry the slabs ready for loading into carts and bringing down to the crofts where they would be built into stacks.

It was back-breaking thirsty work especially in the midsummer heat under a cloudless Persian-blue sky but little Willie MacDonald and his brother Iain were on stand-by with buckets and ladles, ready to fill empty cups with cold spring water sprinkled with oatmeal.

He relived every one of his fifty years as he toiled in the sun frustrated by his lack of stamina yet feeling an urgent need to reconnect with his roots and purge himself of the privileged sedentary life he had grown accustomed to at Shottenden.

By evening, he felt intense pain in his neck and across his lower back and found it uncomfortable standing or sitting.

"You're very restless," Ailsa observed busying herself round the croft before retiring to bed. "Was the peat-cutting too much for you?"

He churlishly refused to answer, feeling the community was pressurising him to return home and run the family croft but one day out on the hill cutting peat was enough to confirm what he already feared; he was physically incapable of running a croft single-handed and had no interest in spending the rest of his life toiling the land of his forefathers.

"Go and get some rest," she urged. "We have another busy day tomorrow and you look as if you could do with a good night's sleep."

The short night that followed brought Angus little comfort. Curled up in his childhood bed, he tossed and turned unable to sleep thanks in part to the repetitive sound of a corncrake rasping in the long grass beside the croft; its irritating, monotonous call continued all night and only ceased when the cockerel on the thatched roof decided to welcome in the new day with exuberant bursts of crowing.

It took Angus a long time to ease himself out of bed but he was determined to walk as far as the bench outside and spend some time to himself contemplating his future.

"Do you mind if I join you?" a familiar voice asked.

He lifted his eyes and gave his mother the weakest of smiles.

The two of them sat side by side, entranced by the turquoise shimmer of the glassy sea and the two panpipe-notes of a cuckoo calling from the woods across the bay. The air was full of bees gathering nectar from freshly-opened wild flowers and the sound of oystercatchers repeated their distinctive 'cleep cleep' from the rocky shoreline.

"Talk to her," Ailsa said eventually, placing her hand lovingly on her son's slumped shoulder. "You have nothing to lose and so much to gain."

Angus grabbed hold of her hand and held it tightly.

"How did you know?"

"It was obvious from the moment you first saw her," came the unexpected reply. "You became a changed man."

He blanched at the thought of having betrayed his innermost emotions to his mother and felt the intimacy between them, deeply unsettling.

"What should I do about it?" he asked, arching his back and wincing with pain.

"Trust your heart." his mother replied getting up to leave. "If she is meant to be, you will find a way."

Angus remained alone reflecting on his mother's words until the pain in his shoulders, arms and legs forced him back to bed.

At ten o'clock an unexpected, cheery 'hello' greeted the new day and Katherine Nicolson entered the croft dressed neatly in her District Nurse uniform and carrying a large leather bag. She had been visiting a first-time mother nearby and decided, on the off-chance, to see if Ailsa were in.

"Anyone at home?" she called, popping her head round the door.

The delight at seeing the minister's daughter must have shown on Ailsa's face because Katherine immediately apologised for not having visited sooner and asked if there was anything she could do to help.

Angus couldn't see Katherine from his box-bed behind the curtain but he heard the two ladies discussing his back, the physical demands of crofting and the unkind way age eventually catches up with everyone. He cowered further under the blankets, ashamed of his feebleness and humiliated by Katherine's presence. He prayed she would hurry up and leave but his prayers weren't answered.

"I can check on him now, if you like," she said helpfully, making her way towards the wooden alcove.

"Mr MacLeod, would you mind if I asked you a few questions?"

Angus hesitantly drew back the curtain and faced the woman whose beauty had captivated his heart, mind and soul. There was no telling what Katherine thought because she showed little emotion and remained totally professional, asking him about his injury and its symptoms.

"It sounds as if you've pulled a muscle," she said with genuine sympathy. "There is very little I can do to help, other than suggest that you keep warm and rest whenever possible. It's important, however, that you move about gently and use the muscles in your back but don't overdo things.

"I expect Dr O'Neal will call round later to give you some pain relief and I'll try and visit you tomorrow to see if things have improved," she added, making for the door.

A few minutes later Angus' mother drew up a stool beside her son.

"Well!" she exclaimed, with a glint in her eye. "The Lord always finds a way!"

Angus wished he could have smiled at his mother's optimism but his mind was full of self-doubt and he struggled to cope with his feelings for Katherine. Having already let the community down by not joining them that morning for another day's peat-cutting, he was reluctant to declare himself to a woman he had only just met.

He lost his appetite and slipped into a reverie during the evening meal.

"Are you still in a lot of pain?" Ailsa enquired cautiously, not wanting to offend.

This time Angus decided to be more gracious and open with his mother.

"No," he confessed. "The pain has eased but I can't get Katherine out of my mind and I've only got a week to sort things out.

"Should I say something?" he asked in despair. "Help me decide what to do for the best! I am out of my depth."

"If it's meant to be, the Lord will provide the opportunity," was all she replied.

True to her word, Katherine called round the next morning and found Angus sitting forlornly in his father's chair, reading a book.

"What are you reading?" she asked innocently.

"'The Power and the Glory' by Graham Greene,"

he replied, adding, "I've only just started so I can't tell you what it's about but it's been on my list of books to read for a long time."

"It must be lovely having so much choice," she said without guile. "Where do you find all the books you want to read?"

Angus told Katherine about his work on the estate, his friendship with Sir Hugh Hollister and the magnificent library at Shottenden. Before long they were talking freely about literature and philosophy, unaware of the passing time.

"I don't want to interrupt you," Ailsa said timidly, "But it's already half past eleven, Katherine."

"Oh no!" came the panicked reply. "I'm late for my next visit! If I get reported I could lose my job. I must go."

She gathered up her belongings and walked briskly to the door, lifting the latch.

"It's been a pleasure meeting you, Mr MacLeod," she added before hurrying out of the croft.

Over the next few days, Katherine visited Angus daily but her visits had become more social than medical until finally she was forced to admit that he no longer needed her help.

"I hope you stay fit and well, Mr MacLeod and have a safe journey back to England."

The thought of losing Katherine was devastating to Angus and he desperately tried to think of something to say that would prolong their parting.

"Could you keep an eye on my mother for me?" he

floundered, embarrassed that his face was blushing. "I leave the day after tomorrow and she is not as robust as she looks."

Katherine turned deathly pale but managed to stay in control of her emotions and assured him that she would do her best.

The following morning, Ailsa called round to the Nurses' Cottage and asked if Katherine would care to join her and Angus for a picnic lunch as a small way of saying 'thank you' for all her help and advice.

"That's very kind of you," she replied cautiously, "but I'm not sure I deserve such a delightful treat — after all I was only doing my job."

"Of course you do!" Ailsa pleaded. "Please say you'll come."

"Well, I've got nothing on this afternoon as it's my half day off but I won't be free until one o'clock. Would two o'clock be all right? It'll give me time to change and bike over from the cottage."

Ailsa agreed to the plan and hurried home to prepare what she hoped would be a memorable picnic. She made up two baskets of food and asked Angus to carry them down to the shore while she took her tartan rug and spread it over the meadow buttercups and orchids. Angus and Katherine sat bashfully in the long grass listening to the lapping waves of the incoming tide, unsure what to say or do. Neither was hungry and instead of enjoying the heat of the afternoon, they appeared tense and reserved.

"Tell me more about Shottenden," Katherine eventually said, picking a blade of grass and twisting it round her finger to avoid looking at Angus.

"What is there to say?" he replied, "other than it's the most glorious estate in England."

"More glorious than Buckingham Palace?" she asked timidly, not daring to look up.

"I don't know," he chuckled, finally beginning to relax. "I've never been to Buckingham Palace but I'm sure Shottenden is much prettier with its cricket ground, walled garden, stables and cottages."

"Not forgetting the library!" Katherine chipped in, remembering Angus' description of the magnificent room.

"Naturally, not forgetting the library!" he added with a smile.

"It all sounds wonderful," Katherine sighed, staring out to sea to avoid his gaze.

"Why don't you two make the most of the sunshine and go for a walk while I clear up," Ailsa suggested, stacking the dirty plates and placing them carefully back in the basket.

CHAPTER 22

"You know my father thinks you're cursed," Katherine admitted with a strained smile as she and Angus walked along the shore, listening to the three-noted call of a sandpiper flying around the water's edge.

"I know," Angus replied, "but if he'd only bother to listen to my point of view, he might not find me quite so wicked."

"I don't think he'll ever change," she said ruefully. "He sees black and white as colours of strength and faith and grey as the colour of doubt and weakness!"

"That's a pity," Angus laughed, "because grey is the only colour I recognise at the moment!"

"Do you ever think we'll tire of this view?" she asked looking out over the causeway towards the Outer Isles.

He didn't answer.

His eyes were firmly fixed on the young woman standing beside him, her long hair blowing wildly in the stiffening breeze.

"Come on!" he said suddenly, trying to break the ice. "Let's play Pooh-sticks."

"What's that?" she asked, laughing at the sight of a man, old enough to be her father, walking carefully over the stony beach to a small wooden bridge that crossed the stream.

"It's a simple game one of the children at Shottenden taught me. I'll teach you the rules later but first things first; wait downstream and when I drop the stick into the water, count the seconds until it reaches you. Whatever happens, don't lose it!"

Katherine did as she was told, amazed that a grown man could get so much pleasure from throwing a stick into the water. His enthusiasm was infectious and she was soon fully involved in the game.

"Am I far enough down?" she shouted up from her position by the water.

"You're fine where you are," he replied. "Don't move any closer to the sea. I'm going to count to three and then I'll release the stick. Are you ready? One — two — three!"

He let go of piece of wood and watched it float under the rickety bridge to where Katherine was patiently waiting at the water's edge.

"Pick it up!" he panicked. "Don't lose it, Katherine! Pick it up!"

She hurriedly grabbed the Pooh-stick and pulled it out of the water. In the stunned silence that followed, Angus got down on one knee and shouted down from the bridge, "Katherine Nicolson of Kilbackie, will you marry me?"

She slid a small gold ring off the Pooh-stick and placed it on the fourth finger of her left hand.

"Yes!" she cried, running up to the bridge and flinging her arms round his waist. "Yes!"

Angus lifted her face and kissed her.

"Before you pledge yourself," he said looking anxious, "I want to be sure you fully understand the sacrifice you will be making by marrying me. No matter what the Kilbackie rumour-wheel says, I have no intention of returning to Skye to run my father's croft. My home is at Shottenden and after we are married, I will be asking you to give up your job and everything that's familiar to you, to move with me back to England.

"It would be a huge commitment and I would totally understand if you felt I was asking too much."

Katherine kept her eyes firmly fixed on Angus' honest freckled face and noticed for the first time that his eyes were the colour of milkwort and his dark hair was streaked with silver.

"If I'd had the courage, I'd have moved away from Skye a long time ago," she sighed, "so living with you in England would be a dream come true."

"Thank you, Katherine," Angus said, stroking her face.

She was about to say something else but he put his finger to her lips.

"I love you, Katherine, more than you will ever know. I love your gentleness, intelligence and compassion and despite our age-difference, I believe I can make you the happiest woman in the world."

She looked down at the ring on her finger and pressed her ruffled hair against his chest.

"I'm afraid I told my mother about my plan," he confessed, "and she insisted you had a ring to wear.

She was so excited, she literally ran to her small box of treasures and took out her mother's wedding ring with instructions that I was give it to you until a more suitable engagement ring could be bought."

"Please don't buy me another ring," she pleaded, wiping away the tears on her cheeks. "If this one has been loved by your mother and grandmother, I will treasure it for the rest of my life."

Angus kissed her hair and whispered, "Everything that's happened to me so far in life has been preparation for this moment, Katherine, and I intend to honour and love you for as long as I live."

She nestled closer to her husband-to-be and felt his arms envelop her.

"I love you too," she beamed, lifting her face towards his.

Before he had time to savour the moment, she added with a smile, "Will you teach me the rules of that Pooh game?"

"Not now," he replied, suddenly appearing nervous. "We must get back to my mother and tell her our good news, then I have the task of formally asking your father for your hand, something I should have done first but I'm afraid I lost my nerve!

"I promise I'll send you a copy of *The House at Pooh Corner* when I get back to Shottenden. It's an enchanting little book and you can read everything there is to know about Poohsticks!"

When Angus asked Donny for his daughter's hand, the minister turned puce and the veins in his ample neck bulged as he worked himself into an apoplectic frenzy.

"Good God, Angus, you are fifty years old and she is only twenty-seven. The idea is preposterous and out of the question. I will never give my consent for my only daughter to marry a non-believer nearly twice her age and, no matter how much you plead or beg, you are never to see her again. Do you hear me — *never?*"

For a brief moment Angus thought Donny was going to have a fit.

"Have I made myself clear?" Donny screamed. "You are never to set foot in this manse again or have any further contact with Katherine."

Donny was an ambitious man, who had worked hard to secure a place at Theological College and much to his surprise he had excelled in Biblical Hebrew and Classical Greek. He loved theology and would spend hours in his study trawling through commentaries, looking up words in *Cruden's Concordance* and examining the minutiae of biblical translation and interpretation. Preparing for the Sunday service could take up to three or four days and preaching was the highlight of his week.

Edith enjoyed the status of minister's wife and found her husband easier to live with now he was sober and focussed. She was dutiful, hospitable and caring and on the rare occasions he sought her opinion, she offered him wise advice.

Donny naturally presumed his daughter would

follow in her mother's footsteps and marry a minister, run the Sabbath school, have a large family and become a highly respected member of the community. Instead, Katherine decided, against her father's wishes, to travel to Glasgow and start a three-year nursing course which she loved. She, too, studied hard and would have returned to Skye sooner had it not been for the outbreak of war.

Donny never understood why his only daughter chose to leave the Manse but when, in 1945, a vacancy for a District Nurse in Rosvaig was advertised in *The Nursing Times*, Katherine decided to apply and was offered the position with accommodation provided in the Nurses' Cottage.

With Angus firmly barred from the manse, the tension in the Nicolson household reached breaking point the next evening at supper when Katherine's brothers, John and Kenny, accused him of devil worship and questioned his virility.

Drunk, ignorant and fuelled with prejudice, their talk became increasingly offensive.

"Stop it!" Katherine begged. "Stop being so vulgar and leave him alone."

"'Stop being so vulgar, you naughty boys!'" they mimicked, childishly.

She appealed to her father for help, but the minister looked on with quiet amusement, unwilling to defend his daughter or his friend.

Katherine could have forgiven her brothers' lewd behaviour but not her father's tacit approval.

His contempt for Angus changed Katherine's life forever.

After supper, she tapped on the minister's study door and walked straight in, without waiting for permission. As usual, Donny was sitting at his desk making copious, detailed notes for his forthcoming sermon. The brass oil lamp, which Edith polished every Monday morning, threw a halo of mellow light against the wall and beside his desk stood a large wicker waste-paper basket overflowing with discarded sheets of paper.

He looked up and smiled at his daughter but his expression soon changed when he saw the fury in her eyes.

"How dare you!" she hissed, hardly able to contain her anger. "How dare you sit at the family table and condone John and Kenny's drunken tirade against the man who not only saved your life but was your best friend.

"You have dedicated your whole life to biblical teaching," she went on, hardly drawing breath, "and have delivered hundreds of eloquent sermons on the wrath of God and his awful judgement but you rarely, if ever, talk of God's compassion and His love for His people. Your mind is so consumed with the terrors of hell that you have forgotten how to love."

The minister looked baffled as she continued her lecture.

"You stood by, while your sons made fun of a good,

honest man, the man I love and have every intention of marrying, with or without your permission."

Donny took a long hard look at his daughter then slowly and deliberately picked up the notes lying on his desk and tore them into little pieces, letting the fragments of paper slip through his fingers onto the floor.

Without uttering a word, he turned his back on his daughter, picked up his pen and started to re-write his sermon.

Katherine slipped out of her father's study and never set foot in the manse again.

The next day, she and Angus announced their engagement and the following Sunday, Reverend Donny Nicolson informed his congregation that he no longer had a daughter.

CHAPTER 23

Shottenden, 1946

"Well I'm blowed!" Hugh gasped, too amazed to form a constructive sentence. "When and where are you going to get married?"

"Ah!" Angus exclaimed, clearing his throat. "That's the problem, Sir Hugh. We'd love to get married on Skye but Donny has forbidden it, so the only other suitable place would be here at Shottenden."

Hugh looked confused.

"Why has Donny, your best friend, forbidden you to get married?"

For a while, Angus looked uncomfortable but then he straightened his shoulders and replied, "Because I am engaged to his daughter, Katherine!"

It was difficult to tell from Hugh's expression whether he was amused or appalled at Angus' choice of bride but he generously held back from commenting and said he would try to find a solution to the problem.

Katherine, meanwhile, had moved out of the manse and was living with her future mother-in-law, Ailsa MacLeod, an arrangement that suited them both.

When Hugh told his mother that Angus had got engaged and that his wife-to-be would be staying at

Shottenden as his guest until her wedding day, he received a hostile reaction.

"If that's what you want, I'll have to go along with it," she muttered gracelessly, "although I fail to see why you go out of your way to help a crofter's son and a minister's daughter, young enough to be *his* daughter, get married. You must be going soft in the head, Hugh."

From the start, Lady Hollister had resented Angus' influence on her son and found it difficult to like him. There was something awkward and tense about his manner and she could never understand why her son enjoyed his company so much. The thought of Angus' bride living at Shottenden for three months was particularly disagreeable to her, but as soon as she saw the extraordinarily beautiful and dignified young woman walk through the door, the cantankerous old lady accepted she might have been a bit hasty in her judgement.

A month after her arrival, Lady Hollister informed her son that once Katherine was married, she intended to offer her a position as her companion.

"What about Daisy?" he exclaimed. "Surely you're not thinking of having two companions."

"Of course not!" she replied impatiently. "Stop interrupting me, Hugh, and listen to what I have to say.

"Daisy came to see me last week and asked for some time off to look after her son, William. I don't know if you remember him, but he was always such a delightful, quiet boy. It came as quite a shock when he volunteered to join the army at the outbreak of war and was sent to Singapore. Poor thing! He was captured by the Japanese and was terribly mistreated by those beastly little men. According to Daisy, the prison guards starved and beat him until he was unrecognisable. Can you imagine? It all sounds simply ghastly.

"Since William's return, Daisy has hardly left his side, fearing he could harm himself at any time. She feeds him nutritious soup in the hope he will start putting on weight but according to Daisy he still only weighs eight stone.

"I've given her a fortnight off but made it clear that a firm decision about her future would have to be made soon."

"Let's see how the next three months work out," Hugh replied, wanting his mother to be as comfortable as possible in the huge rattling house that no longer seemed to serve a purpose.

Lady Hollister's health had recently taken a turn for the worse and she was experiencing severe pain in her leg, so the arrival of a qualified nurse was considered advantageous.

"I don't want to speak out of turn," Katherine hesitated one evening as she was preparing Lady Hollister for bed on Daisy's night off, "but is your leg giving you trouble?"

She paused to gauge the response but was met by a stony silence.

Over the next few days, Hugh noticed his mother was hobbling and insisted on summoning Dr Porter to the house for a consultation. Dr Porter was a tall suave man with immaculate manners and immense charm. He would travel day and night, through wind, rain and ice to visit his patients and no call was ever too insignificant. Renowned as a bon viveur, he effortlessly graced the drawing rooms of the wealthy whose ill-health sustained his lavish lifestyle. As far as he was concerned, a medical qualification was as good as a silver spoon and he had no misgivings commiserating with the sick and associating with their pain—compassion was a financial virtue.

"Good morning, Sir Hugh!" he announced as Huntley showed him into the drawing room. "I'm sorry to hear Lady Hollister is not enjoying her usual good health."

He placed his battered Gladstone bag on the Wilton carpet and stood confidently in front of Hugh.

"A sore leg, you say. Well, well, that's easily put right. Do not concern yourself unduly; we'll soon have your charming mother back on her feet admiring the flowers in the garden and hosting games of bridge."

Katherine and Lady Hollister waited for the doctor in the morning room.

"Good morning, Lady Hollister," he declared cheerfully inclining his head out of deference. "Now what's all this I hear about you having a sore leg?"

Katherine had persuaded Lady Hollister to remove her stocking ahead of the visit to make it easier for the doctor to examine the leg and true to his method of diagnosis, he spent several minutes staring at the ulcer, before concluding that a bottle of Tincture of Iodine and some fresh dressings would soon put things right.

"Thank you Doctor Porter," the relieved lady said, folding back her skirt.

"I'll visit you again in a few days," he said, closing his bag before washing his hands thoroughly. "Don't forget my instructions."

The good doctor left Lady Hollister full of gratitude and after a courtesy glass of sherry with Sir Hugh, he continued on his rounds.

Katherine had watched the visit in horror and when Daisy later described the true extent of the leg infection, she decided something had to be done.

"Lady Hollister," she implored, "Your leg is not healing and I believe you require a dose of something called penicillin, which destroys infection and speeds recovery. I remember a small child suffering from blood poisoning just after the end of the war. Her nurse had heard about penicillin and insisted the little girl was given a dose but the only available stock was kept under lock and key for military use. As all the mine sweepers had left the waters around Skye, the persistent nurse persuaded the doctor to take a vial from the store and give the dying child an injection. The result was extraordinary, because within forty-eight hours the little girl was skipping around the house without a care in the world.

She had been completely cured.

"Please, Lady Hollister; ask Doctor Porter when he nexts visits, to give you a dose of penicillin?"

"I'll do no such thing!" Lady Hollister retorted, clearly annoyed by the story and Daisy's obvious indiscretion. "Now if you have nothing better to do, I suggest you leave the room."

Not long after Katherine's intervention, Lady Hollister was confined to bed with a fever and unable to walk.

Dr Porter continued to visit, oiling her concerns with smooth, well-chosen words, insisting that she was getting better. Eventually, worn down by pain and discomfort, Lady Hollister told her son about Katherine's visit.

"I trust Katherine Nicolson," he replied. "Dr Porter has become greedy and is more interested in his fees than his patients' welfare; It has become apparent that your recovery is no longer of any interest to him but Katherine seems genuinely concerned so I think we should demand a dose of penicillin."

Reluctantly, Lady Hollister agreed with her son and on the doctor's next visit, she requested the miracle cure. Within four days, the infection had totally disappeared and although the ulcer still needed dressing, Lady Hollister was up and about and back to normal.

Unable to show gratitude, she repaid Katherine's courage by ordering Billings, the chauffeur, to take her and Gladys over to Marshall and Snelgrove in Harrogate, where the manager, Mr Elliston, would be expecting them. She wrote a letter to Miss Dyer, her favourite assistant, asking her to help Katherine choose a suitable wedding dress and trousseau, enclosing all her saved clothing coupons.

On the day of her wedding, Hugh stood at the bottom of the stairs and watched in total amazement as a radiant Katherine Nicolson descended Shottenden Park's grand staircase with natural poise and elegance. She wore an exquisite full-length ivory dress with a puddle train and a floor-length sheer veil fastened to her swept-up hair. In her hands she clasped a long trailing bouquet of green foliage, white lilies, gypsophila and myrtle, all of which had been delicately pieced together by Daisy.

"You look absolutely beautiful!" Hugh gasped, placing his arm proudly through hers and leading her across the hallway to the waiting car. "Angus is the luckiest man in the world."

Billings had cleaned and polished the Armstrong Siddeley until it shone and sparkled like Whitby jet. He stood to attention by the open passenger door and took hold of the bouquet as Katherine stepped into the back of the car and settled down on the soft leather seat, arranging her dress and veil around her. Billings placed the bouquet beside her, closed the door and went round to the driver's seat where he waited for Hugh before starting the engine. He drove slowly down the drive to St Thomas's Church which nestled on the edge of the estate.

The simple marriage ceremony took place at three

o'clock on 5th October 1946 and was witnessed by Lady Hollister, Hugh, Gladys, Daisy, Huntley and Mr and Mrs Billings. The service was followed by a wedding tea in the main house.

No-one in Katherine's family thought to reply to the invitation but Ailsa sent an affectionate letter, apologising for not being able to attend the ceremony but wishing them both every happiness in their future life together.

Hugh had arranged for the floral arrangements in the church to be taken to the newly weds' cottage, so when Angus finally lifted his bride over the threshold, they were greeted with a profusion of scented flowers.

"Oh my goodness, Angus!" she exclaimed. "They're beautiful. Was this your idea?"

"No," he said, looking round the room. "Unfortunately the flowers have nothing to do with me but I bet Sir Hugh planned it all."

They held hands and laughed with joy, racing each other up the narrow staircase to the bedroom, where vases of cream and yellow freesias and lilies filled the room.

CHAPTER 24

"Take a seat, Katherine," Lady Hollister requested graciously, smoothing the folds in her peacock blue dress.

The new bride sat delicately at the end of the drawing room sofa and radiated contentment.

"How are finding your new home?"

"I love everything about Shottenden," she replied, "especially our cottage, the lawns and the flowers in the walled garden."

"I'm pleased," the elderly lady said, stroking the satin trim of her dress.

There was a moment's silence when both women appeared lost in thought.

Lady Hollister was the first to speak.

"As you probably know, Daisy has looked after me for many years and been the most wonderful help but ever since her son William returned from Burma suffering from a nervous disorder, she has found it hard caring for us both. Regrettably, she has handed in her notice in order to devote more time to her son and I can't tell you how much I'll miss her.

"I was wondering, Katherine, if you would consider replacing Daisy as my companion.

You've already seen her at work and probably have

a little idea of what is involved but I am now offering you a full-time position."

Katherine looked round the elegant drawing room and out through the long sash windows towards the mature trees bathed in autumn light and smiled.

"I would love to," she replied, with genuine pleasure.

Lady Hollister sighed with relief and clasped her hands together.

"I'm not the easiest person to please," she said truthfully, "but I always reward loyalty and discretion."

It was arranged for Katherine to spend the following week shadowing Daisy, who had agreed to return to work for one last week.

"Whatever you do, don't speak unless you are spoken to and *never* be late," Daisy advised.

"Can you sew?"

Katherine nodded but admitted she had never worked on fine silk or lace.

"I'll give you some off-cuts to practice on," Daisy offered. "It's surprising how much sewing and mending is needed to keep Lady Hollister looking immaculate and fashionable. She hasn't had any new clothes made for a long time which probably explains why she pays so much attention to her current wardrobe. She's a remarkable lady and still as beautiful as ever, even at seventy-four."

Katherine tried to imagine Lady Hollister in her youth and the dazzling life she must have led. It couldn't have been more different than her dour upbringing in the Manse where all forms of entertainment were frowned upon and novels were banned. It was only when she started her nursing course in Glasgow that she discovered the joy of reading and devoured the classics — particularly the works of Tolstoy, Flaubert, Austen and the Brontës.

"Did Shottenden ever host balls?" she asked, keen to learn as much as she could about the place she was about to call home.

"There hasn't been a ball in my time working for Lady Hollister," Daisy replied, "and I started working for her just after the First World War. It's a pity my grandfather is no longer alive, I think you two would have had a lot in common. He was the family's butler for over twenty-five years and had an encyclopaedic memory of everything that took place in the House. The Grand Days, as he called them, were before the Great War when Sir Hugh was a very young man. Apparently they were frivolous times of endless parties, shoots, balls, tennis and cricket matches and once a week, during the winter months, the hunt would meet outside the house."

"I would love to have been a fly on the wall in those days," Katherine sighed.

By the end of the week, she felt more confident and was looking forward to arranging the flowers in Lady Hollister's bedroom, bringing up the breakfast tray, keeping her clothes in order and accompanying her on her weekly visit to Marshall and Snelgrove.

"I gather the terrible weather down south is coming

north," she mentioned as Katherine pinned up her long, grey hair ahead of a morning's game of bridge. "I do hope it won't get much colder. The nights are already freezing and I do so hate the cold."

On 3rd February 1947 the outside temperature plummeted and it started to snow. At first there were only a few large, soft flakes but as the night drew on, the weather deteriorated and the light flurry became a blizzard. Soon the whole estate lay under a thick blanket of snow and was completely cut off from the surrounding countryside.

After seven years of food and fuel rationing, people were weary of having to make ends meet and as the cold snap tightened its grip, Katherine became particularly concerned for Daisy whose family income had been reduced by her decision to stay at home and look after William. To make matters worse, the freezing weather had forced factories to lay off workers and her husband, Bill, had been put on a three-day week.

"I've got to find out how she is," she insisted as she and Angus sat round a log fire wrapped in woollen blankets. "It doesn't seem right that we have plenty of firewood and food from the estate, whilst Daisy's family is probably having to cope with nothing."

After much nagging, Angus agreed to talk things over with Sir Hugh and seek his advice.

"By all means go and see how she is faring," Hugh said, showing genuine concern. "We really should have checked on her days ago.

"You're welcome to take the tractor if you want," he added. "I've been told that there are ten-foot drifts in places."

The next day Angus drove the Fordson as far as he could down the drive before it ground to a halt in front of a huge wall of inpenetrable snow.

"We'll never get through this," he declared, looking at the height of the drift.

"Then we'll have to walk," Katherine replied, defiantly scrambling to the top of the snowdrift and setting off at a steady pace.

"Are you coming?"

Angus banged the steering wheel hard with both fists in a fit of exasperation and leaving the engine ticking over, climbed onto the drift.

The snow crunched and cracked under their feet.

"I'm not as young as you," he panted, "so if we are going to help Daisy, let's go at a pace that won't kill me."

Katherine gave a weak smile and took her husband's hand.

"Why the sudden urge to see Daisy?" he asked curiously.

"It's difficult to explain," she explained, looking him straight in the eye. "I think it's because I see myself in her and know that without you, my life would have been just as difficult."

Angus held her gloved hand and kissed it.

High above the road, they fought their way through the deep snow, ducking under laden branches and stopping to admire the frosty foliage sparkling in the afternoon sun.

"Don't be long," he implored as Katherine approached a row of stone cottages and knocked several times on the door of No. 7. Eventually it was half-opened by a gaunt young man wrapped in a heavy army coat and wearing a pair of mittens, a scarf and a pompom hat.

"Hello! You must be William," she said kindly. "Is your mother at home?"

William cowered behind the door and refused to engage in conversation. He had a tic which jerked his head into involuntary spasms and affected his speech.

"Ahhh Ahhhr," he mumbled, pointing at Angus, who was stamping his feet in the snow to keep warm.

"That's my husband," Katherine explained. "He won't hurt you. I promise you won't come to any harm. Now could you go back indoors and find your mother and tell her that Katherine has come to pay her a visit?"

William continued staring suspiciously at Angus and his eyes refused to make contact with Katherine's. After a few minutes' stand-off, Katherine slipped unnoticed into the house.

"Daisy!" she called. "Daisy, are you there?"

There was a rustling sound coming from the freezing back kitchen and a small head peeped out from under a pile of newspapers.

Daisy's haunted eyes told their own story and with

great tenderness, Katherine lifted her to her feet and held her in her arms.

"Oh Daisy!" she sighed. "I'm so sorry I didn't come earlier.

"I'll do everything I can to make you, Bill and William more comfortable. You can't go on living like this."

Daisy grabbed hold of Katherine's coat and sobbed.

CHAPTER 25

"You can't bring them all here without first asking Sir Hugh and Lady Hollister," Angus said as they trudged back to the Fordson.

"They'd be furious!"

"Lady Hollister might react badly," Katherine admitted, "but I bet Sir Hugh would understand if I explained how I found Daisy swaddled in newspaper, trying to keep warm in a freezing room. Her chapped lips had turned blue and her swollen hands were raw with chilblains. She even had a teacosy on her head."

"Now you're being silly!" he replied, slightly amused.

"No, I'm not," she retorted furiously, "and it's not funny. I'm telling the truth, Angus. Bill and Daisy are destitute."

Angus glanced back at his wife, admiring her feisty spirit as she stood proudly on the drawbar. She had always fought for what she believed in and he loved her for it. As the temperature dropped and the sun sank behind the trees, he could feel the Arctic air slice through his coat and tried to imagine Daisy's daily struggle to survive without fuel or food.

He shivered at the injustice.

"Even if Lady Hollister were to agree to Daisy and Bill staying a few days, I don't think she'd be delighted to have mad William as well."

As soon as the words were out, Angus knew he should have been more tactful.

Once home, he lit the fire, changed out of his wet trousers and hung his socks over the fireguard, resting his frozen feet in front of the hearth.

Katherine took her time preparing a light supper, determined to make her husband pay for his unkind words.

Eventually, she appeared with a tray and and cut a thick slice of white bread for her husband.

"Would you like it toasted?" she asked, refusing to make eye contact.

He nodded, furious with himself for being so crass and hurting her feelings.

She jabbed the end of the toasting fork through the soft dough and held it against the heat of the fire until it had browned on both sides; then she spread the slice with butter and handed it to Angus on a plate.

"Help yourself to cheese or honey," she said coldly.

Neither of them spoke.

"All right," Katherine eventually admitted, desperate to break the ice. "Perhaps I was a bit hasty suggesting Daisy, Bill and William came to stay at Shottenden but you had no right to be so unkind about William."

Angus decided to listen rather than comment.

"Tomorrow morning I'm going to take some food over to Daisy and Bill and as soon as the drive is open, you can take them some logs.

"As for William, I'm going to talk to the Reverend

Hilton to see if he can come up with a solution. There must be something we can do to help."

Angus agreed with his wife's overall plan but pleaded with her to change out of her wet clothes and get dry before delivering another speech.

"I can take your outbursts on the chin," he chuckled, "and love your passionate desire for justice but I can't live without you, Katherine, so hurry up and change out of your wet clothes before you die of pneumonia and break my heart."

CHAPTER 26

Katherine knocked confidently on the vicarage door and was greeted by the housekeeper, Mrs Parker who welcomed her in and on hearing her request, showed her through to Mr Hilton's study.

"Sit down, Mrs MacLeod," the vicar said, showing Katherine to a well-worn floral sofa. "Can I get you something to drink? Mrs Parker is about to make tea."

"Thank you," she replied. "I'd love some."

★   ★   ★

Hubert Hilton was a tall, lean man in his fifties who had, for many years, been vicar of a large industrial parish in the North West but the strain of running a demanding city church had forced him into early retirement.

He had met Hugh quite by chance at Headingley just after the war whilst watching Yorkshire beat Surrey by six wickets. The two men struck up an immediate friendship and when Hubert mentioned he was looking for a position in a quiet country parish where he could continue his research on the effects of intensive farming on wildflowers and wildlife, Hugh declared he had just the job. The living at Shottenden had been vacant since the war and as its patron, Hugh had the right to choose the next incumbent.

He chose Hubert Hilton there and then, an impetuous yet inspirational decision.

Hugh was finding it harder to keep up-to-date with the changes in agricultural thinking and technology following the 1947 Farming Act; whereas Angus continued to read the latest Research and Development which encouraged growers to increase farm production and use more machinery.

He was a strong advocate of progress and reform, which often conflicted with the clergyman's more holistic view of farming.

Fortunately for Angus, Mr Hilton was a calm academic who was only too pleased to talk about a subject close to his heart. As the son of a clergyman from the Lincolnshire Wolds, he had spent much of his youth walking the fields within the parish boundary, making detailed notes of its wild flower, mammal and bird life. After Oxford, he bought a cottage in the village and returned as often as he could to carry on his meticulous research into effects of intensive farming on the local soil, flora and fauna.

He was an active supporter of the recently founded Soil Association and was becoming disillusioned by the post-war agricultural policy encouraging higher yields, more chemical use and bigger machinery.

Over time, he began to notice subtle changes to the countryside around his Lincolnshire home. Ancient hedgerows were being grubbed up to make way for larger fields in which bigger machines could operate more efficiently. Pesticides and fungicides enabled autumn-sown wheat to survive the winter and produce ever greater yields but the early sowing stripped the land of stubble — denying linnets, yellowhammers and corn buntings their winter supply of seeds.

He watched with sadness as plant-rich hay meadows were ploughed up and the water meadows drained in the pursuit of greater food production, driven by generous guaranteed prices and a desire for less dependency on foreign imports.

These areas rich in wild flowers began to lose their unique biodiversity and the clergyman noted a decline in the number of clovers, ox-eye daisies, meadow sweets, yarrows, and agrimonies.

Angus loved listening to the vicar's alternative views on farming, especially as he was so articulate and able to back up his arguments with meticulous personal research.

Mr Hilton's life-mission was to nurture soil and souls and value them equally.

*　*　*

Katherine possessed an aura which fascinated him and while he sat transfixed by her presence, he completely forgot Mrs Parker who was standing patiently by the door, waiting further instructions about tea.

"Mrs Parker, I'm sorry to have kept you waiting." He apologized, shaking himself out of his reverie. "Could I trouble you for one more cup of tea?"

Then, turning to Katherine, he added, "Is there anything I can do to help you, Mrs MacLeod? I presume, looking at the atrocious weather outside, this isn't a social call."

"It's about William Smith," Katherine said cautiously, not wishing to sound like a gossip.

"Ah! William," he sighed. "I've been worried about him for some time."

Katherine recounted the terrible conditions in which the family were living, adding that Daisy was worn out caring for her son.

The vicar looked at the lady sitting on his sofa and admired her for wanting to make the world a better place.

"She is totally devoted to William and won't admit she needs help."

"I know," came the reply. "I've been giving much thought to Daisy and Bill's situation and I think I may have found a solution.

"Malvingborough Abbey is a Benedictine Abbey about twenty miles from here. It specializes in the care of physically and mentally wounded servicemen and its hospital has a first-class psychiatric ward where compassion and wholesome food play an important part in the patient's recovery.

The nuns work in the large walled garden growing food for the Abbey's kitchen and undertake the menial jobs as well as care for the ex-soldiers. It is an inspirational place which could transform William's life and give Daisy a break."

"Would they have a place for him?" Katherine asked.

"I'm not sure but I think it would be a good idea for Daisy and William to visit the Abbey and talk to the Abbess. If you would like, I can arrange an appointment and as soon as the snow thaws, I'll take them there in my car."

Katherine's visit to the vicarage gave her hope and the next day she made her daily visit to Daisy to deliver fresh milk, bread, butter and cheese as well as a few baked potatoes and some cooked cabbage.

This time she had some good news as well.

"When the weather improves, would you like to take William to visit a beautiful abbey where wounded servicemen can find help and healing?

"You don't have to give an answer right now but promise you'll talk it over with Bill and let me know."

Daisy nodded and hungrily took the food out of the basket, broke the soft white loaf in three and handed the largest portion to her son, who was sitting expressionless in an armchair. The snow was still too deep to bring logs for heating and cooking but Katherine's compassion and practical help was sufficient to keep the small family alive.

CHAPTER 27

The harsh winter had made Daisy realise that she could no longer cope with William on her own. Giving up her job had been an implusive act of love but it had put immense financial and emotional strain on Bill, who returned home every evening to find an exhausted wife battling to care for their withdrawn son. He grieved for the child he had lost and resented Daisy's obsessive commitment to him. No matter how hard he worked, he knew there was little chance the William he had loved so dearly would ever return.

"I can't do this any more, Bill," Daisy confessed after supper one day in late May. "I really thought I had enough love to make him better; a bit like when he was a child. Do you remember when he fell over and cried and a kiss from Mummy was all it took to make things better? It was so simple back then but now I seem to be making things worse, and it isn't fair on you or William."

Bill listened to his wife, relieved that she was finally recognising the cracks in her steely determination. They discussed their options but he left Daisy to introduce the idea of visiting Malvingborough Abbey to William.

"I'll call in and have a word with the vicar to see if he's still willing to help," she said, remembering his earlier offer.

"Good idea," he agreed, delighted his wife had finally come to her senses.

Mr Hilton was only too happy to ring the Abbey and arrange an appointment.

On the day of the interview, Daisy flung open her bedroom window and breathed in the sweet scent of newly-mown grass. June was her favourite month and her garden was full of roses, delphiniums and stocks.

She had already prepared William for the visit and when Mr Hilton drove his Austin 8 round to No. 7, he saw Daisy waiting for him on the front door-step with her arm affectionately round her son, who was holding his head in his hands.

"Is everything all right?" he asked, stepping out of the car.

"No!" replied Daisy, trying to hold back the tears. "Everything's not all right. William's refusing to go."

"Come on, young man," the vicar encouraged gently. "There's a good chap. There's nothing to worry about. Your mother thought a little outing would be a treat for us all."

William looked up at the tall man towering over him and started to scream. "Don't take me away from my mother! I don't want to leave her and go to prison."

Mr Hilton appeared shocked at the unexpected outburst and no amount of coaxing would make the traumatised young man change his mind. As William's cries turned to whimpers, he clutched his twitching head with the palms of his hands and started swaying from side to side.

"We're going nowhere until you fetch Katherine!" Daisy told the bewildered clergyman. "She's the only person William will listen to and I'm afraid without her support, he won't come with us."

"Don't worry," Mr Hilton reassured Daisy, "I'll drive over to the cottage to see if I can find her."

Katherine arrived an hour later to find William in a state of heightened anxiety and Daisy still perched on the edge of the front step, looking at the end of her tether.

"Thank goodness you've come," she blurted out, seeing her friend approach. "It's William. He's having one of his flashbacks and is scared Mr Hilton is going to take him to prison. He won't move from here."

Katherine squatted down to William's level and took his hand gently in hers, coaxing him with soothing words as she had done so often before with her patients.

"William," she whispered softly. "Everything is all right. No-one's going to hurt you. Mr Hilton thought you'd like to go for a short drive in his car, that's all. Shall we all go together? You, your mum and me. I'm happy to come as there's someone I'd like to see on the way. Perhaps we could all pay her a visit."

William's heart rate slowed down and finally he stopped snivelling.

LUCY MONTGOMERY

"Come on!" she encouraged. "Let's go for that ride in the vicar's car."

Malvingborough Abbey was a fine Georgian house set in mature gardens on the outskirts of Rippleton, a small market town about an hour's drive from Shottenden. Its large, sweeping lawns reached down to the river Ripple which flowed serenely under vast weeping willows. Although only a short distance from the bustling town centre, the Abbey remained an oasis of calm.

The Abbess greeted her guests warmly, graciously ignoring the fact that they were two hours late. She explained that a meeting had been arranged for William to spend some time with Roger Whitman, a fellow Japanese POW who had worked on the Burma—Siam Railway.

Under the watchful eye of Sally Walters, a specialist nurse trained to observe signs of tension and anger, the two men met in a small study and stared at each other in silence. Roger thrust his hands in his pockets and jingled the loose change whilst eyeing William over the top of his glasses. William, on the other hand, refused to uncross his folded arms or look Roger in the face.

During their time together, Nurse Walters noticed how William slowly began to relax in the company of someone who could empathise with the unspeakable terrors he had endured in Burma. She gave the two men a large jigsaw puzzle to complete, in the hope they would begin to trust each other and eventually start to talk about their different experiences.

"I'll leave you two in peace to finish the puzzle," she said as she opened the study door to leave the room. "I'll be back soon."

She walked down the corridor to the Abbess' office and knocked on the door.

"Come in," the Abbess responded in her clear efficient voice.

"May I have a private word?"

The nurse ignored Daisy and Katherine who were sitting straight-backed on hard chairs, hoping for good news. Daisy rested her handbag on her lap and clutched the handles so tightly her bony knuckles turn white.

As the Abbess left the room, the two friends glanced at each other and Katherine raised her crossed fingers.

"I think William's psychiatric troubles are curable even though psychological damage is not an exact science," the nurse whispered to the Abbess, handing over her report. "He is definitely withdrawn and suffering from apathy and anxiety but I believe he is one of the lucky ones and could make a full recovery if he spent more time in the company of other Japanese POWs."

The Abbess scanned the report and thanked the nurse.

"His mother will be thrilled with your findings," she enthused, heading back to her office.

Nurse Walter's reasonably optimistic prognosis was relayed to Daisy, who immediately started crying

with relief and clasped her hands together in a show
of gratitude.

"Can I see him?" she asked, nervously.

"Of course you can! If you follow me, I'll take you
to him."

The ladies walked into the study where William
and Roger were talking quietly and putting together
the final pieces of the jigsaw.

"Don't rush," the Abbess told them, showing Daisy
and Katherine a comfortable sofa where they could
sit and wait. "We're in no hurry."

When the puzzle was finished, Roger shook
William's hands and smiled, obviously delighted by
their mutual achievement. After he left the room,
William walked over to the sofa and sat beside his
mother.

"If you could trust us and not be afraid," the
Abbess told him, "I think we could help you. Would
you like to stay here for a few months?"

Daisy gave her son's hand a squeeze, encouraging
him to take the chance.

You could have heard a pin drop as everyone waited
for his reply. He shuffled uncomfortably on his chair,
aware of all the eyes focussed on him.

Instead of giving an answer, he gazed out of the
window into the walled garden, where men his age
were hoeing vegetables in a beautiful, ordered,
peaceful world.

He knew exactly what his answer would be.

CHAPTER 28

"What's this?" Katherine asked, looking at the large box on the floor.

"I've no idea but it's cluttering up my kitchen," Gladys complained, busily rolling out the pastry for a Bakewell tart. "You couldn't do me a favour and tell Sir Hugh that a large package has arrived for him."

Katherine sensed Gladys' annoyance and went to find Sir Hugh.

She knocked hesitantly on his study door and waited for a response.

"Come!" came the husky reply.

As Katherine entered the room, Hugh lowered his copy of *The Times* and stretched his back to allow oxygen to flow more freely into his scarred lungs.

He smiled.

"Is anything wrong?"

"No, Sir Hugh," she replied, softly. "Gladys asked me to say there's a large box for you in the kitchen."

Struggling to his feet, he grabbed hold of a silver-topped walking stick to steady himself.

"Could you ask Angus to meet me in the kitchen?" he asked, swaying slightly before regaining his balance. "I want to show you all something."

Angus arrived just as Hugh had finished apologising to Gladys for the mid-day disruption.

LUCY MONTGOMERY

They broke open the crate and threw handfuls of
the protective wood shavings on the floor, much to
Gladys' annoyance.

Inside the crate was a 9" Pye television, set in a tall
walnut veneer cabinet. It was the latest addition to Sir
Hugh's growing collection of electrical gadgets. He
was fascinated by modern technology and had already
bought a gramophone, a Brownie camera and a Bush
radio as well as having a telephone system installed in
the house.

His mother had been vehemently against
modernising Shottenden and accused Hugh of
reckless spending when he added a new bathroom to
each main bedroom but she soon forgave him when
he bought her a range of luxury French toiletries and
some soft white towels for her birthday.

The purchase of a washing machine, steam iron,
Aga and a large fridge was the final straw. Lady
Hollister considered all the changes unnecessary
and she refused to speak to her son for a whole week
but Hugh knew that fewer staff members made
labour-saving devices essential and if the Estate
were ever to be sold, it needed to be equipped for
the modern age.

"Perfect!" he exclaimed, patting the newly-acquired
piece of furniture. "Now all I have to do is work out
where to put it."

"Put what?" Gladys asked, looking down at the
packaging cluttering her floor.

"The television, Gladys. It's a television and next

Saturday we are all going to sit down in the drawing room to watch the marriage of the Princess Elizabeth to Philip Mountbatten," he replied, rubbing his hands together with glee.

"Would you and Johnny mind taking the television into the drawing room?" he asked Angus, clearly delighted with his latest purchase. "It's quite heavy."

Hugh led the way and looked round the room trying to decide where to put his new toy.

"I think it would be best in the corner by the drum table where everyone can see it. We can run the aerial lead through the window casement and up the side of the house to the chimney," he said, explaining to Johnny and Angus how the television worked and then he left them to set up the aerial.

After much trial and error, the fuzzy interference on the screen disappeared and was replaced by clear black-and-white moving pictures with sound.

"We've done it, Sir Hugh! It's working!" they cried, delighted with the results even though they had no idea how the pictures arrived on the screen.

On Thursday 20th November 1947, the Shottenden estate workers and domestic staff gathered in the grand entrance hall just before eleven o'clock, unsure why they had been summoned.

A visit to the house was almost unheard of and most of the staff waited nervously in the hall, expecting the worst.

As the clock struck eleven, a relaxed, smiling Sir Hugh entered the hall.

"Thank you all for coming," he said with genuine warmth. "Before we go in, I want to assure you that this is a social gathering and has nothing to do with work."

There was an audible sigh of relief from the men who stood uneasy in their darned socks.

"After all the sacrifices and hardships of the past eight years," Hugh added, trying not to sound pompous or patronising, "I felt it right to celebrate the King's happiness and toast the young Princess' future."

Hugh was determined to make the Royal Wedding a memorable occasion and had ordered the log baskets to be filled and the fires lit. Each member of staff was welcomed personally into the warm, comfortable drawing room and handed a glass of chilled champagne.

The awkward silence amongst the workers confirmed Lady Hollister's worst fears when her son first told her about his plan to host a television viewing in the drawing room.

"It's a terrible idea, Hugh," she reprimanded, tossing her stylishly coiffured head to one side. "You'll humiliate everyone and receive no thanks for your hospitality. Don't expect me to join in your little charade."

In many ways, Lady Hollister was right. The staff shuffled uncomfortably on the Wilton carpet and gazed nervously at their opulent surroundings. Unsure what to do or say, the ladies made an attempt to sip their champagne politely, relishing the sweet taste and sparkling sensation on their tongues, whilst the men downed the bubbly liquid in one gulp.

Hugh picked up a tray and collected the empty glasses, aware that every eye in the room was watching him.

"Please, do sit down," he said, terrified his plan to bring the estate together was turning into a disaster. "I'll switch on the television."

There was a deathly hush followed by an astonished gasp as images of the King and the Princess appeared on the small screen. The little 9" box seemed to be drawing everyone together just as Hugh hoped it would.

The Shottenden staff watched spellbound as the Irish State Coach, escorted by the Sovereign's Escort of Household Cavalry in full ceremonial uniform, clattered under Admiralty Arch and passed down Whitehall into Parliament Square.

The good-tempered crowd, fifty-deep in places, waved flags and streamers and countless home-made periscopes glinted and sparkled in the winter sun.

On arrival at Westminster Abbey, the Gothic masterpiece consecrated in 1269, the young bride stepped out of the carriage with great composure and serenely ascended the steps to be greeted by the Dean of Westminster outside the Great West Door of the Abbey. The roaring cheers of thousands of enthusiastic onlookers mingled with the sound of peeling bells, creating a glorious cacophony.

Katherine stared in awe at the mass of tiny crystals

and seed pearls embroidered onto the heavy silk wedding gown. Its delicate thirteen-foot silk train hardly seemed to touch the ground as Princess Elizabeth paused ahead of walking down the nave on her father's arm.

The uniforms, outfits, tiaras and flowers exuded glamour and wealth and offered a weary and exhausted nation a glimmer of hope.

Hugh watched intently as the heir to the throne held the hand of the son of an exiled minor royal and felt the dawn of a more just and egalitarian society had begun.

Shottenden had never hosted such an extraordinary occasion before and never would again.

CHAPTER 29

Shottenden, spring 1948

William had been away from home for nearly eight months and was making steady progress but the Abbey's distance from Shottenden made it impossible for Daisy and Bill to visit him.

Mr Hilton had offered several times to take them in his car but they always refused.

"I don't want to owe him a favour," Bill said proudly and Daisy agreed.

Malvingborough Abbey sent them regular reports on William's slow recovery and hinted that he might be ready to return home at the end of April.

Daisy desperately wanted to see her son again but was worried that his return would put paid to her new-found independence.

She had started working at Davidsons, the local haberdasher's, which Mr Davidson had run with his wife for over thirty years. He was a neat, dapper man in his late fifties with thick grey hair, dark eyes and olive skin. He could easily have been mistaken for a foreigner but his family had lived in the area for generations and although there were rumours about his grandmother and a French circus performer, they were never substantiated. The most striking thing about Mr Davidson were his large, sticking out ears which appeared out of proportion to his face.

He lived a quiet, unassuming life above the shop with his wife, Rebecca, until her untimely death. Her passing left him totally bereft and without her care, he began to lose interest in the business and his appearance. Nobody had the heart to tell him about the bad atmosphere in the shop so he limped on much as before until one evening whilst checking his monthly takings, he realised just how serious things had become.

Mr Davidson had the sense to confide in his daughter who encouraged him to place an advertisement for an assistant in the post-office window.

Much to his surprise, he received ten replies.

Daisy was by far the best candidate. Well-dressed with an engaging smile, she was keen to learn and showed a natural aptitude for maths.

Simon Davidson employed her on the spot and before long she was running the shop, allowing him to spend more time with his daughter and grandchildren. Freed from the restraints of work, he took on a new lease of life and began visiting the social club where he met Anthea Eastburn, the recently widowed wife of the local bank manager.

Anthea was a respected, fearless woman who defied her peers by making appearances at the club on her own. She had served the community as deputy head teacher of the local primary school for many years, was a member of the Parochial Church Council and Brown Owl to the Shottenden 1st Brownie Pack. It was in her role of Brown Owl that she persuaded Daisy to become the pack's Tawny Owl, a job she loved and under the leadership of these two strong 'Owls', the pack flourished and grew to over thirty girls, drawing in children from a wide area.

1948 was a year of hope for Daisy and she was determined to make the world a more caring place. Drawing inspiration from the glamour of the royal wedding, she decided to re-introduce maypole dancing on the village green and asked Johnny if he knew where the pole had been put for safe-keeping during the war. He wasn't sure but thought it might have been tucked away somewhere in the cricket pavilion.

She asked Katherine to help her look for it.

"It's not here!" Katherine said, rummaging through the junk at the back of the pavilion. "Are you sure this is where Johnny put it?"

"That's what he said," Daisy replied. "Let me have a look. After all, I know what I'm looking for."

Daisy squeezed past Katherine and moved some of the furniture out of the way. Chairs and tables had been stacked higgledy-piggledy and were in danger of toppling over.

"It doesn't look as if anyone's been here since 1939," she said, "and the last man to leave must have been in a dreadful hurry. It's total chaos."

"Take care," Katherine cried, as Daisy crawled under the furniture hoping to find the pole. "The chairs look as if they could fall at the slightest touch."

"They're fine!" Daisy replied. "The stacks aren't as dangerous as they look. They're quite sturdy."

Katherine left Daisy to continue her search and, sniffling and sneezing, she waited outside on the pavilion steps. She had always been sensitive to dust but this time she felt faint and nauseous.

"I've found it!" Daisy spluttered through the clouds of dust. "Gosh, this place hasn't been swept for years."

She staggered out of the room and into the fresh air, patting down her clothes and ruffling her hair.

"Are you all right?" she asked, looking concerned. "You've gone as white as a sheet."

"I'll be OK in a minute," Katherine replied unconvincingly. "I think it's the dust; it always affects me."

"Are you well enough to give me a hand?"

"Of course!" came the hesitant reply.

The two ladies hauled the filthy twelve-foot pole across the veranda and down the steps onto the grass. Apart from needing a fresh coat of paint, it looked in perfect condition.

"Johnny mentioned they used an old wooden cart wheel as a base," Daisy said. "I wonder where it is?"

Instead of answering, Katherine ran behind the pavilion and threw up.

"Come on, Katherine," Daisy insisted. "I'm taking you home to bed. We can look for the wheel another time."

CHAPTER 30

At ten o'clock on Saturday 1st May 1948, Lady Hollister stood on the cricket pavilion steps dressed in a floral, silk dress and matching hat and declared the Shottenden May Day fête open.

"Let the festivities begin," she announced in her rather stilted way.

The fête committee had worked hard to set up a variety of stalls round the green, including a coconut shy, splat the rat, guess the weight of the cake and tombola.

The Mothers' Union and St Thomas's Church volunteered to run the flower, produce and tea tents and, much to Anthea's delight, the Brownies were asked to sell raffle tickets in aid of the village hall and the British Legion. She handed out the different coloured books to the Elves, Gnomes, Imps and Pixies at the Friday meeting.

"You must all be immaculately turned out in your uniforms on fête day," she told a circle of cross-legged girls, eagerly looking up at her. "Shoes polished, tie-pins gleaming and dresses crisply ironed. Now remember; a strip of five tickets costs thrupence so how many strips would you need to sell for a shilling?"

The Sixers thought a while and replied, "Four."

"Well done," Anthea congratulated her pack.

On the immaculately-mown village green, the maypole's brightly coloured ribbons fluttered in the spring breeze and twenty-four excited Brownies gathered round Anthea and Daisy.

"Now you all know what to do," Brown Owl instructed, "so take up your positions, keep calm and enjoy yourselves."

The girls had changed out of their uniforms into party dresses and one by one they filed onto the green, took hold of the end of a ribbon and stepped away from the central pole. Standing back to back in pairs, they waited patiently for the Morris Men to start playing the opening bars of 'The Keel-Row' before skipping and weaving their way round the pole until they had completed the plait.

Parents, villagers and friends on tartan rugs and striped deck chairs clapped in time to the music and applauded the girls' performance, crying "Encore! Encore!"

"What should we do?" Daisy asked anxiously. "Should we do an encore?"

"Why not!" Brown Owl replied. "The girls have practised hard over the past few weeks and deserve all the appreciation they can get."

When the dancing was over, Daisy sat on the grass and watched the Shottenden and Hillingfield cricket teams saunter across the Green towards the pavilion, ready for the match.

Hidden in the shadows, deep in thought, stood Katherine MacLeod.

"Hey! Katherine," Daisy called out, kicking off her shoes and stretching out her legs. "Come and sit by me and enjoy the sunshine."

Katherine glanced at her friend but said nothing.

"Don't hide away in the shade on such a beautiful day. The sun will do you good — especially as you've been looking rather peaky recently."

Very slowly, Katherine made her way towards Daisy but it was clear by the look on her face that she was feeling out of sorts.

"I'm hoping to turn these chunky, white things into lean, bronzed ones," Daisy laughed, pointing to her legs. "What do you think my chances are?"

Katherine gave the merest hint of a smile but before she could reply, Daisy added, "Don't worry, I know the chances are nil but at least I can dream."

Katherine remained unresponsive.

"Come on," Daisy cajoled. "Let's go and have a cuppa, then you can tell me what's on your mind because something's definitely not right."

She held out her hand for Katherine to pull her up, then, lacing up her shoes, they walked side by side to the Scout marquee and joined the short queue.

"Two teas, please," Daisy said as they finally reached the green Beryl cups on the trestle table by the urn.

The friendly volunteer picked up a large teapot and poured out two cups of tea.

"Sugar and milk are at the end and don't forget to help yourselves to cake."

Daisy and Katherine sat at a rickety card table in the corner of the marquee and sipped the hot tea.

It tasted good.

The sweet scent of narcissi in a jam jar on the table and the Victoria sponge made Daisy hungry and despite Katherine's continuing silence, she was determined to enjoy herself. She prodded a morsel of cake with her fork, raised it to her mouth and let the butter, sugar and jam slowly melt on her tongue.

Katherine's eyes never left the table.

"I'm pregnant," she whispered, not daring to look up.

"That's wonderful news!" Daisy replied, determined to keep the atmosphere light. She dabbed the corners of her mouth with a handkerchief and held onto Katherine's hand. "When's it due?"

"I'm not sure. It's still early days but I think around Christmas."

"Even better, a double celebration," Daisy added. "I bet Angus is thrilled. He'll make a wonderful father."

"He doesn't know," Katherine whispered, so quietly that Daisy wasn't sure she'd heard correctly. "You're the first person I've told."

"But surely you should tell Angus about the baby? After all, it isn't every day a man of his age becomes a father for the first time."

Katherine looked slightly embarrassed and a little hurt.

"I didn't mean to be unkind," Daisy blurted out,

aware that her comment might have been taken the wrong way. "It's just that Angus is a bit older than most first-time fathers.

"Is there something else you're not telling me?" she asked, cautiously.

"No, everything's fine, it's just that I feel so sick and next week Angus is returning to Skye to see his mother and if I tell him about the baby, I know he'll worry about me and cancel the visit. The last thing I want is for Ailsa to be hurt by not seeing her son, especially as she hasn't seen him since Murdo's funeral. I'm so fond of her and wish we didn't live so far away.

"Do you think I'm right keeping the pregnancy from him? After all, he's only going away for ten days."

Daisy didn't feel in a position to advise but instinctively thought Angus should be told so he could pass the good news on to his mother.

Her thoughts were distracted by a group of Morris Dancers jingling their way across the front of the tea tent to take up their positions. The accordion and fiddle struck the opening bars of the English folk song 'Country Gardens' and in one swoop, the group hopped enthusiastically from one foot to the other, clashing their batons and waving white hankies in the air.

Right at the back of the crowd, Daisy caught a glimpse of a familiar face.

"William!" she cried, leaping to her feet and leaving her half-finished cup of tea and slice of cake. She ran out of the tent and through the crowd to reach her son.

"Why didn't you tell me you were coming?" she asked, holding his cheeks in the palms of her hands.

"I only knew yesterday," he said, embarrassed by her public demonstration of joy. "There wasn't time."

"Do come and say hello to Katherine. We're having tea and I know she'd love to see you again."

"Would you mind if I went home," he replied, choosing his words carefully. "I only came to find you and let you know I was back. Don't let me keep you from your friends, I'm fine on my own."

Daisy examined her son's face and noticed how frightened he looked.

She held her head up high and whispered proudly, "Of course you can go home, but on one condition."

He looked surprised. "What's that?"

"That I come with you!"

For a fleeting moment, she saw his old familiar smile return and knew that Malvingborough Abbey had turned his life around and given him hope.

"Give me two minutes and I'll be back," she chirped. "I just need to tell Anthea that I'm going home."

She ran back to the Brownies who were sitting in their May Day party dresses looking very serious.

"How are we going to get our uniforms?" they asked, watching the Shottenden and Hillingfield players spill in and out of the pavilion ahead of their match.

Brown Owl was flustered and annoyed with Daisy

when she explained that William had unexpectedly returned and she needed to go home with him.

No raffle tickets could be sold until her Brownies had changed back into their uniforms and with the departure of Tawny Owl, there would no-one to help Anthea retrieve the girls' uniforms from the men's changing room.

Much to her relief, she saw Simon Davidson unfolding his deckchair nearby, ready to watch a relaxing afternoon of cricket. He glanced momentarily in Anthea's direction and caught her subtle beckoning movement.

"What's up?" he asked, unsure how to cope with all the little eyes gazing up at him.

"Nothing," Anthea lied, trying to sound positive. "It's just that Daisy has gone back home to be with William and the girls' uniforms are in the pavilion which is now occupied by the cricket teams. I'm not sure what to do. We can't sell any raffle tickets until the girls are back in their uniforms."

"Ah ha!" he said, scratching his head and smiling. "I can see your problem."

He scanned the faces surrounding him and closed his eyes. There was a hushed silence whilst he thought of a solution.

"I've got it!" he cried, making everyone jump. "You need another wise owl to replace Tawny."

The Brownies looked perplexed, not sure what he meant.

"I can't be Tawny Owl, can I, girls?" he guffawed,

"because she's gone home. Why don't I become Long-Eared Owl, just for this afternoon."

There were shrieks of laughter from the pack and a jaw-dropping gasp from Brown Owl who couldn't believe what she was hearing.

"Listen carefully to what Long-Eared Owl has to say," she said, trying to suppress her giggles.

"Well, ladies! If you wait here, I'll fetch your uniforms for you," Simon exclaimed, climbing up the pavilion steps.

CHAPTER 31

Shottenden, May 1948

Angus returned to Kilbackie as planned, leaving Katherine alone at home. After much deliberation, she decided not to tell him about the pregnancy, preferring to wait until she was totally certain and he was back home, but two days before he was due to return, there was a knock on the cottage door.

It was Hugh.

"Do you mind if I come in?" he asked, stooping to clear the low lintel.

Katherine wiped her hands on her apron and welcomed him in.

It was the first time he had been inside her cottage since he had filled it with flowers on her wedding day and he was pleased to see she was taking a pride in keeping it clean and tidy.

"Is everything all right?" she asked nervously. "Something's wrong, I can tell by your voice."

The colour drained from her face and she began to sway.

"Come and sit down," Hugh encouraged, supporting her gently by the elbow. "I'm afraid I have bad news."

She lowered herself into a comfortable armchair

and raised her eyes, pleading for Hugh to confirm all was well.

"I have just received a telephone call," he began, as a wave of despair swept over him.

Katherine's eyes filled with tears and her shoulders slumped as she placed a hand on her unborn child.

"He's dead, isn't he?" she wailed. "Please, Hugh, don't lie to me. I need to know the truth. He's dead, I know it."

She tried to get out of the chair, believing the dreadful news would go away if she acted normally.

"I'll put the kettle on," she whispered, struggling to her feet.

"Sit down, Katherine," Hugh said, with great tenderness. "I'll get us both a drink."

She allowed herself to fall back into the chair and let the tears roll freely down her cheeks.

"What happened?" she asked, as Hugh made his way into the kitchen.

"No-one is sure," he replied. "Do you take milk and sugar?"

"Just milk," she sniffled.

He ignored her reply and added two teaspoons of sugar. The kettle began to whistle and he poured the water into a pot and carried the tray into the front room.

"Apparently he was walking home from Kilbackie Island across the causeway when he stumbled and hit his head on a boulder. He was found dead in the water with a head wound."

Katherine looked incredulous.

"He can't have been on Kilbackie Island," she exclaimed. "Everyone knows Major Urquhart is paranoid about privacy and Angus would never trespass. It isn't in his nature."

Hugh looked uncomfortable and was unable to give her any more information. All he could do was assure her he'd try to find out more and keep her informed.

Over the next twenty-four hours, shock and grief left Katherine so withdrawn and listless that Lady Hollister became concerned.

"Go home," she urged, with surprising insight, "and get some rest. I'll ask Gladys to check in on you later. Is there anything I can do to help?"

Katherine shook her head sadly and walked back home across the lawn with her ears deaf to the sound of birdsong, her eyes blind to the beauty of the herbaceous border and her body cold in the warmth of the sun. Lifting the latch, she entered a chilly emptiness and made her way up to her bedroom where she slipped, fully dressed, into the marital bed.

"Oh God!" she sobbed, "how will I ever cope without Angus?"

After two days, Gladys reported to Lady Hollister that Katherine hadn't eaten and was still bed-bound.

"Is there any way you can persuade her to eat something, no matter how small?" the old lady asked, clearly worried about Katherine's deteriorating health.

"I read somewhere that an invalid's desire for food depends on the way it's presented," Gladys replied.

"Would your Ladyship allow me to experiment with a few ideas to try to tempt her to eat?"

"Do whatever you think best," came the positive reply.

Gladys went down to the kitchens and began to prepare small jellies enriched with port wine, lemon juice, cloves and cinnamon and set them in ornate biscuit moulds. She turned the jellies out onto an exquisitely hand-painted botanical plate and decorated them with tiny violas from the garden. On the tray, next to the plate of jellies, she placed a vase of deep red Bishop of Llanduff dahlias from the walled garden.

The presentation was stunning and arriving at the cottage, she entered Katherine's bedroom and sat beside her bed, waiting for her to stir.

"I'm not hungry," she complained, turning her head away from the food.

"Have a look at the scarlet dahlias I've brought you," Gladys said, lifting the vase to make it easier for Katherine to see. "Aren't they beautiful? They're named after the Bishop of Llandaff which I believe is a town somewhere in Wales."

Katherine glanced over at the vase and caught sight of the plate of decorated jellies.

"Try one," Gladys said, coaxing her to eat but with little success. Eventually, however, charmed by the beauty of the plate and the smell of the warm spices, Katherine attempted to sit up and taste a jelly which melted in her mouth and slipped into her empty stomach.

Before long, she had finished the plate of delicacies, slumped back onto a soft pile of pillows and closed her eyes for a couple of hours.

"Are you awake?" whispered a familiar voice.

"Daisy!" Katherine sighed drowsily, turning towards her visitor. "You've come!"

Daisy perched on the edge of the bed and held Katherine's hand tightly in hers.

"I'm so sorry," she sniveled, her voice shaking. "I would have come to see you sooner but we've only just returned from a short visit to the Abbey as William was keen to see Roger Whitman again. I can't think of anything to say that will lessen your pain. I'm just so dreadfully sorry. What happened?"

Katherine recounted what Sir Hugh had said, repeating that Angus could never have stumbled on the causeway and hit his head. He was far too careful and had no reason to be on the island in the first place. Nothing made sense.

Daisy listened attentively and made no comment but eventually plucked up the courage to speak.

"Did you…?" she started, but couldn't continue.

"Did I what?"

Neither of them spoke.

"You were going to ask if I ever told Angus about the baby, weren't you?" Katherine whispered.

Daisy nodded.

"I didn't," came the faint reply and overcome by grief and guilt, she wept.

CHAPTER 32

Ailsa's short letter arrived on 20th May 1948, stating that the Reverend Donny Nicolson would be taking Angus' funeral on Tuesday 25th May at two-thirty in Kilbackie Church.

Katherine showed the letter to Hugh.

"Would your mother give me some time off to attend the funeral?" she asked, unsure whether she was due any holiday.

"You don't need to ask," Hugh replied in earnest, "because I'm going to take you. I'll get Billings to drive us to Skye and you can stay with Ailsa for a few days and attend Angus' funeral."

"You're not serious!" Katherine replied, with a mixture of disbelief and excitement. "It's hundreds of miles away."

"Well," he blurted out, "I can't let you travel on your own and I won't let you miss your husband's funeral, so what other option do you have?"

It was agreed that Hugh, Katherine and Billings would set off after an early breakfast on 22nd May, taking with them a picnic lunch prepared by Gladys for the journey.

The car purred its way through the uplands of Lancashire and Westmoreland and crossed the Scottish border at Gretna Green where they stopped for lunch. Katherine found the journey surprisingly comfortable and whenever she felt tired, she could curl up on the back seat with a travel rug and sleep.

For Hugh, the journey was a dream come true.

The First World War had dashed his hopes of becoming an all-round cricketer and the mustard gas had robbed him of a prodigious sporting talent, yet he never complained. He adopted a positive approach, content to sit in his library and reflect on the crowning glory of his undergraduate years; the University Match at Lord's on 8th July 1912 when he captained the Cambridge team and won by three wickets.

With his cricket life over, Hugh channelled his energy into motoring. He first came across the Alvis Speed 20 at the London Motor Show back in May 1933 and was determined to buy one. The four-seater saloon was described as distinctly fast in acceleration and speed, with a comfortable body and good all-round vision. It had an exceptionally steady steering action with little roll or wheel bounce.

Hugh chose Billings to be his chauffeur as he was the only man on the estate meticulous enough to maintain the vehicle's engine.

"I won't let you down, Sir Hugh," he had said, thrilled to have been asked. "Your car will be kept in perfect working condition and will always be immaculately clean."

The Alvis skirted Glasgow, crossed the Clyde and took the Great Western Road north towards Luss on the banks of Loch Lomond, following the narrow twisting road sandwiched between the deep, clear water of the loch and steep wooded slopes.

Billings drove with care and confidence, accelerating to top speeds when the road was clear and slowing down when the surface was rough or visibility was poor.

"Let's stop here by the loch," Hugh suggested, as they drove into Luss village. "I always think of Loch Lomond as the gateway to the Highlands even if others disagree. It's where I start to get excited about the next stage of the journey."

Katherine was pleased to get out of the car and stretch her legs. The sun was shimmering over the vibrant blue loch and as they walked past a row of identical sandstone and slate cottages towards the narrow sandy beach, they saw a large pleasure steamer moored at the end of the pier, waiting for the final passengers of the day to embark.

"Isn't this a wonderful spot?" Hugh raved, relishing the view and obviously delighted to be back in Scotland. Although he still looked pale, there was a hint of colour in his cheeks and his tousled hair made him look much younger.

Katherine's light clothing was no protection against the cool breeze blowing off the water and she began to shiver. The breathtaking beauty of the mountains unnerved her, making her loneliness even harder to bear. A slow, debilitating panic overwhelmed her and she struggled to fight back the tears.

"Don't cry! Whatever you do, don't cry!" she told herself, digging her finger nails into the palms of her hands.

"Is everything OK?" Hugh asked, with concern.

"Can we go back to the car?" she muttered, turning her back on the view. "I'm cold."

Hugh seemed to sense her unease and suggested they went straight to the Loch Lomond Arms where he had already booked their rooms. Once there, he left their luggage with the girl at reception and ordered tea in the lounge. The arrival of sandwiches, scones and cake beside a warm log fire soon restored Katherine's composure and she began to relax and appear less troubled.

"You're looking much better," he observed, passing her a smoked salmon sandwich and topping up her cup with tea. "While we're here, I want to apologize for the inconsiderate way I behaved just now."

Katherine looked bemused, unsure what he was implying.

"There I was, admiring the view, without giving a thought to the dreadful loneliness you must be feeling without Angus. I'm so sorry. Will you forgive me?" he asked, with genuine remorse.

She smiled and gave a weak nod.

"I promise there will be no more unscheduled stops and I'll get you up to Skye in time for the funeral."

His apology lifted Katherine's spirits and she settled back in the chair, determined to enjoy the delicious tea laid out before her.

The next morning, after an early breakfast, Billings drove the car on to Tarbet and took a right fork through Glen Falloch, past the majestic waterfall at Falls of Falloch and on to the remote village of Crianlarich which lay in the shadow of Cruach Ardrain, one of Scotland's many Munros.

Crossing Rannoch Moor, a vast eerie wilderness of blanket bog, small lochs and rocky outcrops, he pulled over onto the verge to give Katherine a chance to stretch her legs and catch a glimpse of the grouse, red deer, snipe and golden plovers that roamed, soared and flew across the empty landscape stretching far into the distance towards Loch Laidon and Kinloch Rannoch.

The only sounds in the silent emptiness were the haunting cries of curlews and the plaintive 'peeee-uus' of buzzards.

By the time they reached the Invergarry Hotel, Katherine was exhausted and spent the rest of the afternoon in bed. When eventually she appeared for a light supper, her face was drawn and pale and she had dark shadows under her eyes.

"Are you all right?" Hugh asked, as he stood up and held the chair for her to sit down. "You're looking very pale."

"No, I'm not all right," she replied, in despair. "I feel awful and don't know what to do."

"Are you ill?" he asked.

Her eyes filled with tears and she had to bite her bottom lip to stay in control.

Fiddling with her wedding ring, she lamented, "I just feel miserable and want Angus back."

Katherine had been determined to stay strong and positive for the sake of her baby but sleepless nights, recurring nightmares and panic attacks had begun to take their toll on her nerves and even though she was putting on a good performance, she felt she could shatter at any moment.

She was haunted by the fact that Angus had died without knowing about his child and her greatest fear was losing his baby.

In the long, lonely nights, she craved the warmth of his touch and sobbed into the pillow, hammering the mattress with her clenched fists.

Everything seemed so unfair.

Hugh's damaged face looked at her with great understanding and she wondered whether he, too, suffered agonising moments of loneliness.

"What are you going to eat?" he asked, looking at the menu. "I think I'll go for the lamb." Katherine chose the hake and after the order had been taken, she slipped into a dreamy trance, thinking about Angus.

During the meal, she pushed pieces of fish round her plate with a fork and hardly ate a thing. "It's no use, Hugh," she muttered, with tears in her eyes. "I've lost my appetite. Would you mind if I went back to bed?"

"Of course not!" Hugh said, handing her a large white folded handkerchief with the monogram

HACH sewn in the corner. "You go off to bed. We can talk about things in the morning."

Katherine got up from the table, took the handkerchief and wondered what the intials AC stood for.

CHAPTER 33

Shottenden and Skye, 1948

When Katherine appeared the next morning, Hugh was already sitting at the breakfast table, reading about the Hoover Company's new washing machine factory in Merthyr Tydfil.

"How did you sleep?" he asked, putting down his newspaper to give her his full attention.

"Well," came the reply, much to his relief.

The waitress came over to take Katherine's order.

"A cup of tea and some toast, please," she requested.

"That's not enough to keep you going," Hugh exclaimed. "Especially as you didn't eat anything yesterday evening. Try some porridge, I can heartily recommend it."

Reluctantly, Katherine added porridge to her order and waited.

Hugh slowly folded his newspaper and looked at Katherine who sat nervously on the opposite side of the table. She found the intimacy of meal times awkward, even though Hugh's impeccable manners never made her feel uncomfortable or embarrassed.

On the contrary, his attention to detail and his ability to care for her made him the perfect friend and travelling companion.

When breakfast arrived, he carefully explained the day's schedule, pointing out that she could make any changes she wished.

"I was wondering if you would like Billings to drive you tomorrow from our hotel in Portree to the Manse so you can spend some time with your family before the funeral. He could then pick you up from the cemetery and bring you back to Portree where I thought we would spend a couple more nights ahead of returning home."

"Aren't you coming to the funeral?" she asked, looking terribly disappointed.

"In the circumstances, I don't think that would be a good idea," he replied.

"Please come," Katherine pleaded. "My father will have told everyone that my marriage to Angus was a sham and without your support, I can't face all those faces staring at me."

"Katherine," Hugh stated in earnest. "Listen to me. Even if your father has turned the whole community against you, your reputation will only sink further if you arrive at your husband's funeral in a chauffeur-driven car, accompanied by an unmarried English baronet. It's just possible people may think we had something to do with Angus' death."

Katherine looked horrified and twisted the end of her cardigan in her fingers whilst staring blankly into the distance.

"Why are you doing all this to help me?" she asked,

bringing her eyes nervously back to focus on Hugh. "After all, I'm only the wife of your stockman."

Hugh chose to ignore this rather cheap, self-pitying comment.

"Because I loved Angus," he replied without hesitating.

"He was my dearest, most loyal friend and the brother I never had. He made my past bearable, my present joyful and my future exciting, and I miss him terribly."

Hugh's moving choice of words deeply affected Katherine and she pulled out the large hankie to wipe her nose.

"Please come with me to the funeral," she implored, trying to hold herself together.

"I can't," Hugh insisted. "You need to go on your own for Angus' sake. Go to the funeral, hold your head up high and show everyone that you are the same beautiful, dignified person they all knew and loved. I shall be waiting for you in the car when it is all over."

She accepted Hugh's plan but with one amendment.

"Could Billings drop me off and pick me up at Ailsa's instead of the Manse? It's only a short walk to the church and I haven't seen her for such a long time."

As soon as Katherine entered the croft, Ailsa MacLeod threw her arms round her daughter-in-law and wept.

Speaking in Gaelic, the distraught ladies held hands

and shared their grief and pain. Ailsa ran her knarled fingers over Katherine's wedding ring.

"I see you're still wearing my mother's ring," she beamed, showing her deep pleasure. "Did Angus never buy you an engagement ring?"

"No," Katherine replied, placing her hand over Ailsa's. "This is the only ring I wanted. It means the world to me and I think of you every time I look at it."

The old woman kept hold of the ring and sank into reverie.

"Have you seen your Aunt Mairi yet?"

"No, I came straight here. Why? Is she all right?"

"She's fine. It's just she was so disappointed not to have been invited to your wedding. She would have moved heaven and earth to be there for you. She is always asking after you when we meet."

Katherine looked horrified.

"I sent everyone in the family an invitation; in fact I clearly remember putting them all together in a small package and posting them to the Manse," she replied indignantly, recalling how hurt she had been when no-one had answered. "How could she think I'd not invite her, especially when she's the aunt I'm closest to."

As she spoke, it began to dawn on her that her father must have destroyed all the invitations out of spite and none of them were ever delivered. She found it hard to believe that a father could stoop so low to destroy the happiness of his only daughter.

"Perhaps you'd better have a quiet word with her while you are here. How long are you staying?"

"I've got to leave straight after the funeral," Katherine replied. "It's only the shortest of visits because Sir Hugh has to get back to Shottenden but I'll try and make time to visit Mairi although it may be difficult."

"What's Sir Hugh like?" Ailsa asked. "Angus always spoke highly of him but never really said much, so it's difficult to know what sort of person he is."

"He's unlike anyone I know," came the truthful reply. "He's a generous, courteous gentleman, always looking for ways of helping others, with a first-class mind and before being gassed in the Great War, he was a keen sportsman. He used to hunt, shoot, fish and play cricket but he no longer enjoys good health and although he would never admit it, I think he is in constant pain. His grandmother comes from Applecross and he's proud of his Highland connections. It was while staying with her in the school holidays that he acquired his deep love of natural history, especially ornithology.

"He's a good man, Ailsa, and was like a brother to Angus."

Ailsa seemed content with Katherine's reply.

There followed a long pause.

"Ailsa," Katherine mused, releasing her hand, "before we leave for the service, I have something to tell you."

Angus' mother looked lovingly into Katherine's

eyes and said calmly, "You don't have to tell me, Katherine, I already know. You're pregnant!"

"How do you know?"

"It's called female intuition, and I also know that you're are suffering because you never told Angus about the baby."

Katherine stared in disbelief, trying to hold back her tears.

"Don't cry," Ailsa implored, clasping her hands. "When Angus came to visit me, he talked about wanting a child. I told him that I was certain you were pregnant and he believed me. Stop punishing yourself and be at peace because Angus knew he was going to be a father before he died and he was ecstatic."

She moved away from her daughter-in-law and dragged a chair over to the dresser.

"What are you doing?" Katherine asked, watching in alarm as the elderly lady climbed onto the wooden chair. "For goodness sake, Ailsa, come down and let me help. I've got enough problems without you falling and breaking a leg."

Ailsa did as she was told and stepped back onto the floor.

"I'm far more concerned about my unborn grand-child then these old bones," she conceded, tapping her legs. "Could you fetch that brass and enamel clock from the shelf up there and promise me you'll be careful?"

Katherine had to stretch on tiptoe to lift the clock

from its pride of place on top of the dresser. She handed it to Aisla.

"Thank you," Aisla said. "I want you to take this clock back to Shottenden and give it to my grandchild for his or her baptism. Like the ring, it belonged to my mother and holds many precious memories. I was told that its ticking represents the beating of a loved-one's heart, so perhaps you could pass this story on to the next generation.

Katherine took back the clock and once again embraced Angus' mother.

"I'll leave it here on the table and pick it up before I go," she added, thoughtfully. "I don't think my father would appreciate a clock ticking during one of his funeral services!"

She slipped her hand through her mother-in-law's arm and together they walked out into the cool Highland air.

The welcome they received outside the church was subdued but more generous than either had expected. The only person to keep his distance was Katherine's father who stood inside the tiny church lobby waiting for his flock to file past. Ailsa and Katherine found themselves at the back of the queue and when they reached the minister, he had no words of comfort for either of them. His initial reaction to Angus' death was to refuse to take the funeral but this decision had infuriated Edith.

"You will do no such thing," she expressed with

passion. "Angus was a good man and saved your life. He is also the husband of our only daughter and you have no right to deny him a Christian burial."

"How dare you question my judgement!" raged Donny. "Angus' constant refusal to attend church denies him the right to be buried in hallowed ground."

Edith held up her hand to stop her husband speaking.

"Enough!" she scolded. "I don't want to hear another word from you, Donny. I agreed with your decision not to marry Angus and Katherine because of the absurd age gap but I will not let you deny our son-in-law the burial and blessing he deserves.

"If you betray your friend in death, I will leave you and return to Bedford to look after my parents. I have put up with your intimidation for over thirty years and now the children have left home, I am free to do as I please."

Donny looked stunned and fearing his wife would actually carry out her threat to leave, he reluctantly agreed to take the service.

Katherine watched nervously as her father dragged his artificial leg slowly and painfully across the floor and climbed the steps into his pulpit. He looked pale and gaunt, as if weighed down by a burden too heavy to bear. When finally, he reached the top, he closed the small pine door and took out a large handkerchief to wipe the sweat from his brow. The theatrical performance that followed was a masterclass. He placed the palms of his hands firmly together and locked his zealous gaze on those waiting expectantly below.

Katherine kept her head bowed and closed her ears to her father's words. She had heard him preach so many times in the past and knew that Angus would be judged, condemned and sentenced to a life in hell within half an hour.

She also knew that her father would weigh her on the scales and find her wanting.

The luke-warm reception she received before the service evaporated into the mist as she and Ailsa made their way up the hill to the cemetery where Angus was to be laid to rest next to his father. A pair of golden eagles circled high above the graveyard as the coffin was lowered deep into the peaty Kilbackie soil.

"In the sweat of thy face shalt thou eat bread, till thou return unto the ground; for out of it wast thou taken: for dust thou art, and unto dust shalt thou return."

When the burial was finally over, Katherine took her mother-in-law's hand and returned to her croft.

"Come back with us. Please, Ailsa, come back with us. I can look after you at Shottenden and once the baby arrives we can be a family."

Ailsa looked lovingly at her daughter-in-law.

"I can't," she replied. "I belong to Kilbackie. It's where I have lived all my life and where my husband and son are buried. I can't leave them now, Katherine. My only comfort is that I'll soon be joining them and when I do, I promise I'll tell Angus that I was right about the baby."

Katherine picked up the French clock, lifted the latch and turned her back on Kilbackie forever.

"Take me back to Portree," she pleaded with Hugh, who was waiting patiently for her in the car. "I need to get away from here and never return."

Hugh looked at her distraught, drawn face and questioned his decision not to attend Angus' funeral. After all, their lives had been intricately bound for over thirty years and Angus was the only person Hugh had ever truly loved and trusted.

"Wait here a moment," he instructed Billings. "I won't be long."

He slipped out of the car and walked slowly back to his dearest friend's childhood home. Inside, he found Ailsa staring passively at the thick stone walls, unable to take in the enormity of her loss.

Hugh sat next to her on a small stool and waited for her to say something. Eventually she glanced up and mouthed, "Sir Hugh?"

He nodded.

"Your son was the finest man I've ever met," he said, placing on her lap a photo of Angus standing in the yard with his Jersey cows. He was looking relaxed and was smiling at the camera, with tousled hair and rolled-up sleeves.

The old lady picked up the photo and caressed her son's face with her fingers; then she kissed the photo and held it up to her wrinkled cheek.

She was too lost in grief to respond to Hugh's loving gesture but he knew how much the photo would mean to her and with a heavy heart, he returned to the car.

Billings drove the Alvis cautiously down the croft's stony track, taking care not to damage the suspension. The car's clearance wasn't great and some of the ruts were particularly deep but once it reached the road to Portree, the surface became smoother and the car began to pick up speed.

Suddenly, out of nowhere, a woman ran out in front of the car, waving her arms wildly in a state of agitation, forcing him to brake.

"What's going on, Billings?" Sir Hugh asked, settling back into his seat after being thrown forward by the emergency stop.

"I'm not exactly sure," he replied. "There's a lady on the road trying to stop us continuing our journey."

The lady in question was Mairi Nicolson.

She ran round to the passenger side and pounded on Katherine's window with her clenched fists.

"Katherine!" she panted. "Katherine! I need to speak to you."

Katherine opened the door and the two women flung their arms round each other.

CHAPTER 34

Much to everyone's surprise, Katherine's brother John had been arrested immediately after Angus' funeral and charged with his murder which he vehemently denied. He was denied bail and sent to Inverness prison, where he ranted on about his innocence. When no-one listened, he stopped co-operating and refused to speak.

Hugh decided to extend his time in the Highlands in order to visit John in prison to see if he could learn more about what happened to his friend but felt uneasy leaving Katherine alone so soon after the funeral.

"Will you two be all right tomorrow if I go and visit John?" he asked that evening after supper. "I've booked Mairi into the hotel for a couple of nights and thought you might enjoy spending some time together."

"Kind, considerate Hugh," Katherine thought to herself, smiling for the first time in a long while. "Always putting others before himself."

Billings drove Hugh to Portersfield prison, leaving the two women happily talking in Gaelic, the language which calmed Katherine's fears and helped her relax.

"Hello, John," the Colonel announced, stretching out a hand to greet the hunched prisoner who had been escorted into a waiting room.

John remained seated with his head down, nervously rubbing the hem of his prison shirt between his thumb and index finger.

"Are you being well looked after?"

No response.

"John," Hugh confided, "I have come over from Portree to try to find out what happened to Angus on the Kilbackie causeway. Can you help me?"

The young man sitting opposite him kept silent and Hugh decided not to ask any further questions, allowing John time to relax in his company.

"It's Colonel Hollister, isn't it?" came a meek, hesitant voice.

"That's right, John, I'm Colonel Hollister and I knew Angus and your father many years ago in France."

"You were gassed, weren't you," he whispered. "I heard about your bravery. You didn't deserve that bad luck."

Hugh chose not to reply.

There was a long pause, but curiously both men seemed at ease in each other's company.

It suited them to reflect.

"I didn't do it, Colonel," John blurted out. "I didn't kill Angus."

"I believe you, John," the Colonel assured him, "but you need to tell me exactly what happened. I'm here to help you."

"I've already told the police what happened but they don't believe me," John replied indignantly. "I followed Angus onto the island because I wanted to know what he was up to. Ever since he returned to Kilbackie, he'd been acting strangely, visiting the island and the house every day, bringing with him a notebook and a pair of binoculars."

"Go on," the Colonel urged.

"Major Urquhart, who owned the estate, died a couple of months before Angus' father, and his widow went to live with her niece in Glasgow, leaving Kilbackie House and the island uninhabited. The prize-winning Shetland herd and several hundred sheep have already been sold in Portree Market and, as far as I know, the whole estate is up for sale.

"Angus knew the Major valued his privacy and even though the island and house were empty, he would never have trespassed on the land. That's why I followed him."

"When did you last see him?" the Colonel asked.

"I last saw him around two o'clock, looking round the house and making notes."

Hugh sat and reflected on John's account.

"Think hard," he continued. "Are you absolutely sure there was no-one else on the island at the time?"

John shuffled uncomfortably on his chair and kept his head bowed.

"You saw someone else on the island, didn't you, John, and you don't want to mention his name."

Silence.

"Who else was on the island, John?"

"I can't be sure," came the weak reply.

"You can't be sure of what?"

"Oh God!" John cried and began to weep.

Wiping his eyes on his sleeve, he whispered through choking tears, "I let him die."

The Colonel crossed his arms in a relaxed manner and looked straight at John.

"Take your time and tell me in your own words exactly what happened."

"I needed to get back home before the tide turned, so I crossed the causeway and hid in a ditch to wait for Angus. I was furious with him because of the gossip and sniggering I had had to endure after my sister's engagement was announced. The huge age gap was considered a joke and I hate being laughed at. Angus never arrived."

John drew a breath and continued, "Peeping over the top of my hiding place, I saw him on the island arguing with a man who was waving his arms in the air and shouting. I was too far away to hear what was being said but it didn't look good. Angus appeared to stay in control and walked away from the man towards the causeway but the man followed him, shaking his fist. Finally he stopped, cupped his hands and shouted something but I still couldn't hear what he was saying. Whatever it was, Angus had no intention of responding because he carried on walking. Eventually the man got closer to him, lifted a rock and hurled it at the back of his head. I don't know if he intended to harm Angus or just give him a fright but whatever his motive, Angus slumped to the ground and didn't move."

"What did the man do next?" Hugh asked, trying to stay calm.

"He dragged Angus to the edge of the causeway and left him there."

"Why did you say you left him to die?"

"I could have gone back to save him but I didn't. The tide had started to come in and I panicked."

"Did you see the man cross the causeway?"

John crossed his arms on the table and buried his head deep into their fold.

The only sounds in the room were the muffled cries of despair.

"Did you see who hit Angus?" Hugh repeated urgently.

"I deserve to die," John spluttered. "Just leave me alone, sir, and let me hang."

Hugh was at a loss to know what to do. His time was nearly up and yet he was so close to obtaining the truth. John was inconsolable and unlikely to say another word. He had been pushed to the edge and was close to breaking.

The prison guard looked at his watch. "Time's up, sir."

Hugh slowly stood up, keeping his eyes firmly fixed on John. He then turned his back on the broken figure and left the cell, asking to speak to the prison governor.

"Tell him Colonel Sir Hugh Hollister wishes to speak to him," he ordered calmly.

Pulling rank was not in Hugh's character but a

man's life was at stake and he felt obliged to use the only trump card he had left to save John.

"If you'll wait here, Sir Hugh, I'll see if I can find him."

Half an hour later, a tall, well-dressed man approached Hugh and introduced himself as the Governor.

"What can I do for you, Sir Hugh?" he asked impatiently, deeply resenting being summoned by a military baronet.

"I'd like the opportunity to spend another hour with John Nicolson and I'd like him to be given a cup of sweet tea and a biscuit."

"Would you like us to sing him a lullaby as well?"

"That won't be necessary, sir," Hugh replied with regimental authority. "Mr Nicolson has one of the finest voices in the Highlands and is quite capable of singing himself to sleep."

The Governor looked Hugh up and down and stared into his scarred face.

Hugh didn't flinch.

"MacKay! Fetch two cups of sweet tea and some biscuits and take them to Cell No. 4 for Nicolson and Colonel Hollister. They are to be left alone for an hour to enjoy their little tea party. Is that clear?"

"Yes, sir!" MacKay replied.

The Governor shook Hugh's hand and disappeared back down the corridor.

CHAPTER 35

On 15th December 1948, everyone was seated in the festive drawing room, waiting for tea.

The huge sparkling Christmas tree dominated one corner of the room and hanging from the mantlepiece were swags of holly and ivy. The glowing light from the candles lit up the graceful furnishings and historic portraits surrounding Lady Hollister who was reading the latest copy of *The Tatler*. Katherine walked restlessly round the room trying to stop her large bump and swollen ankles from aching.

"Do sit down and relax," Lady Hollister remarked curtly, without bothering to look up from her magazine. "All this pacing up and down is making me feel quite giddy and I'm sure an agitated mother can't be good for the baby."

Katherine meekly did as she was told and settled down on the edge of a chair while Gladys went around discreetly laying the table and Mairi drew the thick curtains, shutting out the gloomy half-light of a wet afternoon.

Katherine had finally told Hugh about her pregnancy during their stay in Portree and much to her surprise, he was delighted.

At his insistence, Mairi returned with them to Shottenden and replaced Katherine as Lady Hollister's companion. She took up her new position with cheerful optimism and made the role her own, treading agilely between quiet submission and firm assertion.

Gladys was putting the finishing touches to the table when Hugh entered the drawing room, waving a piece of paper in his hand.

"It's here!" he announced breathlessly. "It's all here! I've just received confirmation that John has been released. Apparently the trial collapsed due to a lack of reliable evidence."

Mairi stared at Hugh for a moment in disbelief, then smiled as he nodded in her direction to assure her it were true. Katherine, however, went deathly pale, grabbing hold of the arms of the chair.

"What's the matter?" he asked. "I thought you'd be pleased."

"I *am* pleased," she declared, looking at Mairi. "We all knew John had nothing to do with Angus' death but with him in the clear, the question still remains. Who killed my husband?"

She took in a gasp of air and let out a sharp cry of pain.

"Are you all right?" Mairi asked her as Hugh's expression changed from triumph to horror.

He struggled to find a few meaningful words to ease Katherine's pain but his mouth dried up. Nervously, he stood by, fingering the loose change in his trouser pocket whilst Mairi gathered Katherine into her arms and comforted her in Gaelic.

Gladys remained dutifully poised by the afternoon tea table, unsure whether to pour Lady Hollister's tea or leave. She looked for guidance but had become an invisible player in the unfolding drama.

Lady Hollister finally made it clear she had had quite enough of the disruption to her afternoon and announced rather imperiously, "I shall take tea in the library."

Rising with exaggerated dignity, she swept out of the drawing room like a fragrant goddess, followed, at a discreet distance, by Gladys, carrying a fully laden tea tray. The four o'clock aromas of salmon, egg, freshly baked scones and strawberry jam lingered awhile before dispersing in the winter chill.

"Come on, Katherine," encouraged Mairi. "It's time to get you home."

By this time, Katherine was kneeling on all fours, trying to control the pain by taking in long deep breaths.

Mairi noticed a small wet patch on the drawing room carpet.

"Katherine, we must get you into bed as soon as possible," she urged in Gaelic, with more than a hint of urgency. "Don't worry about anything, I'll make sure everything is cleaned up."

This assurance persuaded Katherine to get up and start the slow walk back home where everything needed for the baby's arrival lay neatly stacked on the kitchen table.

Mairi wasted no time in taking charge.

She lit the lamps and fire and stripped Katherine's

bed, covering the mattress with a large rubber sheet and plenty of newspaper.

Katherine, in the meanwhile, had changed into her nightdress and was steadying herself on the dressing table, clutching her back and letting out low moaning sounds.

"I won't be long," Mairi assured her niece as she finished tucking in the sheets and plumping up the pillows.

"There now, everything's ready. You can lie down and get the weight off your feet."

Katherine slipped between the cool sheets, trying to control the pains gripping her body.

"Thank you, Mairi," she whispered. Exhausted and embarrassed by the afternoon's events, she sighed and repeated the words, "Thank you."

Mairi held her hand and smiled.

"We are so fortunate living at Shottenden," she exclaimed, looking at Katherine surrounded by fresh bedlinen in a cosy room warmed by a roaring fire. "Where else would we receive so much for so little!"

Mairi busied herself with the preparations, placing a large enamel bowl and a jug full of warm water beside the fire. Dragging the bedside table to the end of the bed, she meticulously arranged the soap, cotton wool, scissors, more newspaper, cotton thread and nappies on the top. She hung the towels and blankets over a wooden clothes rack to air and warm in front of the fire.

"I'm just going to put the kettle on," she told

Katherine, who was left clutching her pillow as wave after wave of excruciating pain rippled across her back. "I don't think you'll have long to wait."

Alone in her bedroom, Katherine reflected on the years Angus, Hugh and her father spent together in the Great War, witnessing and experiencing terrible suffering. They returned home weighed down by anger, despair, cynicism and pain and now Katherine was bringing a new life into the world. She was determined to face up to the challenge and make Angus proud of her.

She drew on her reserves and concentrated on the birth of their baby.

Relentless contractions clamped the unborn child in a vice-like grip and sent her swollen body into spasms, yet throughout her ordeal she never uttered a sound.

The only noise in the room came from the reassuring ticking of Ailsa's clock on the mantelpiece.

The midwife arrived about six-thirty and made her way upstairs. After vigorously washing her hands, she examined Katherine and told her that her labour was nearly over.

Mairi continued cooling Katherine's face and neck with a wet flannel while singing haunting Gaelic songs, whose melodies wove through the pangs of childbirth.

The baby arrived with relative ease and immediately started to cry, much to everyone's relief. The midwife nimbly tied the umbilical cord and cut it with a pair of scissors. She then washed the blood off the baby's face and swabbed both eyes with warm water, before wrapping it in a warm blanket and handing the bundle to Katherine.

"It's a boy," she announced. "You have a little son."

Katherine gazed down at the tiny child and kissed his forehead with such tenderness that Mairi and the midwife stopped what they were doing to watch.

Mairi managed deftly to wipe and dry the rubber sheet before re-making the bed and propping Katherine up against the pillows.

"Have you thought of a name yet?" she asked, tucking in the sheets.

"Tavish Angus MacLeod," Katherine replied, cradling her newborn son.

Mairi looked surprised.

"Why Tavish?" she asked.

"In England," Katherine confided, "all churches are named after saints and St Thomas's Church here at Shottenden opened its doors to me and Angus when we wanted to get married. I've never forgotten the kindness we received on our wedding day and have chosen the English form of Tàmhas for our son."

"Tavish Angus MacLeod," Mairi repeated lyrically. "I like it."

Many visitors entered the cottage over the next few weeks, including Johnny Mitchell, whose parents had recently died. His visits increasingly coincided with Mairi's visits and it wasn't long before everyone knew the two of them had formed a close attachment.

Both Hugh and Mairi were asked to be Tavish's

godparents and he was christened by Hubert Hilton at a small private service in the Anglican Church of Saint Thomas, Shottenden.

Katherine took the French clock off the shelf in her bedroom and placed it next to Tavish's crib. Once a week she would wind it up and feel Ailsa's loving presence in the room. She trusted Ailsa to keep Tavish's birth a secret and apart from Mairi, no-one from Kilbackie knew of his existence and she was determined to keep it that way. She and her son needed a fresh start.

The day after Tavish's christening, Johnny bent down on one knee in Shottenden Woods and proposed to Mairi Nicolson.

CHAPTER 36

Shottenden, spring 1953

One warm spring afternoon, Hugh made his way across to Katherine's cottage, where she was sitting on a rug, making a daisy chain for Tavish, now a sturdy four-year-old.

"Hugh!" Katherine exclaimed with obvious pleasure. "How lovely to see you! Would you like a drink?"

He nodded and sat cross-legged on the grass to help Tavish complete the daisy chain, while Katherine brushed down her dress and went indoors to put the kettle on.

"He's looking really well," Hugh called out to her as she disappeared through the door. "He's such a splendid little chap."

Katherine poked her head round the door and smiled.

"Thanks!" she said. "He seems to be getting more like Angus every day. He'd have been so thrilled to have a son."

A few minutes later, she returned carrying a large tray and poured out the tea. Tavish picked up the long daisy chain and placed it on his mother's head, announcing, "You're the Queen of Shottenden!"

There was an awkward pause before Katherine laughed off the comment saying, "Don't be silly, Tavish. There's no such person as the Queen of Shottenden. You've been listening to too many fairy tales!"

Tavish didn't argue but it was clear he had grown bored of playing with daisies and soon he disappeared indoors to find some toys, leaving Hugh and Katherine to finish their tea in peace. Hugh ran his hands over the grass and picked a few daisies but was in no mood to start another chain. Katherine noticed his hands were shaking and he seemed uneasy.

"Is everything all right?" she asked.

"I'm fine," he replied, a little too quickly.

"Hugh, tell me the truth!" she continued. "I've known you for six years; long enough to know when something isn't right."

He put down his empty cup and reached out to hold her hand but Katherine drew it away, terrified he was about to declare his love.

"I'm dying, Katherine," he confessed quietly.

She sat bolt upright and looked him in the eye. This was not what she was expecting.

"I don't believe you," she gasped. "It can't be true."

"I'm afraid it is. My Harley Street consultant confirmed this lunch-time that I have cancer and only a few months to live; that's why I need to talk to you," he continued, once she was composed enough to lift her head and listen. "I've asked Mairi to babysit for Tavish this evening, so perhaps you could come over to the house and have dinner with me. Mother will be out playing bridge so we will be left alone."

Katherine thought hard about Hugh's invitation to dinner.

Now that Mairi was looking after Lady Hollister, she rarely went back to the house and missed its beauty and elegance.

"I don't know," she said.

"I'm afraid you have no choice," he declared, kindly but firmly. "I've arranged everything and won't take 'No' for an answer. Mairi and Johnny will be here at seven o'clock this evening so I'll expect you at seven-thirty. If Tavish needs you at any time, Johnny will let us know."

Hugh had nothing further to say – he needed time and space to come to terms with the prognosis.

CHAPTER 37

Katherine picked out two dresses and laid them on the bed, trying to decide which one to wear. The formal, teal silk dress with elaborate embroidery and a gold belt had been a present from Lady Hollister and she had only worn it twice, both times at Shottenden for Christmas.

The other dress was more casual but was her favourite. Its coral colour highlighted her delicate skin and the floaty lawn cotton made her feel slim and graceful.

She chose the coral one and sat in front of her dressing table adding a few dabs of face powder and some lipstick, then brushed her long hair and pinned it up loosely.

It had been a long time since she last took an interest in her appearance and was surprised at the pleasure it gave her.

"Can I come up?" called a voice from downstairs.

"Shhh! Tavish is asleep and I'm in the bedroom. Make yourself at home, I won't be long."

Mairi settled down on the sofa and waited. She could hear the floorboards creak as Katherine tiptoed into Tavish's room and kissed him gently on the forehead before making her way downstairs.

Her entrance into the front room left Mairi speechless.

"What's the matter?" Katherine asked.

"I don't know how to put this," Mairi replied with astonishment, "but you look absolutely gorgeous! Have you put on some makeup?"

Katherine held her hands up to her blushing cheeks and tried to rub off the powder with the back of her hands.

"Leave it," Mairi continued. "Whatever you're wearing suits you. I've never seen you look so radiant."

The gushing compliment only increased Katherine's embarrasment.

"I'll go and wash off the powder," she stuttered, on the verge of tears.

"You'll do no such thing!" Mairi replied, patting the sofa. "Come and sit down here next to me and tell me what's going on."

"What do you mean 'going on'?" Katherine enquired, feeling particularly self-conscious. "There's nothing 'going on'."

She picked up her coat and made her way to the front door.

"You know Hugh's in love with you, don't you?" Mairi commented as Katherine opened the door to leave.

The words slammed her chest, causing unbearable pain. Hugh had become her unexpected patron since Angus' death, allowing her to stay in the cottage and receive his wage, at least for the time being. She trusted him totally and believed his generosity towards her was the act of a gentleman but now Mairi was suggesting his interest in her had strings attached and she would have to choose between returning his love or leaving Shottenden.

She put out an arm to steady the tremors racing through her body.

"What are you talking about?"

"Exactly what I've just infered," came the calm reply. "Hugh Hollister is in love with you, Katherine, but he's too shy to tell you."

"It's not true," Katherine shouted, not caring if her denial woke Tavish. "It's always been Angus he loved, not me."

"Then I'm sorry for speaking out of turn. You go off and have a lovely dinner and I'll keep an eye on Tavish. Johnny will be along soon, so if there is a problem, I promise he'll come and fetch you."

Katherine paused to regain her composure, then walked out of the door, brushing her dress against a wisp of honeysuckle as she went.

She made her way across the lawn towards the house which had inspired her ever since Angus first described it on Skye.

"Tell me more about Shottenden," she would say. "How big is the house and does it really have electricity?"

Angus would answer her questions patiently, pleased to talk about the place he loved.

Katherine decided against using the front door,

preferring to enter via the kitchen where Mrs Davies was tidying up and Gladys was adding the finishing touches to dinner.

"You off out?" Gladys asked, looking at Katherine. "I hope it's somewhere nice. We don't see you dressed up these days which is a pity because you look wonderful. Whoever you're meeting is a very lucky man!"

She exchanged a quick smile with Mrs Davies and continued working.

"I can't stop to chat right now," Gladys prattled, straining stock through a piece of muslin.

"Sir Hugh has an important guest for dinner and wants the meal served promptly at eight o'clock."

The homely aroma of tender lamb, rosemary and crunchy roast potatoes filled the warm kitchen. Prepared carrots, cauliflower florets and shelled peas from the kitchen garden lay on a large, wooden board, ready to be tipped into a saucepan of boiling water and a gravy jug, full of meat juice, stood resting on a spotlessly clean, scrubbed table.

Katherine watched with increasing embarrassment as her dinner was being prepared before her eyes.

Cutglass bowls of fig and pear compôte, freshly hulled strawberries and a blancmange decorated with pansies and cream stood on the dresser and for the first time since Angus' death, Katherine found Shottenden's excess unsettling.

"I just wanted to see how you both were," she stuttered, "but obviously this isn't a convenient time. Another day perhaps?"

"That would be lovely," Gladys agreed, taking the joint out of the oven and preparing the roux for the gravy. "We haven't seen you for such a long time. How's Tavish?"

"He's fine," Katherine replied, heading towards the back door.

She made her way across the scullery courtyard to a low wall hidden behind an outshed and collapsed in a crumpled heap.

"Another day," she whispered.

The sun sank below the treeline and it started to get cool. Katherine pulled her coat tightly round her shoulders and walked aimlessly towards the woods where she was certain no-one would find her.

CHAPTER 38

"What on earth has happened to you?" Johnny asked, putting his lamp down beside Katherine, who lay motionless on the ground in Shottenden Woods with her head buried in her arms. The mellow glow of the paraffin lamp illuminated the blue tint of her pale complexion and the purple tone of her lips.

"Come on," he coaxed, lifting her frail body effortlessly in his arms. "It's time to get you safely back home. We've been looking for you everywhere and Sir Hugh is beside himself with worry."

Katherine tried to speak but Johnny stopped her.

"Shhhh!" he whispered gently. "Don't waste your energy trying to talk. You can explain everything in your own time, once you've warmed up and had something to eat."

Katherine closed her eyes and relaxed in Johnny's strong hold.

"Tell me one thing before I get you home," he made her promise. "Have you been harmed in any way?"

Katherine shook her head and Johnny appeared satisfied with her answer.

He cradled her exhausted body in his arms and walked back to the cottage where Mairi and Hugh were waiting anxiously in the front room.

"She'll need your help," he informed his wife. "Her clothes are wet through and she's in shock."

Mairi left Hugh pacing up and down the room and followed her husband to the bedroom where she took hold of Katherine's pale, limp hand.

Speaking in Gaelic, she coaxed her niece to take off her damp clothing.

"The sooner we get you dry and warm the better," she said, unbuttoning the flimsy cotton dress and replacing it with one of Angus' heavy work shirts. Katherine began to relax, enveloped in the tangible memory of her husband and she slipped compliantly into bed and closed her eyes like a child.

"Will she be all right?" Hugh asked, rubbing his damaged eyes and muttering, "I've been such a fool! Such a fool!"

"She's very distressed and cold, but she'll be fine," Johnny replied. "I don't know how long she'd been in the wood but I expect it was several hours."

"I'll make up a hot water bottle and sit with her for a while longer," Mairi said. "Johnny, could you fetch Tavish from his room and carry him back home? I think, in the present circumstances, it would be better if he spent the rest of the night with us."

She turned and looked at Hugh.

"There's nothing more that can be done until the morning, Sir Hugh. Why don't you go home and get some rest."

When Katherine woke up, it was already daylight and outside her window a song thrush was singing at full volume. Far away she could hear a mower sweeping across the main lawn, releasing pungent smells of freshly mown grass.

It was four-thirty in the afternoon!

She tried to sit up and call out but the effort of lifting her head made her giddy and, finding no voice, she slipped back under the warm bedclothes.

Beside her, on the bed, lay an envelope addressed to Katherine MacLeod in familiar handwriting but she didn't feel strong enough to read it.

She called out in a faint, husky voice, "Mairi, are you there?"

There was no reply.

"Mairi! Can you hear me?"

Nothing.

Katherine started to panic, having no idea where Tavish was. Cautiously, she pushed the blankets to one side and slipped out of bed, steadying herself on the bedside table before reaching for her dressing gown which was lying over a chair, warmed by the afternoon sun.

Sounds of laughter and irrepressible giggling came from her front room below. Step by cautious step, she descended the stairs and pushed open the door just wide enough to see Johnny balancing Tavish on his feet and whirring him in the air like an aeroplane.

"More! More!" the little boy giggled as the game became increasingly rough.

When, finally, he landed gently back on the floor,

he flung himself against Johnny's muscular chest and hugged him.

"That was fun!" he laughed and added innocently, "I wish you were my daddy, Johnny."

Mairi was sitting on the sofa, knitting a jumper. She looked at her husband, who glanced helplessly in her direction.

"Your daddy was a very special man, Tavish," Mairi revealed, "and you should always be proud of him. Johnny can never replace your daddy but he will always love you and look after you."

Katherine turned away and tiptoed back up the stairs, tears trickling down her cheeks.

She picked up the letter on her bed and after much hesitation, slipped it unread into the back of her Bible. There was a creaking sound on the landing and a knock on the door.

"Are you awake?" Mairi asked softly.

"I'm just getting dressed, won't be long," Katherine replied, fastening the zip of her floral dress and pulling on a cotton cardigan. The coral dress, which had so changed her appearance the previous night, lay crumpled in a corner of the room.

There was another knock on the door.

"Is it safe to enter?"

"Come on in, I'm dressed now."

Katherine was sitting on her bed, adjusting the straps of her summer sandals and looking terribly pale, with red blotchy cheeks and puffed bloodshot eyes. Instead of greeting her friend, she remained seated, struggling to do up the buckles with trembling fingers.

Mairi stood in the doorway, finding it difficult to believe that the person in front of her with slumped shoulders and lank hair, was the same Katherine MacLeod who had looked a picture of health the night before. She had known her niece all her life and even though there were thirteen years between them, she had always admired the way Katherine had fought for what she believed in.

Something was crushing her spirit and Mairi was determined to find out what it was.

"How are you feeling?" she asked hesitantly, not wanting to intrude.

Katherine looked exhausted and kept her eyes focussed on the floor.

She had nothing to say.

"Sir Hugh was in a desperate state when you went missing," Mairi explained. "He blamed himself for your disappearance and frantically put together a team of volunteers to search the entire estate. It was fortuitous that Johnny had a hunch you'd be in the woods and found you reasonably quickly."

Katherine appreciated Mairi's concern but wished she would go away.

"What's the matter?" Mairi persisted, trying to get the bottom of her niece's pain. "Is it Sir Hugh?"

Katherine looked horrified by the suggestion.

"Why do you always have to talk about Sir Hugh?" she cried, becoming agitated. "It has nothing to do with him, so kindly drop the subject and leave the room. I'd like to spend some time on my own."

Mairi looked deeply hurt, never having heard Katherine speak so abruptly.

"Would you like me stay with you this evening until Tavish is asleep?" she asked timidly.

"No, it's all right." Katherine replied, slightly more gently. "You and Johnny have done more than enough and I need to sort myself out and spend some time alone with my son."

Mairi left the bedroom as quietly as she had entered, calling down to Johnny that it was time to go home.

Katherine could hear Tavish running enthusiastically towards the couple as they prepared to leave. There were squeals of excitement as Johnny lifted the young boy high in the air and placed him on his shoulders.

"Who's the King of the Castle?" he roared.

"I am!" shouted the small boy. "I'm the King of the Castle!"

Katherine could hear her son being lowered back onto the floor.

"You be a good boy and look after your mother for us," Johnny instructed.

"I will," came the breathless reply, "but I wish I was going home with you."

CHAPTER 39

After the final hymn the congregation stood in their pews, waiting for the robed choir to process down the aisle to the vestry. Katherine gazed at the sun's rays streaming through the East window, lighting up the sixteenth-century altarpiece which depicted Jesus the Good Shepherd tending his flock by a deep blue river.

The painting never failed to move her and reminded her of Kilbackie.

After the benediction, she picked up her gloves, bowed modestly towards the stained-glass window and, holding Tavish's hand, edged her way out of the pew. She walked across the flagstones to the South porch where there was a short queue waiting to greet the vicar.

Fortunately, Hugh was nowhere to be seen.

Her restless mind focussed on a simple piece of paper pinned to the notice board at the back of church, 'Malvingborough Abbey, the way to serve'. There followed a brief description of its work and a quote saying: 'God seeks us — with joy and awe we need only say 'Yes'.'

"I see you've found the poster I put up," Daisy noted, making her way towards Katherine. "The Abbess asked if I would publicise her work and, of course, I willingly agreed. Without them, I don't think William would be with us today. Do you remember the state he was in when he first returned from the Far East?"

Katherine thought back five years to the time when William entered the Abbey as a traumatised, deeply-scarred soldier and re-emerged nearly a year later as a thoughtful, well-balanced young man. The Abbess put the transformation in his life down to patience, love and prayer.

"Did I tell you he's got a job as an apprentice at Wilson's Garage on the Garston Road," Daisy gushed, then whispered, "I shouldn't really say this in church, but he's courting Dorothy Davies from Battenbourne. Do you know her?"

Katherine shook her head.

"She's such a sweet girl. Bill and I are keeping our fingers crossed, if you know what I mean!"

Katherine had become anxious and depressed since Hugh had told her about his cancer.

Mairi checked in on her from time to time and continued to take a keen interest in Tavish, speaking Gaelic and singing to him her favourite childhood songs but, apart from these occasional visits, she saw no-one.

"I haven't seen you for such a long time," Daisy complained. "Why don't you pop round on Wednesday. It's my afternoon off."

Katherine tried to think of an excuse but couldn't think of one so she reluctantly accepted the invitation.

"Excellent!" Daisy replied. "See you Wednesday and don't forget to bring Tavish."

As Wednesday drew closer, Katherine became increasingly tense and short-tempered, snapping at Tavish for no reason. He sensed her anxiety and whined for attention which irritated her even more. They drove each other into an ugly shouting match which only ended when Tavish screamed, "I don't want to live with you any more, I want to live with Mairi and Johnny because they love me!"

Katherine was horrified by her son's outburst and shut down her emotions to save herself from total collapse. She 'ummed' and 'ahhed' whether to cancel her visit but in the end she decided to go as Daisy was her only true friend.

"Come on in!" Daisy said, ushering them into the front room where tea was already laid out.

"Take a seat!" she motioned. "I've brought down some toys from the attic for Tavish. I don't know if he likes soldiers and cars but there're plenty of them here in these boxes. They used to belong to William so I'm afraid they're rather old and battered."

"What do you say?" Katherine nagged, as Tavish took out a handful of soldiers and lined them up against the skirting board.

"Thank you, Daisy."

"I was really sorry to hear about Sir Hugh's illness," Daisy sympathised, pouring out a cup of tea. "He is such a courteous man, always offering wise advice and never judging unfairly. I have a lot of respect for that man and many happy memories working for his mother, even though she could be very difficult at times.

"Did I ever tell you about the time she refused to go downstairs to play bridge until I found the tiny bow that had fallen off the blue silk petticoat she wanted to wear. I assured her Ladyship that no-one would notice it was missing but she refused to listen and insisted the bow be found. In the end, I had to cut a small strip of silk from the hem of one of her blue evening dresses and make up a new bow. When I presented her with the finished garment, she tossed her head imperiously to one side and declared rather grandly, 'I no longer wish to wear that slip. Could you find me another one?'

"I was furious but held my tongue and did what she asked!"

Katherine sat rigidly on the edge of her chair, staring at her son as he raced cars round the room. She showed no emotion and made no comment.

"What's the matter?" Daisy asked sympathetically. "You're my best friend and you've hardly uttered a word since arriving. You've a face as long as a fiddle and I know I'm not a very good storyteller, but you could at least have smiled at the story of the lost bow."

Katherine looked at her friend and gave the weakest of smiles.

Eventually she spoke.

"Did you know Shottenden is going to be taken over by something called the National Trust?" she said impassively. "They're keeping on a few estate workers but I'll have to look for somewhere else to live."

Daisy looked at Katherine and wondered what was tormenting her; it had to more than she was letting on.

"No, I haven't heard anything about the National whatever taking over the estate but I've often wondered what would happen to Shottenden if Sir Hugh were no longer around. Don't worry about having nowhere to live, Katherine, you can always come and stay with us!" Daisy replied, enthusiastically. "It'd be such fun to have a child in the house again and Bill and William always love seeing you. You could stay in our spare room, even if only for a short time. Whatever happens you mustn't leave Shottenden. I couldn't bear it."

Katherine thought long and hard before answering.

"Oh! Daisy! I don't know what to say," she replied with affection.

"How about 'Yes!'" Daisy insisted, her eyes shining.

"I can't!" Katherine sighed. "I can't move in with you even though you are my dearest friend, and I know Tavish and I would be happy with you."

"Why ever not!" Daisy exclaimed. "What's got into you, Katherine? What on earth's the matter?"

"I can't explain," came the anguished reply. "Without Angus, I don't belong here any more. I feel like a stranger in a foreign land, Daisy, and can't settle. My heart and soul belong to Skye but it's robbed me of my happiness and my future and I can never go back.

"I've decided to write to the Abbess of Malvingborough Abbey to offer my services as a nurse for as long as they will have me. I need to work, Daisy and find peace."

"What about Tavish?" came the shocked reply.

"If it is God's will, then Tavish will come with me."

"But, Katherine, you can't take Tavish away from here and spend the rest of your life in obscurity."

"I can," she replied, "and I will."

Three weeks later, Tavish heard the postman's bicycle ride up to the front door and saw an envelope drop through the letterbox. He tore down the hallway and picked it up, proudly presenting it to his mother who was sitting in the kitchen having breakfast.

"What have you got there?" she asked.

"A letter!" he cried, waving the white envelope wildly in the air. "You've got a letter, Mummy."

Katherine held out her hand and took the envelope from her son and placed it on the table.

"Who's it from?" Tavish asked, his eyes glinting with excitement.

"Never you mind," his mother replied. "Now off you go and play with your trains, I'll be with you in a minute."

Fortunately for Katherine, Tavish decided to be obedient and ran into the front room, leaving her nervously turning over the envelope. She got up from the table and put the kettle on, restlessly pacing up and down, waiting for the water to boil. She picked up the envelope several times but hadn't the courage to open it.

Tavish soon came running back to the kitchen "Come and play with me," he demanded. "I want you to play with me."

"I want doesn't get," Katherine replied. "And, how about a few P's and Q's?"

"Please come and play with me," he repeated with a grin, shaking his hands up and down with excitement.

"All right, I won't be long. Give me a moment to read this letter and finish my drink."

The small boy dutifully returned to the front room, leaving Katherine staring at the envelope until finally she had the courage to slit it open and pull out a crisp white sheet of headed notepaper belonging to the Abbess of Malvingborough Abbey.

It was rare for Katherine to receive a letter and as she read through its content, she became deeply moved by the power and beauty of the writing. The effect of the warm, encouraging words was overwhelming and for the first time since Angus' death, she saw a glimmer of hope.

The one sentence at the bottom of the page would change her life for ever.

'It is with deep regret that we are unable to accept children and therefore cannot offer a place for you and your son, Tavish.'

Katherine crunched the letter in her fist and hurled it across the room.

CHAPTER 40

Even though Katherine had vowed never to step inside Shottenden following the unfortunate dinner incident, she changed her mind when Mairi informed her that Sir Hugh's health was failing fast and he wished to see her once more before he died.

Katherine felt she should heal the rift between them and had no desire to deny Hugh his dying wish so, on the appointed day, she took the path across the lawn to the front door and rang the bell. She braced herself for the farewell meeting which, much to her embarrassment, was to take place in his bedroom.

"Come this way!" the nurse said, leading her across the familiar hall and up the main staircase. "Sir Hugh's expecting you."

Hugh's bedroom was surprisingly elegant and airy, with five long sash windows forming a classic curved bay. Half-drawn curtains shaded his bed from direct sunlight and freshly cut flowers from the walled garden added colour and scent.

Surrounded by plumped pillows and crisp, well-pressed sheets, he lay near the edge of a large four-poster bed. His translucent skin had turned a sickly grey and even with the help of oxygen, he was struggling to breathe.

At first, Katherine thought she had arrived too late

but once accustomed to the dim light, she noticed his chest was heaving gently up and down with every shallow intake of breath.

She drew up a chair beside the bed and rested her arm on the small bedside table, carefully avoiding the vase of fragrant sweet peas. Through a half-open window, she could hear the distant bleating of sheep in the parkland and the song of skylarks rising ever higher towards the heavens.

Hugh looked awful.

"You'll have to put your ear close to his mouth," the nurse told her. "Sir Hugh is totally blind now, and his voice is very weak."

Katherine was ill-prepared for the weeping sores that covered his watering eyes. She blushed a deep crimson as she moved her head closer to his mouth and smelt his foul, acrid breath. She wanted to gag and run away from the fine man whose life was slowly ebbing away but, for Angus' sake, she put her feelings to one side and gently caressed his sunken cheeks with her soft, warm fingers.

"You've come!" he whispered in a quiet hoarse voice, reaching up to hold her hand. "You've come!"

"Yes, Sir Hugh!" she replied with affection, "I've come."

"Did you read my letter?" he rasped, keeping hold of her hand.

She shook her head but realising he couldn't see her answer, she added, "I was too afraid."

"Don't be afraid," he gasped, taking in small

breaths of oxygen before continuing. "It says every-thing you need to know."

He paused, waiting to take in sufficient oxygen to be able to finish what he wanted to say.

"Angus was my soulmate," he sighed, "and my future. Without him I have no desire to live, but you have Tavish to look after, Katherine, and I have done everything within my means to secure your futures."

His head rolled to one side and the nurse, who was never far away, wiped the watery tears out of his infected eyes.

"Sir Hugh is exhausted," she remarked firmly but kindly. "I think you should leave now."

Katherine kept hold of his hand.

"Just a few more minutes," she entreated. "I promise I won't tire him."

She stared down at Hugh as he lay peacefully waiting his end, surrounded by beauty, protected by privilege and well-cared for by nurses. He wanted for nothing, was widely respected by his tenants and yet his death seemed so unbearably lonely.

Shottenden House appeared eerily quiet as she descended the grand staircase and cautiously crept along the corridor towards the room Angus had called 'his sanctuary'.

She needed to draw closure and say farewell to the magnificent library that had transformed her husband's life and given him so much pleasure. On entering the room she was astonished to see the shelves stripped bare and all the books placed in open

tea-chests stencilled with the words 'Kilbackie House'.
It was clear that Hugh had ordered the entire contents
of his precious library to be packed up and sent to
Skye ahead of the National Trust taking over.

"Oh Hugh!" she cried. "What have you done?"

The sight of the dismantled library and Hugh's
emaciated body strengthened Katherine's resolve to
change her life before it finally spiralled out of
control. She searched the crates for a large book
which would never be missed and eventually came
across the 'Fungi of Australia' which seemed to fit
her plan perfectly. Moving quickly for fear of being
discovered, she slipped the book under her coat and
walked out of the imposing front door with her head
held high.

Johnny and Mairi had offered to take Tavish home
with them, promising to return him washed, fed and
ready for bed at six o'clock.

She looked at her watch - it was just before five.

She had a whole hour to herself.

Back home, she sat at the kitchen table, opened the
reference book half way and began cutting out a
large, square secret compartment in which she could
hide the items she wished to send back to Kilbackie.
Satisfied with the finished product, she moved to the
sofa and started to read Hugh's letter.

"My dear Katherine,"

*"Forgive me for the thoughtless way I handled this
evening. The dinner invitation was meant to provide me
with an opportunity to discuss your future but I never made*

this clear and left you feeling threatened and afraid, for which I am truly sorry.

"Can we be friends again?

"What I am about to write is sensitive and private but I trust your discretion and know the information will go no further.

"Shottenden is badly in debt and the tax owed after my death will officially make it bankrupt. I have arranged an 'Acceptance in Lieu' with the Exchequer and when I am no longer around, the National Trust will take over and run the estate on behalf of the nation. The deal will preserve the house, its gardens and parkland and maintain the farm as a viable business but, regrettably, it means you will have to vacate your cottage and find alternative accommodation.

"As far as my mother is concerned, she will live in a small grace and favour flat in the main house for the rest of her life and all the necessary arrangements for her future well-being are in hand.

"I have led an exceptionally privileged life and when the Kilbackie Estate came on the market, I bought it with private funds and sent Angus back to look over the estate to see if it were somewhere you could both call home.

"His death destroyed this plan and I will never recover from the shock of losing the finest man I have ever had the privilege of meeting. I am tormented, knowing I unwittingly sent him to his death, and there are many times I find my guilt too heavy to bear. Death, when it comes, and I hope it comes soon, will be a relief.

"I have no fear of dying and believe all will be forgiven in the after-life.

"I have placed Kilbackie House, its buildings and land in trust for Tavish until he reaches the age of twenty-five. The trust will be managed by three trustees: the Reverend Hubert Hilton, my godson; the Reverend Alasdair Mackie from Gairloch; and my solicitor, Mr Simon Knowles of Knowles, Barton and Waghorn in Richmond. After my death, I want you to contact Mr Hilton who will offer you wise advice and have your best interests at heart. He is an honourable man who can be trusted to be discreet and keep all discussions private.

"I have also set up an annuity for you, giving you financial security for the rest of your life.

"After Angus' funeral, do you remember I went to Inverness to interview your brother, who had been arrested for Angus' murder? He told me he was innocent but refused to say what he had seen that fateful day, apparently fearing the truth more than the hangman's noose.

"I made a pact with him, promising to engage the best defence lawyer in the land if he told me exactly what happened.

"John said very little at first but eventually broke down and told me everything and, however hard you find the truth, I feel you should finally know what happened to your husband.

"Your brother followed Angus onto the island hoping to give him a 'good hiding' for humiliating the family but after downing a bottle of whisky, he wasn't in a fit state to start a fight and decided to return to the mainland to sober up.

He found a sheltered grassy patch high up above the causeway and settled down to wait for Angus' return.

"He didn't have to wait long before he saw Angus strolling back towards the causeway, followed by an agitated man, shouting and waving his arms wildly in the air.

"Angus continued walking, showing no sign of fear and never once quickening his step.

"His pursuer's pronounced limp made it difficult for him to keep up and determined not to let Angus get away, he picked up a stone and threw it with all his might. It struck the back of Angus' head and he slumped to the ground where he remained motionless. We shall never know if the culprit intended to harm Angus or just frighten him but the impact of the blow was catastrophic.

"The man looked round to see if he had been spotted and then dragged Angus's body down to the lower slopes of the causeway, leaving it to the mercy of the incoming tide.

"It was a brutal act of cowardice, witnessed by your brother who remained hidden in the grass until all was clear.

"By the time John had made his way down to the water's edge, the rising tide was beginning to lap at Angus' body. John rolled Angus over as he was lying face-down on the sand. He thought he heard a moaning sound and was going to take his brother-in-law's pulse for signs of life but the sight of the deathly white face staring back at him terrified him so much, he fled the scene without even checking."

Katherine could read no further.

She was too shocked to finish the rest of Hugh's letter. Although she now knew who threw the stone that killed her husband, she had no wish to see his name written on paper.

Images of Angus, floating in the cold waters of the Minch, would haunt her forever.

Her distress was interrupted by a sharp knock at the door.

"Hello! Is anyone at home?"

She folded the letter and quickly replaced it in her Bible, intending to finish it later.

"I'm in the front room, Daisy. Come on through."

Daisy looked at Katherine and raised an eyebrow.

"I'm fine," Katherine replied. "Really I am! I've just been over to the House to see Hugh. Did you know he was blind and needs oxygen to breathe?"

Daisy nodded.

She walked over to the sofa and sat down next to Katherine, resting her gaze first on the Bible then on Katherine's face.

"Are you sure that's the only reason you look as if you've seen a ghost?" she enquired.

"Yes," came the abrupt reply.

It was rare for the two friends to be awkward in each other's company. Katherine had no desire to open up in front of Daisy and Daisy decided that now wasn't the right time to question her friend about her obvious unhappiness.

She stood up to leave.

"I only popped in to see how you were. I'm on my way to see Gladys with some sage from the garden."

Katherine appeared to perk up. "If you're going to

the House," she said, easing herself off the sofa and walking towards the kitchen, "could you return this book to the library for me?"

Daisy took the book and looked at the title.

"You're up to something, Katherine," she surmised, wagging her finger as she spoke. "You are as transparent as a piece of glass and I can read you like the cover of this book. 'Fungi of Australia' — what's that all about?!"

Katherine looked at her friend and beckoned her back to the sofa.

"Could you spare me a few minutes before seeing Gladys?" she begged, looking at her watch. "I've got a letter for you to read and a plan I want to share with you."

CHAPTER 41

Hugh Hollister died a week after Katherine's visit and his funeral was an event no-one would ever forget.

Not in over thirty years had Shottenden been seen in its full glory. Lady Hollister was determined to bring the place alive one more time before it ceased to be a family home and was taken over by the National Trust.

She ordered her son's body to be taken from his bedroom and placed in a silk-lined oak and brass coffin, draped in the Union flag and adorned with flowers from the walled garden. Cautiously and with great reverence, the six pallbearers chosen by Lady Hollister carried the coffin down Shottenden's main staircase and out through the front door for the last time. The deathly silence was shattered by the pitiable yapping and whining of Tats, who scampered aimlessly round the pallbearers as they eased the coffin into the hearse.

Billings bent down and picked up the bewildered dog in his large hand, stroking her to calm her down before lovingly placing her on a rug in the front footwell of the Alvis. Here the little dog seemed to sense her master's presence and curled up contentedly.

Lady Hollister, dressed in a spectacular black outfit with a neat veiled hat, sat regally on the back seat of the car and exuded a beauty that belied her eighty years. She gazed out at the members of staff who had lined the drive with their heads bowed out of respect for the noble man who had weathered the political and economic storms of the inter-war years, endured unbearable pain and worked tirelessly to bring stablility and prosperity to their lives.

The long slow march of a lone piper in full MacKenzie Highland dress playing 'Lord Lovat's Lament' filled the air with evocative memories of the Applecross Peninsula where Hugh had spent so much of his youth learning about crofting and natural history.

Katherine soon regretted taking her place in the line. The piper's lament took her straight back to Kilbackie where she and Angus only managed to spend a few days together before he returned to England. She recalled every precious moment; the feel of the summer breeze that blew across the Minch, the first touch of his hand on her neck, the sound of the stream that carried her ring, the peeping sandpipers darting across the rocky shore, the warmth of the sun on her bare arms and the smell of his skin. The pipes seemed to draw from her the unresolved emotions she had tried so hard to suppress and it wasn't long before she became overwhelmed with grief, having lost the two people she loved most. A future without Angus and Sir Hugh was more than she could bear.

By the time the hearse reached St Thomas's lych

gate, the Highland music had ceased and been replaced by the monotonous tolling of a solitary bell which rang out from the church tower. A military Guard of Honour from the Cameron Highlanders stood to attention as the coffin was lifted out of the hearse and placed on the shoulders of six serving officers. After the service, Colonel Sir Hugh Hollister, the last owner of Shottenden Park and patron of St Thomas's Church, was taken to his family plot and laid to rest next to his father.

A bugler sounded the Last Post and the Reverend Hubert Hilton gave the final blessing.

The last thing anyone was expecting at the beginning of the service was the announcement that Lady Hollister would be hosting a reception after the funeral.

All were welcome.

Katherine chose not to attend but Daisy was curious to see who would be there and later she called in to describe the occasion to her friend.

"You should have been there, Katherine," she babbled, looking flushed and trying to control the excitement in her voice. "It was the most incredible experience ever! There was so much champagne, endless cups of tea and more food than anyone could eat. Waiters and waitresses had been hired specially for the event to give the domestic staff a day off and the house was full of the most beautiful fragrant flowers. I've never seen anything like it in my whole life.

"Officers, gentlemen and ladies talked effortlessly

to villagers and staff, and Lady Hollister seemed a different person. She was totally animated and utterly charming to everyone."

Daisy was annoyed at the way Katherine listened but remained cooly detached.

"I didn't have to call in and tell you all about it," she protested, rather hurt by Katherine's continuing aloofness. "Now I wish I hadn't bothered. You've put a damper on what was a wonderful party and if you're going to be so grumpy, there's no point me staying."

With a toss of her head, she left the room and headed home in a huff.

Without the security of Shottenden, Katherine began to lose her reason for living and stopped eating. She spent most of her time in bed with her eyes shut. Housework and cooking ceased to give her pleasure and she was convinced her son no longer loved her.

Things came to a head one evening when William returned home from work and noticed a small bare-footed child, lightly dressed in shorts and a tee-shirt, walking aimlessly along the road with his hands in his pockets.

He stopped and crouched down to the child's level.

"What are you doing out here on your own, Tavish? Where's Mummy?"

"Mummy's asleep and won't wake up," the child replied. "I'm hungry and I want Daisy."

William placed the tiny hand in his and together they walked back to his home, entering the house just as Daisy was taking a pile of ironing upstairs to the airing cupboard.

"Tavish!" she shouted with alarm. "What's happened? Are you all right?"

The little boy could only repeat what he had told William.

"Mummy won't wake up and I'm hungry."

"Here, take this," Daisy requested, passing the pile of fresh laundry to her son, "and tell your father I'm going over to Katherine's so if I'm not back in time, you'll have to get your own supper."

She took her coat off the hook, gathered Tavish in her arms and ran out of the house, leaving William standing bemused in the hallway.

Tavish wrapped his arms tightly round Daisy's neck and refused to let go.

"I want Mummy," he wailed.

"Shhhh now!" Daisy whispered, trying to sound calm. "Everything's going to be fine."

The side door was already open when Daisy arrived at the cottage. She stepped inside and placed Tavish gently on the floor, stretching her aching back.

"Where's Mummy?" she enquired.

"In bed," came the tearful reply. "I tried to wake her up but she wouldn't open her eyes."

"Run along and play with your toys whilst I check your mother's all right," Daisy said, giving the boy a hug and sending him on his way. "If you're good, you can have a biscuit."

She ran up the stairs and found Katherine just as

Tavish had described, lying in bed with her eyes closed. The curtains were half-drawn and dusk was closing in, cloaking the room in gloom.

"Katherine, wake up!" she pleaded, shaking the apparently lifeless body.

Daisy placed her ear next to Katherine's mouth and then felt her pulse. She was breathing, albeit shallowly.

Her bedclothes smelt of stale sweat and unwashed skin.

"What have you done?" Daisy sighed, sniffing the contents of the glass on the table and dabbing her finger in its contents.

It was tap water.

Katherine stirred and squinted though half-opened eyes.

She mouthed, "I'm so sorry, Daisy."

"Don't apologise to me, I'm the last person you need to apologise to. Just tell me what's happened."

"I'm too sad to keep going," came the unexpected reply. "I promise you I haven't done anything bad but all I want to do is sleep and forget the pain that's crushing me."

"But you're the strong one, Katherine," Daisy choked, stroking her cheek. "You're the one we all look up to."

"Not any more," she sighed, closing her eyes.

"Listen carefully," Daisy urged. "I'm going to give Tavish a bite to eat and put him to bed, then I'll phone Bill and tell him I'm staying with you tonight. We can talk later."

Katherine gave a weak nod and turned her head to face the wall.

"Come on young man," Daisy urged, ushering Tavish into the kitchen. "It's time we got you something to eat. How about a spam fritter, then stewed apple and custard?"

"Mmmm!" he replied. "I'm really, really hungry. Can I have the biscuit you promised me?"

Daisy rummaged in the cupboards looking for something to eat but all she could find were a few wrinkled apples, some cold potatoes and a jug of sour milk.

"There aren't any biscuits," she commiserated, "but I'll bring some tomorrow."

Tavish seemed content with the answer but it was clear that he wasn't being properly fed or cared for.

"And today," Daisy announced, waving a wooden spoon in front of the small boy's face, "I'm going to conjure up a delicious meal…after three now…

"One, two, three ABRACADABRA!"

Tavish squealed with delight as Daisy threw the apples into the air and caught them one by one. She laid them neatly in a row on the table and took out a sharp knife from the kitchen drawer. She then chopped the cold potatoes, tossing them into a hot, dry frying pan.

Without butter or dripping, they made a miserly supper but at least the potatoes were hot and slightly crispy.

While he devoured the potatoes, she cored the

apples and cooked them in a small amount of water until they had softened into a puree.

"Now, let's see if we can find something to go with your apple," she suggested, looking at his empty plate.

Right at the back of a cupboard she found a small tin of sweetened condensed milk.

"Could you open the drawer under the table in front of you, Tavish, and pass me the tin opener?"

He found the opener and handed it to Daisy who wound the metal handle round and round until the lid separated from the tin.

"Perfect!" she said, spooning out a generous amount of sticky, sweet cream onto the apple sauce.

"This is deeeelicious!" Tavish cried, licking the bowl to make sure every trace of dessert had been eaten. "Can I have some more?"

"There're only two spoonfuls left but I'll definitely bring you lots of things to eat in the morning."

Once he had changed into his pyjamas, brushed his teeth and wiped his face with a flannel, he went to say goodnight to his mother.

"Night night Mummy," he whispered in Gaelic, flinging his arms round her neck and kissing her. "I love you."

Back in his own room, Tavish picked up Humpty, his teddy, and slipped into bed, quickly falling into a deep sleep.

Daisy tiptoed back into Katherine's bedroom and sat on the edge of her bed, waiting for her to find the courage to talk.

"I loved Angus so much," she sighed. "He didn't deserve to die the way he did."

She heaved herself up into a sitting position and placed a pillow behind her back. Daisy noticed the dark rings round her eyes and her downcast look.

"It's not fair. Tavish will never know his father and I face the rest of my life without the only man I truly loved."

She paused to wipe her nose.

"Did I ever tell you he was murdered?"

"No," Daisy replied, "but I guessed as much from the letter you showed me."

"I've reached the end," Katherine sighed, "and want to close my eyes forever and slip away. I hardly dare admit it but I envy Hugh being at peace and free of his struggles."

"Nonsense!" Daisy said, shocked at the depth of Katherine's depression. "Life is never fair but you are still young and for Tavish's sake, you need to survive and take back control of your life. I don't mean to sound unfeeling, Katherine, but you aren't the only widow having to bring up a child on her own. There are thousands of war widows out there facing a lonely future and struggling to cope."

Katherine stared down at the red eiderdown and thought hard before whispering, "I need to get Tavish back to Skye where he belongs, but I can't take him there."

CHAPTER 42

Early the next morning, Daisy looked in on Katherine who was sleeping soundly.

"Wakey, wakey!" she called out, drawing back the curtains and opening the window to let in the damp, morning air. "How are you feeling, today?"

Somewhere in the inaudible response, Daisy only caught one word 'Tavish'.

"Don't worry about him," she replied, "he's still fast asleep. Let's get you fresh sheets and a change of clothing before I have to leave for work. I've run a hot bath, so all you have to do is get out of bed and soak your body."

Daisy helped support her friend across the room to the bathroom. Days of inactivity and almost nothing to eat had weakened her constitution; her limbs were now as slender and pale as bean sprouts and her unkempt hair hung in tangled clumps over her shoulders.

She could barely stand but somehow she managed to lower herself into the tub and then sat pinched and tense, with her knees bent high under her chin. She stared at the taps and started to shiver as cool air wrapped round her naked body. Daisy took a china jug and gently poured water over Katherine's hair and protruding shoulder blades, working a bar of soap into a lather and lovingly massaging her body and head. The lapping sound of water and cleansing feel of soapsuds helped Katherine relax and she turned her sad face towards Daisy and mouthed the words 'Thank you'.

"Will you be all right if I leave you for a few minutes?" Daisy asked. "I want to change your bed."

Katherine gave a weak nod and slipped under the water, feeling its healing qualities revive her. Five minutes later, Daisy returned with a large towel and a fresh set of clothes. She knew Katherine would be returning straight to bed but felt it important she made an effort to dress for the day.

The bath and new sheets had noticeably energized Katherine, bringing colour to her cheeks. She even attempted a smile as she lay back in bed and enjoyed the fresh lemon-scented smell of her hair.

"I've got to go to work now," Daisy said, "but don't worry about Tavish, I'll wake him up and get him dressed, then take him over to Mairi's. Between us we'll look after him until you feel stronger."

With Tavish skipping merrily beside her, Daisy made her way across the Park to Mairi's cottage. He chattered childish nonsense the whole way and although she had no idea what he was talking about, it was encouraging to hear his enthusiasm for life and to know that his mother's worsening depression didn't seem to be affecting him.

"Come in! Come in!" Mairi welcomed her visitors, giving Tavish a hug.

He beamed back and gabbled excitedly to her in Gaelic, telling her about his mother and how he had met William on the road.

Daisy watched in amazement as the beauty of their language and soft lilt of its rhythm drew them close together, surrounding them with an aura of tranquillity. She now understood what Katherine had meant when she talked about the power of Gaelic shaping her life.

"I knew things were tough," Mairi admitted in English, "but I had no idea she had reached such a low ebb. Why don't you leave Tavish with me for the day and perhaps we could talk this evening when you've finished work. I'll pop round to see Katherine later on to make sure she's eaten something."

"You'll have to take food over with you," Daisy suggested. "All there was in the house yesterday evening were a few cold potatoes and some apples which I gave Tavish for supper. The kitchen cupboards were empty."

"Poor wee mite," Mairi sighed, bending down to Tavish's level. "You must be famished. Let's go into the kitchen and see what we can find. How about some cornflakes and a glass of milk and if you're really hungry, I might be able to find some bread, butter, eggs and bacon. How does that sound?"

"Delicious!" came the hungry reply.

"Please, Daisy, don't forget the biscuit you promised me," Tavish added impishly.

"I won't. I'll make sure you have one before

bedtime. Now I must dash or else I'll be late for work. Thanks for helping me, Mairi."

When evening came, Mairi only had bad news for Daisy.

"I called in to see Katherine this afternoon and she was still in bed having eaten nothing all day. She looked terribly thin and pale and pleaded with me to leave her alone. I don't know what to do, Daisy. She was full of dark thoughts."

"I think we should ring Dr Porter and arrange a home visit," Daisy suggested.

At eight o'clock that same evening, Daisy and Mairi met the doctor at the cottage and showed him up to Katherine's bedroom.

Dr Porter was a compassionate man with a round head, thick black wavy hair and a portly stomach. Known for his sociability and fondness of whisky, he was devoted to his patients and would think nothing of leaving a dinner party early or getting up in the middle of the night to visit the sick or assist at a home delivery.

He examined Katherine thoroughly and asked if she could describe the thoughts that were troubling her.

She couldn't put her feelings into words and remained silent.

"I need to phone Mr Meredith, the Mental Health Officer, for a second opinion," he explained to Daisy and Mairi. "As far as I can tell, she's suffering from a bout of severe melancholy and needs to be admitted to Summerdale Mental Hospital."

"You can't be serious!" Daisy snapped. "Katherine's not like that! She's the sanest person I know and totally unsuited for a mental asylum."

"You're probably right," the doctor replied, shaking his head sadly, "but what's the alternative? Neither of you can look after her full-time and without specialist help she will probably starve herself to death. The best thing you can do is to care for her little son while she's away. What's his name by the way?"

"Tavish," Daisy replied.

"Tavish," he repeated, with sorrow in his voice. "What a terrible thing to happen to one so young."

A few days later, Katherine woke up in the acute admissions ward at Summerdale Mental Hospital, having no idea how she got there. The drowsy effects of the sedative had begun to wear off and she felt deeply depressed and incredibly alone.

The room was three quarters full of women of all ages, shapes and sizes; some wandered aimlessly round the ward muttering to themselves while others shook violently or rocked to and fro on their beds, screaming.

Katherine found herself in a living hell for tormented souls.

She turned onto her side and closed her eyes.

At six-thirty in the evening the meal bell rang and a nurse woke her up.

"Come on, Mrs MacLeod," she purred in a soft patronising way, "you've had a nice long sleep and the doctor says you are well enough to join us for supper."

The ward gradually emptied and Katherine reluctantly joined the end of the queue which led into an impressive refectory, full of wooden tables, each set for twenty patients. Overwhelmed by the sheer number of women in one place, Katherine followed a dark plump lady of about fifty who briefly turned round and winked at her, revealing an extraordinary pair of alert, blue eyes. Behind the wide-open hatch a bored expressionless cook ladled some watery stew into a bowl with one hand, then added a spoonful of thick glutinous mashed potato with the other. She passed the bowl over to Katherine who took it and continued down the line until she found herself standing alone in the large, bustling room. Unsure what to do next, she caught sight of the blue-eyed lady who winked at her again and beckoned her to sit down.

Faced with a bowl of unappetizing food, Katherine lethargically pushed the lumps of potato around with her spoon but ate nothing.

"You new here?" the plump lady asked.

Katherine nodded.

"You'd better eat up or else there'll be trouble!" she warned with a knowing look. "They have ways of keeping us all well fed in here."

The fat in the cooling gravy was beginning to solidify.

One of the warders on duty in the refectory stopped when she saw the untouched food in Katherine's bowl.

"Hurry up and finish your stew," she threatened. "We don't tolerate fussy eaters."

Katherine listened but did nothing and at the end of the meal, her food remained untouched.

Back in the ward, she was getting ready for bed when a nurse walked briskly in, carrying the supper she had left uneaten in the refectory.

"I believe this is yours," she quipped, placing the bowl on the chair beside Katherine's bed.

The smell of cold stew reached the back of her throat and made her retch.

"I'll leave it here for you to finish," she taunted. "If it is still there in the morning, we'll have no choice but to force feed you and that isn't a pleasant experience, I can assure you. Now be a good girl and eat your supper. The night sister has been told about your food and will keep an eye on you to make sure you don't do anything foolish like attempting to flush it down the toilet."

Katherine ignored the warder's warning and drew the blanket over her head to try to shut out the sound of coughing and grunting.

Her nerves were shredded and she couldn't sleep.

"Let's have a good look at you," a voice spoke from the end of her bed the next morning.

She peeped out from under the sheet and saw the warder who had previously tried to make her eat.

"You still haven't eaten anything, I see," she tut-tutted. "I warned you, Mrs MacLeod."

A quarter of an hour later, Katherine was escorted

to a side room and told to lie down on the bed. Unaware of the danger she was in, she meekly obliged and before she could take in her new surroundings, she felt her arms, feet and head being forcibly held down and a man lean across her body, ramming his chubby fingers into her mouth, forcing open her jaw.

Everything happened so quickly, she didn't have time to stop the assault by clenching her teeth.

She struggled to free herself from the unexpected brutality of being force fed but the restraining hands kept her firmly in their grip.

Her cry for help never found its way past four feet of rubber tubing pushed through her left nostril.

She splutted and choked as nourishment was poured through a funnel into her stomach forcing her to vomit over her clothes, face and hair. The action of being sick made her body and legs arch convulsively, the acidic taste of the regurgitated liquid burned her mouth and the agonizing pain in her nostril made her eyes smart.

She pleaded with the warder to allow her to wash the vomit off her hair and clothes but her request was denied.

Back on the ward, she railed against a system that had forced her away from her son but hadn't the energy to voice her protest.

Slowly, as the weeks went by, Katherine became more institutionalized and submissive, inhabiting a lonely, alien world in which she ate just enough to keep the feeding tubes away.

She believed the doctors when they told her she was a wicked person, totally unfit to be a mother and eventually, worn down by hunger and a feeling of abandonment, she signed the official papers agreeing to give Tavish up for adoption.

After three long months isolated from the outside world, Katherine received her first visitor.

"Good God! Katherine!" the visitor raged, seeing her friend shuffle head bowed into the visitors' room. "What have they done to you?"

Katherine lifted her pale thin face and looked directly into Daisy's horrified eyes.

"You've come!" she whispered. "I always knew you would."

She stretched out a matchstick arm and grasped the hand of her dearest friend.

"Don't tell me what they've done to you in this awful place," Daisy retorted. "I don't think I could bear it. Just hold my hand and know you haven't been abandoned."

The warmth of Daisy's grasp gave Katherine hope.

"I don't have very long," Daisy whispered with a sense of urgency, "but I thought you'd want to know that Tavish is well and living happily with Mairi and Johnny.

"Did you know they have adopted him?"

Katherine mouthed the word, "Yes".

Daisy reached in her pocket and brought out a crumpled piece of paper.

"This is from Tavish," she smiled. "Go on, open it."

Shaking with emotion, Katherine unfolded the paper and saw a coloured drawing of a smiling face with the words 'I love you' written at the top.

"I helped him a bit!" Daisy added, grinning with delight.

"Even though he lives with Mairi and Johnny, he still comes over to my house for tea every now and then."

Katherine kissed the picture and tucked the paper down the front of her dress when no-one was looking.

"Thank you!" she breathed, placing her hand over her heart. "This means so much to me."

She sounded tired and weak and seemed startled at the sound of her own voice.

"Could I ask you to do me a favour?"

"Of course you can!" Daisy replied. "Tell me what you want and I'll try and help."

"On my bedside table you will find my Bible," Katherine instructed, "and hidden near the back is the letter I gave you to read just before Hugh died. Could you take it to Mr Hilton and explain that I am temporarily interned in Summerdale and cannot make the necessary arrangements for Tavish's future? It is very important that you deliver the letter to him in person."

Daisy assured her friend that she would pick up the letter that evening and take it straight to the vicarage.

"I'll be back as soon as I can," she promised, "but in the meantime, stay strong and know that I'll do everything possible to get you out of this dreadful place."

CHAPTER 43

Daisy knocked on the Mr Hilton's door and was warmly greeted by the clergyman.

"How lovely to see you again!" he exclaimed, ushering her into his cold spartan study where open books and sheets of paper lay scattered across his desk. The only other furniture in the elegant Georgian room was a huge bookcase overflowing with books of all shapes and sizes, and neatly stacked down one side of the study were more piles of papers, surplus books and magazines.

Daisy took a seat and gazed out of the window. Clumps of bright green snowdrop shoots were beginning to poke through the grass under a mature beech tree and the dead stems of last year's perennials lay rotting among the mulched leaves in the herbaceous border.

"You've a lovely view of the garden from this window," she declared.

"I'm glad you like it," he replied enthusiastically. "This is my favourite room in the vicarage and I never tire watching the seasons change from my desk.

"How's William?" he went on, showing genuine interest.

"He's fine," she replied proudly. "In fact, you might be hearing from him soon as he's just got engaged to

Dorothy Davies and wants to get married at St Thomas's."

"That's wonderful news!" the vicar replied. "Please pass on my warmest congratulations to the happy couple.

"Now, what can I do for you?"

Daisy explained that she had just returned from visiting Katherine in Summerdale and been asked to bring him a letter.

She opened the clasp of her handbag and pulled out the beautifully hand-written envelope.

"You should have seen her, Reverend!" she blurted out, handing over the letter. "She was terribly thin and pale with black circles under her eyes and a haunted stare that looked straight through you.

"Just before her committal, Katherine mentioned that Sir Hugh had passed Shottenden over to something called the National Trust and she was going to lose the right to remain in her cottage. Did you know about this?"

The clergyman nodded and asked if she knew what was in the letter.

Daisy replied that she had read it although she didn't really understand it.

"It talked about something called a trust and Kilbackie where, I think, Katherine and Angus came from. It also mentioned a farm, something about Tavish reaching twenty five and Angus' accident but I think you'd better read the letter for yourself, Reverend, because you'll understand it better than me."

The Mr Hilton put on his glasses and pulled Hugh's letter out of its envelope. Daisy watched as he read and re-read each word with care, then folded the letter and left it on his desk.

"Does it make any sense to you?" she asked.

"Yes, Daisy, it does," he replied kindly. "You've done Katherine a great service by bringing me the letter. I think I can help her."

"Can you?" Daisy enquired, desperate for someone to take an interest in Katherine's hopeless situation. "I can't help feeling Malvingborough holds the key to her unhappiness," she added. "I know you're a busy man, Reverend, but do you think you could find out if the Abbess ever received her letter and, if so, what was in the reply?"

Mr Hilton had always admired Daisy's pluck and assured her that he would do his best for Katherine.

Daisy left the vicarage confident that, at last, progress was being made.

A few weeks later, she received a telephone call from the vicar with some interesting news.

She made her way over to see him and once again was shown into his study.

"Please, take a seat," he said, in his usual courteous manner. "Would you like a cup of tea?"

She shook her head.

"Since our last conversation," he continued, "I have spoken to the Abbess, who was kind enough to fill me in on her correspondence with Katherine.

"The contents of the letters are obviously

confidential but I thought you'd like to know that the Abbey has a strict policy of never accepting children."

It took a moment for the full impact of this statement to sink in.

"Oh poor Katherine!" Daisy sighed, burying her head in her hands. "Now I understand everything.

"Do you think the Abbess would reconsider her application if she knew Tavish had been legally adopted?"

"She might," agreed the vicar, "but there's no guarantee. Would you like me to ask?"

"More than anything in this world! Would you really be able to do that to help her?"

Within a month of the vicarage meeting, Katherine received her second visitor.

The Abbess was a remarkable, quietly-spoken lady of about sixty, whose gentle manner hid a steely determination to help the sick and injured servicemen in her care. Her lined face bore the serenity of someone who had struggled through life but was now at peace.

She wore a simple black tunic and veil, white bandeau and wimple and sat straight-backed on a wooden chair in the visitors' room, waiting to hear what Katherine had to say. In the stillness of their surroundings Katherine began to open up.

She described her husband's death and her son's adoption and how important it was that he should grow up on Skye and fulfil the dreams of his father and Sir Hugh Hollister.

Instead of offering advice, the Reverend Mother remained seated and listened patiently to Katherine's outpouring of suffering and pain.

"Skye lies deep within our souls," she reflected. "We are hewn out of its volcanic rock and moulded by its wind and rain. The sea mist that swirls across the Minch runs through our veins and the cries of the birds and the rhythm of crofting life shape our language.

"Society has judged me harshly by taking away my son and silencing my voice; it has condemned me to a lunatic asylum and caused me great pain but it can never extinguish the hope that burns within me."

The Reverend Mother continued listening in silence and when Katherine had finished speaking, she stood up and before leaving the small room, clasped Katherine's hands firmly in hers, kissed the top of her bowed head and blessed her.

CHAPTER 44

"Wake up!" a voice whispered loudly.

Katherine half opened her eyes to see who was standing by her bed but it was too dark to recognise the face behind the voice. She pulled the thin blanket up over her head, wishing to be left alone.

"Now!" hissed the voice, this time shaking her. "Get dressed and follow me."

It was pitch black in the small room Katherine shared with four other women and the voice sounded threatening, so she fumbled for her clothes which were folded neatly on the wooden chair next to her bed and began to dress.

"What's the time?" she yawned.

"Five-thirty," the warder replied. "Now hurry up."

Katherine had no idea why she had been singled out so early, especially as she had always tried to live discreetly in the shadows and never draw attention to herself.

"Are you ready?" came the voice again, but this time more sharply.

"Yes," she murmured.

"Good, then follow me."

The warder led her into an empty side-room, assuring her that someone would be along soon. Katherine sat on a hard plastic chair and stared up at the high window, watching the dawn break through a ruby sky. There were no pictures or magazines in the room to distract her and apart from the six o'clock rising bell and the six-thirty breakfast bell, she was unaware of the passing time.

No-one came to visit her and as the minutes turned to hours, she began to feel faint.

Finally, three hours later, a nurse popped her head round the door and from her surprised look, it was clear she wasn't expecting Katherine to be there.

"I'm so sorry," she apologised. "I didn't mean to disturb you. I was looking for Dr Atkinson. Have you seen him by any chance?"

Katherine shook her head.

The young nurse stood clutching a wodge of papers and looked nervous.

"I'm new here," she added innocently, "and Dr Atkinson asked me to meet him in the interview room at nine o'clock. I'm already really late and I haven't the slightest idea which room he meant. Are you sure you don't know where he is?"

Again Katherine shook her head, adding, "On your way out could you tell someone that Katherine MacLeod is still waiting in Room 14? I seem to have been forgotten."

"Oh! You poor thing," the young nurse replied brightly. "Of course I will. In fact, I'll go immediately, that is if I can find my way around the labyrinth of corridors. I had no idea Summerdale was so big. To be honest, I'm a bit nervous walking around the asylum on my own, knowing there are so many nutters around."

Katherine turned slightly pale and the nurse looked at her in horror. "I say, I'm frightfully sorry. You're not one of them, are you? It's so difficult to tell who's mad and who's sane in this place — I'm really sorry if I've offended you, I didn't mean to be unkind."

She left, too embarrassed to wait for Katherine's reply, but not long after her departure a warder popped her head round the door.

"Mrs MacLeod?" she enquired. "This way, please."

She led Katherine into the long dimly-lit corridor known as 'The Tunnel of Hell' where patients were mysteriously taken at night, their terrified screams piercing the Victorian walls and chilling the blood of those trying to sleep.

"You're needed in the end room," she said, leaving her to walk the full length of the corridor on her own.

Having had nothing to eat all morning, Katherine felt light-headed and slightly nauseous and her legs were shaking so much they eventually crumpled under her and she fainted.

No-one came to her aid in the immediate silence that followed, then much to her relief, she heard footsteps running towards her and felt herself being scooped up into a warm embrace.

"I promised I'd come for you, Katherine, and now I'm taking you home."

A shrill voice shouted from the far end of the corridor.

"Leave that patient alone and come back to the visitors' room at once! The public are not allowed into the main part of the hospital. If you don't do as you're told, I'll call Security."

Daisy took no notice of the threat and gently helped Katherine to her feet. Together they struggled to the end room where Mr Hilton was waiting for them.

He used all his charm and diplomacy to calm the Senior Warder and explained that Katherine was ill and the sooner she were off the premises and in the care of a doctor, the better for all concerned. Calling Security would only delay her discharge and complicate matters.

The Senior Warder confirmed that Katherine was very weak and in urgent need of care. Bearing in mind the exceptional arrangements that the Abbess and Mr Hilton had made for her future support, he agreed to break with protocol and sign the papers to fast track her release.

At eleven o'clock on 9th April 1954, Mr Hilton, Daisy and Katherine walked out of the hospital into the bright, spring sunshine.

Katherine gave a sudden gasp.

"Is the walk to the car too much for you? We could easily bring it up to the door to save you the effort."

"No, no, I'm fine," she assured them, pointing to the carpet of daffodils spread across the well-kept lawns. "Angus always used to quote his favourite poem to me whenever we went for a spring walk at Shottenden. If I remember rightly its last lines were:

'*And then my heart with pleasure fills, And dances with the daffodils.*'

"I can't tell you how good it feels to be free."

"Is it all right if I drop you both off at Daisy's house?" Mr Hilton asked, driving his Austin 8 carefully through the narrow country lanes. "It's just that I've got a few parishioners to visit before lunch and the Park is slightly out of my way."

"That'll be perfect," Daisy replied, thanking the vicar for everything he had done to help secure Katherine's release.

Once back home, Daisy tidied the cushions on the sofa and told Katherine to make herself comfortable.

"There's so much to tell you, but first things first, let's have something to eat. I've done a bit of baking in your honour. I hope it's all right."

Katherine appeared subdued and distant, unable to converse or make eye contact. She also looked desperately thin and tired.

Daisy poured two mugs of sweet tea and put the homemade Battenberg cake on the table.

"Have some," she urged, cutting a couple of small slices. Much to her delight, Katherine took one, peeled off the marzipan and started to eat it.

"I've forgotten how delicious marzipan tastes!" she said, licking her lips and taking a sip of tea. "You are clever, Daisy, remembering that Battenberg is one of my favourite cakes."

She took a small bite out of the yellow square and savoured its sweetness.

"We don't have much time," Daisy noted, looking at her watch. "Mr Hilton will be returning later this evening to take you to Malvingborough Abbey where you can start to rebuild your life and be safe. He has talked to the Abbess and explained everything and she has agreed to accept you now that Tavish has been adopted.

"You have him to thank for your freedom and the Abbess to thank for your future and that's not all," Daisy confessed. "I hope I've done the right thing, Katherine, but I've invited Tavish for tea, even though legally you are not supposed to have any contact with him. If Mairi ever found out, I would be in terrible trouble so please don't let me down."

Katherine perked up and for the first time since leaving the hospital, showed some response.

"It's a huge gamble but I knew it was probably the last chance you'd ever have to see your son again. Do you promise me you'll stay out of sight and only view him through the half-open door? There must be no contact of any kind."

Katherine nodded and smiled with her eyes.

"How about a bowl of soup and some bread to build up your strength ahead of his arrival? I don't want you keeling over when Tavish gets here in two hours' time."

Katherine sat beside Daisy at the table and struggled through half a bowl of vegetable soup and a slice of bread and butter.

"Is that all you're eating?" Daisy exclaimed, wiping her bowl clean with a crust of bread. Katherine was too exhausted to explain how the force-feeding had damaged her throat, making it painful to swallow.

At three-thirty, they heard a knock on the front door and Katherine quickly hid herself. Tavish had grown since she had last seen him but he still had Angus' black hair and piercing blue eyes. He gave Daisy a huge hug and waved Mairi goodbye.

"What would you like to do before tea? Shall we play Snakes and Ladders?"

"Yes! Yes!" the little boy cried with excitement, running to the cupboard and taking out a rather battered box covered with pictures of green and yellow snakes and red ladders.

He opened the board and picked up the four counters and dice.

"Can I be red?" he asked, placing his counter on the edge of the board.

"Of course you can," Daisy replied. "If you're red, I'll be blue."

The counters ran up the ladders and down the snakes until eventually the red counter reached the last square.

"I've won! I've won!" he cried enthusiastically. "I'm the champion! Can we have another game?"

"One more," Daisy smiled, "and then you must play on your own while I get tea."

The second game of Snakes and Ladders finished with another victory for Tavish. He was ecstatic.

"Can I play with William's toys until tea-time?" he asked, finding the wooden box of cars in the corner of the room. "I promise I'll be careful with them."

"As you've asked so nicely," Daisy replied, relieved that he was happy to play on his own. "Why don't you get out the box of soldiers as well?"

She slipped into the kitchen, passing Katherine on the way.

"Are you OK?" she whispered, fearing the sight of Tavish would prove too much for her.

Katherine nodded, her eyes shining with pride.

"Don't forget, Tavish mustn't see you. You do understand?"

Tavish tucked into his favourite cheese and tomato sandwiches, followed by homemade chocolate crispies, and then asked if he could have some more. Daisy hadn't the heart to deny him food especially when she remembered the starving little boy she had rescued when Katherine was too ill to care for him.

"Just one more crispy and then we must wipe your hands and face. They're covered in chocolate."

Ignoring his groans, she cleaned him up and suggested he drew a picture for Johnny and Mairi.

"Mairi says I'm to call them Daddy and Mummy now I live with them," he let on. "Do you think Daddy would like a picture of a tractor?"

Katherine grasped the door handle to steady herself as she slid down onto her knees, listening to the child she had given away prattle contently about his new life; every innocent word struck a raw nerve. She longed to gather up her son in her arms and smother him with affectionate kisses, reminding him how much he was adored. He would never understand the intense love that had created him and the enlightened thinking that had given her and Angus the confidence to bring a child into the world.

Hidden and voiceless, Katherine could only dream that one day Tavish would discover the immense wealth of knowledge hidden within the pages of Hugh's library at Kilbackie.

"I'm sure he'd love you to draw a tractor," Daisy replied, fearing Katherine's reaction as she watched her son effortlessly embrace his new life. She hoped she hadn't made a big mistake in inviting him over.

She willed Mairi to hurry up and collect the little boy so she could spend a few more valuable moments alone with Katherine.

By the time Mairi arrived, Tavish had drawn a bright red tractor and written his name in bold round letters at the top.

"Mummy! Mummy!" he cried, running up to Mairi. "Look, I've drawn a tractor for Daddy!"

"Has he been good?" asked Mairi, lifting the small boy up to get a closer look at his drawing.

"He's always good," Daisy replied, ruffling Tavish's hair. "You know how much I love it when he pops over for tea. He's welcome any time."

"Wow!" Mairi exclaimed, as Tavish pointed out the power take-off and hydraulic lift. "That's brilliant, Tavish! Who taught you all those complicated words?"

"Daddy," he giggled with delight. "He knows everything about tractors."

It was obvious from the way Tavish spoke that he had spent a lot of time with Johnny and shared with him a love of farming.

"Have you got a minute?" Mairi asked, settling nervously on one of the comfortable armchairs. Daisy nodded and sat down beside her.

"Johnny and I are moving to Skye," she announced, so quickly that Daisy hadn't time to take it in before Mairi continued. "It's all rather hush-hush at the moment but unbeknown to us, Hugh bought the entire Kilbackie estate and left it in trust for Tavish. The trustees have been in touch and asked if we would consider moving into Kilbackie House and running the farm on Tavish's behalf until he reaches twenty-five. It is a dream come true for Johnny, who's always wanted to farm on his own and it means I will be returning home to be near my family."

The news left Daisy speechless but eventually she asked the only question that interested her.

"And what about Tavish, is he going as well?"

"Of course he is!" came the swift reply. "He's our son and we're moving back to where he belongs. He's not English you know, Daisy."

Daisy took this comment as a veiled criticism and it hurt.

"When are you going?" she asked, feeling that Mairi was getting above herself.

"Next Friday. Obviously we'll come and say goodbye before we leave. I know Tavish will miss you but we are moving back to Kilbackie to be a family. If ever you, Bill or William wish to visit Skye, you'd be more than welcome to come and stay with us; we'll have lots of room."

CHAPTER 45

"I'm sorry, Katherine, but who does she think she is — Lady Kilbackie? She hasn't even set foot in the house and she's already behaving as if she owns the place."

Katherine gave the faintest of smiles.

"Don't be too hard on her, Daisy. Mairi is a good woman and will make a great mother and, most importantly, Tavish loves her and adores Johnny. It's a dream come true for her to live in Kilbackie House and I know Johnny will work hard to make a success of the estate on Tavish's behalf. She may have come across a bit superior but her heart's in the right place. I should know; after all, she is my aunt."

"Everything's changing," Daisy sighed, "and I don't like it. Shottenden without Hugh is hard enough to accept but life without you around is going to be unbearable. It's not too late to change your mind, Katherine. You could still come and live with us until you find somewhere permanent."

Katherine reached for her friend's hand.

"I've spent hours, days and weeks in the asylum thinking about my future, Daisy," she concluded, "and I want to return to nursing. Now I am free, I can work tirelessly trying to make a difference to the tormented minds and broken bodies of our servicemen.

"*You* know my reasons for not returning to Skye, so my move to Malvingborough Abbey is final."

"And Tavish?"

"One day I hope he'll understand what I've done for him and find it in his heart to forgive me.

"As for me, I keep most of my anger for my father who had everything he ever wanted; a loving wife, three children and a position in the church and yet he remained hell-bent on destroying his best friend's life and with it, my happiness. My father's a vicious murderer and yet I'm the one having to serve his life sentence.

"I bear no grudge against Johnny and Mairi but there is a part of me that will always yearn to feel the Highland rain on my face, to touch the wild heather on the moors and hear the curlews call in the still damp air down by the shore, but I know now this will never be.

"I am only thankful that my son, my darling Tavish, will experience all these wonders for himself."

The peep peep from Mr Hilton's car broke Katherine's impassioned speech.

"It's time I went," she explained with great dignity. "Don't worry about me, Daisy, I know I have made the right decision. I'm at peace and will serve the Abbey to the best of my ability."

She embraced her friend affectionately, walked through the front door and withdrew from the world.

Ask Not How

Book Two of The Corncrakes of Skye

Lucy Montgomery

Having moved to Kilbackie, Johnny enthusiastically runs the farm whilst Mairi looks after Tavish, fearful that his true identity might be discovered.

Tavish is bullied by his cousin, Allan Nicolson, but he finds solace learning how to sail with the mysterious Sandy Campbell. Why does Sandy spend so much time sailing around the small isles and will Allan's hatred of Tavish spoil his chance of staying at Kilbackie?

On his retirement, Donny is replaced by one of the Estate's trustees, Alasdair MacKay, a charming clergy-man who pays particular attention to Hugh's library.

Bill and Daisy finally decide to visit Johnny and Mairi at Kilbackie, bringing with them William, Dorothy and their daughter, Sally.

Much to Mairi's horror Tavish, falls in love with Sally.

The Cuban Missile Crisis, the Hippy Movement and the Vietnam War all weave their way into the lives of those living on Kilbackie.

Is Tavish strong enough to keep his parents' dream alive?

ISBN 9781901870688